GENEVA

GENEVA

RICHARD ARMITAGE

faber

First published as an original audio book by Audible

This edition published in the UK in 2023
by Faber & Faber Ltd
The Bindery, 51 Hatton Garden
London EC1N 8HN

Typeset by Faber & Faber Ltd
Printed in the UK by CPI Group (UK) Ltd, Croydon, CR0 4YY

*This is a work of fiction. All of the characters, organisations and
events portrayed in this novel are either products of the author's
imagination or are used fictitiously*

Trigger warning: This book contains scenes pertaining to
dementia that some readers might find distressing.

A CIP record for this book
is available from the British Library

ISBN 978–0–571–38438–9

2 4 6 8 10 9 7 5 3

For Mum, who taught me anything was possible,
if you put your mind to it.

PROLOGUE

A shard of ancient granite thrusts upwards through the white origami folds of the Swiss Alps, piercing the low-hanging cloud. A kestrel soars high above the summit of the most iconic mountain in Europe, the Matterhorn. To the north-west, a high-altitude lake lies in a deep valley carved by glaciers. The cities of Montreux and Lausanne are busy with travellers moving across the network of autobahns like veins carrying vital blood to the principal body, the shining city of Geneva. A melting pot of winter thrill-seekers, millionaires and bright minds, all of them ready to take on the late-November evening. But up here in the majestic stillness of the peak, the silent air holds the kestrel in suspension. Caught in a passing updraught, the span of feathers ripples in the freezing air. The bird begins to turn in a spiral, descending towards the pine forest below. Everything is calm, everything quiet, the mirror-still water of the distant lake glowing in the fading light of the winter sun.

The crack of a gunshot blasts through the silence, shattering the calm. The kestrel sheers away. The trees shudder and release a flock of fleeing birds in a cloud of powder snow. A pair of mountain chamois leap from the undergrowth in startled flight.

Deep in the forest, a woman sprints over the freshly packed snow, weaving through the trees in desperation. Hot breath pumping out into the freezing air as she climbs hard. The runner groans in exhaustion, but she must not give up. She pushes forward, struggling against the deepening snow that slows her with

1

each passing step. She has to keep going; it can't end here. Pulling at pine branches to propel herself forward, she risks a glance backwards. Her pursuer is nowhere in sight, but she knows they won't be far behind. She isn't safe, not yet.

Her forearm has been grazed by the gunshot. Drops of her fresh blood hit the snow and spread like ink on a blotter, a trail that could lead them to her. She rolls sideways over a cluster of rocks and conceals herself beneath the boughs of a pine tree, heavy snow bending the lower branches to provide cover. She lies still, her body pressed to the trunk, breathing hard, straining to hear.

The crack of a second shot punctures the air. Splinters explode from the trunk of a tree just to her left, raining snow and shards of bark over her. She lets out a shriek of desperation and pounces like a wild animal from her hiding place back into the open. She has already come so far, she has already fought so hard, she refuses to fail now. Heart pounding, lungs bursting, legs burning, she must keep pushing on to safety.

A third gunshot rings out, ricocheting off the granite cliff to the right of her. They are further away, falling behind. Good. Forcing herself onwards, she pushes deeper between the trees, blindly smacking pine branches out of her way, needles scratching her skin. The snow is up to her waist now, but she wills her body to fight through the pain. With every gasping breath, she is one step closer to freedom.

Finally, she reaches open ground, a sloping plateau of rock. But the surface is of compacted ice, and she loses her footing almost at once. She tumbles forward, desperately trying to gain purchase and control her fall. Her feet stop just as the rock face falls away to nothing. An updraught from the valley a thousand feet below catches her, billowing in her coat, and for a second she is held, her arms spread and her spine flexing like a snake to counter the fall. She hangs, suspended between life and death.

The jagged tip of the Matterhorn, like a broken finger, is poised to choose her destiny. Somewhere far above, the kestrel calls. The cry of her daughter's voice is high in the air, and in that moment, she knows: this is it. Every moment she has lived, every face and every feeling meld into one as her heart pounds in her chest like a drum.

Breathe. Breathe.

CHAPTER 1

SARAH

A sudden jolt, blinding light pierces my eyelids, and I swallow down my claustrophobia. I try to calm my breathing as my stomach lurches. I bite down hard. The sound is deafening and my fists are clenched at my side. I lie still and try to block out the noise. I'm trapped, forbidden to move, not even one muscle. Breathe: In . . . and . . . hold. Oh God, I need to get out of here.

Hard plastic presses into my shoulder blades and pelvis. I am meat on a slab. Suddenly, the whirring vibrations stop, and I'm plunged into silence and darkness. Is it over? My body starts to slide, cold air enveloping me as I'm carried towards the light. I hear the door open, followed by footsteps. Then, a voice.

'Sarah, there's a malfunction with the machine. Are you OK to stay where you are for a few minutes? I'm just going to reboot the system, but we'll have to re-scan. I don't want to risk compromising the result. I'm so sorry about this.'

'It's OK, Karima, I'm fine.'

I'm really not fine. Not fine at all.

The slab that I'm lying on continues to move, spitting me out from the MRI chamber. I sit up and try to regain my calm. At the end of the room there is a window into the control area, and I see my husband, Daniel, leaning over the computer, studying something on the screen. He stands with his arms folded as Dr Karima Falka returns. Daniel catches my eye and offers me a reassuring smile, but he can't disguise his sadness. This day is

5

something neither of us was ready for. A few moments later, Karima returns to the scanning room.

'OK, we're back on. Can you lie down again for me, Sarah?' Her soothing Scottish accent reassures me. As I obey, a crackle of static electricity sends a shock wave up my spine.

I flinch; my voice is tight. 'Is Dan OK?' There is a pause. Maybe she didn't hear me. 'Karima?'

'Yeah . . . he's . . . good. You're doing really well. Not too long now and we'll have you out of here.'

The door closes and I feel that ominous magnetic hum of the MRI chamber gathering speed as the slab slides back into the void. My toes curl, and once again I'm plunged into the jaws of the machine.

Whatever happens, babe, I'll take care of Maddie – you and Maddie. We'll get through this.

Of course, Daniel had already jumped to the worst-case scenario. I had a more optimistic view, but that's us in a nutshell: poles apart. He's a worrier. I just don't think in the same way. I truly believe this will be OK. I have to. But things have started to happen that can't be ignored. First, it was simple things like driving to the supermarket and forgetting which vehicle was mine in the car park. I spent half an hour walking around randomly clicking the key fob. 'Of course, the red Audi.' Then there was the time I forgot to pick Maddie up from school. I wrote it off as 'just one of those things', but if I'm completely honest with you, and I have never told another soul this, when it happened, I had forgotten I had a daughter. That utterly terrified me. And then I couldn't remember the name of my hometown, the place where I grew up. It's Barnsley, by the way; I looked it up. More recently, it's the headaches, migraines that feel like someone has my head in a vice. That's when I retreat into the darkness. That's when the

6

thoughts invade like a snake wrapping itself around my neck and whispering poisonous lies into my ears, making me doubt myself and my life.

Dan and I both knew what all the symptoms meant; we both recognised the signs of dementia. Unfortunately, we know about it all too well because my dad was diagnosed with Alzheimer's in 2018. It was Dan who joined the dots on Dad's symptoms first. Being a professor at the London College of Neurology has its twisted perks, I guess. And now it might be happening again. To me. I'm a scientist too – well, I was before, but it's hard to know who I am now without the data, evidence and facts to guide me through each day. Critical thinking and problem-solving were fundamental to my identity, but now basic strands of thought are becoming hard to grasp, and I feel spent and spare. Early retirement does that to a person, I think. I mean, I'm not even fifty yet, but I just had to stop. And let's be honest, I definitely ended on a high. When I look back at what I've achieved, I feel proud. I did something significant. But there's a whole second act to figure out now, and maybe I'm about to pay the ultimate price for the intensity of the first.

I had worked on a prototype gene therapy to combat Ebola back in 2013 during an outbreak in West Africa, but it wasn't cleared for use in a population. And then, well, epidemics die out naturally, and the research money suddenly disappeared. The pharmaceutical industry is a fickle master. But when the disease reared its ugly head again in 2018, we were ready to put our work into action, and that's exactly what me and my team at Oxford University did. I didn't expect the Nobel Prize. I didn't feel that I had done anything monumental like Alexander Fleming or Marie Curie; those who place the stepping stones ahead of us so that we can all tread the path. So, when it happened, I found it embarrassing, especially as it was a team effort and I was being singled out. That's why I declined the invitation to the Nobel awards ceremony in Stockholm.

I'm not one for publicity, and I hate fuss; it was all too much. I was very happy to deliver lectures, write my thesis and be a published scientist, but that's my limit, and all I wanted to do at the end of it all was take a break. Many of my colleagues couldn't understand it; I don't think Daniel could either. As well as the pound signs, I think they view a Nobel Prize in Physiology or Medicine like an Oscar for science: a doorway to fame, fortune and a lifetime of public speaking, standing ovations and whatever else your heart desires. To be honest, I just felt burned out, and all I wanted to do was read thrillers, plant daffodil bulbs and bake cakes with Maddie for my dad.

When I was finally released from my work, and the care homes opened their doors after Covid, I'd been absent for two years, and Dad didn't know who I was. I can't begin to tell you how devastating that felt.

Mum passed away a few years ago, and soon after, we realised Dad wasn't coping living on his own. The melted Tupperware on the electric stove that had nearly set the house on fire, along with the junk hoarding and the newspapers we found in the freezer, were pretty strong indicators he needed full-time care. We found him a place we could afford near to us: a home from home in the Home Counties. To my amusement, Dad didn't really fit in. He expected a full English with bread fried in an inch of bacon fat for breakfast. Instead, he got muesli and oat milk. Try putting that down in front of a Barnsley FC supporter and Premier Foods middle management retiree and watch it fly. He sounded off. Walking into Hartford Gardens over a year after we had last set eyes on each other, I was desperate to feel my dad's arms around me again. But in that moment when he looked up at me after that long-awaited hug, stared at me intently for a second and said, 'You're new here, aren't you?', I shattered. He didn't recognise me.

When you are consumed with work, 'family' sometimes feels like background music; something you collapse into at Christmas and Easter, or the occasional birthday barbecue. It grounds you and allows you to exhale a little. When I woke up after lockdown, all that had gone. I'd lived through it efficiently, working hard, relocating Dad, saying goodbye to the house I grew up in, but actually, stopping for that big breath was a shock. I couldn't open my eyes wide enough for what they needed to see because so much had fallen out of view, lost forever. My mum, my childhood and my whole life were held in my dad's memories.

I panicked. How the hell could I salvage what was slipping through my fingers? I know many other people have had to go through the same thing, watching the cruel decline of the people they love, so I'm not going to wallow in self-pity. But I decided something there and then. I decided to make more memories with Maddie and Dan. Then I would take those stories to Dad, planting new seeds in the hope that the roots would grip memories from his past and haul them up to the surface and into daylight again. But perhaps now I need to make memories for another reason. If the worst is true, I don't want Maddie to forget me, to forget who I was.

The MRI machine decelerates, and I exhale. The ordeal is over. I peel my naked backside from the slab and roll off. I'm starting to dress when Karima breezes in, all positive energy.

'We'll get these results to you quickly, Sarah, don't worry. I'm going to change your current prescription for the headaches. This one isn't a painkiller but an enzyme blocker. Works slightly differently. They should keep you a bit more balanced, but they can sometimes be a bit "buzzy".'

'Sounds like a party.' She laughs and gives me that shoulder clasp, the one weighted with pity.

'Just let me or the Prof know if you aren't sleeping and we'll change the dosage, or I'll give you a course of Zopiclone.'

'Thanks for doing this, Karima, off the record, so to speak.' I pull on my trousers as Dan gives me a thumbs up through the glass.

'Anything for the Prof. You'd have been on a six-month NHS waiting list if Daniel hadn't worked his magic. Mum's the word.' She taps a forefinger to her nose. Another perk of Daniel's position is having access through the back door. The thought of cheating the system appals me; I'm not that person. But I just did it, so I guess I am.

I fix a smile on my face and try to anchor myself to who I am. I am Sarah Collier: fun mum, award-winning scientist, dedicated daughter, awesome wife. As the facts start to fall into place, the smile begins to feel more natural, and I make my way out of the room towards the open arms of my husband. I know how this story goes; we've been here before, after all. But perhaps this time things will be different. Maybe it won't be as bad as we think; maybe the results of the scan will be a reason for hope.

Anyway, I'd rather know the truth than be kept in the dark.

CHAPTER 2

DANIEL

Gazing down from the dizzying heights of my office on the seventh floor of the London College of Neurology, I can see Great Ormond Street Hospital. Several stressed-looking parents are hanging around down there on the street. My fingers clutch the edges of the window frame, which has been painted closed – it's a long way down.

Dr Karima Falka sticks her head around the door to my office; her assistant has been on babysitting duty while Sarah was having her scan.

'Maddie's asking about Pizza Friday. Hut or Express?'

'I think we'll let Mum decide, seeing as she's had a day of it.'

I wink at Karima. She's a good egg, discreet.

'Mads? Come on, sweetheart, get your things. Mum's finished with her test.'

My cheeky little imp bounces around the corner with her Minions backpack strapped to her front, chewing something that has made her lips blue.

'Sarah's just putting her face back on, and I'll get to work processing the test results.' Karima retreats into her office.

'Daddy, where's Barbie?'

'Oh, I think she's manning the phones.' Her favourite doll is slumped on my desk, stiff and vacant. Her hair has been hacked into an asymmetric mess; she looks dishevelled and unhinged. She's grabbed by the foot and stuffed headfirst into Minion World.

Sarah comes out of the bathroom looking a bit more put together than poor Barbie, but I can see her smile is fixed, not quite reaching her eyes. I know when Sarah is putting on a brave face.

'I'm guessing Domino's . . . with extra breadsticks?' It's called comfort food for a reason.

She nods, exhales and cracks a smile. 'We're going to need a vat of wine too.'

On the way home, as the swish of Crossrail accelerates along the back gardens of Chiswick, a wave of nostalgia hits me: our evening walks across Turnham Green for a pint at the Tabard. Golden days, the long summers that turned into autumn. Where did those years go? When you are in your twenties, life feels like it will stay just as it is, with everything in front of you. Then you have a kid and bills to pay, and the treadmill of life begins. The fading evening sunlight turns the sky orange over Windsor; the ancient majestic silhouette of the castle looms in the mist rising off the Great Park. There is melancholy in that changing light, which is interrupted by Maddie singing 'Piece of Me' by Britney Spears, blue mouth wide open, belting out the lyrics. Her dance teacher told her the song is about a doll whose arms are detachable. Maddie makes little funky robot moves and belts out a lyric about resorting to havoc and settling in court. Sarah catches my eye again, and we both burst out laughing. This is where we still live, in these moments, nothing spoken, just a recognition of the funny things in life, the contortions and the whimsy. Maddie is our soul, our heart and our joy. We have laughed so much since she came into our lives because this little angel – well, sometimes she's a little devil – is everything to us.

'Pizza Friday' means eating on the couch with an old movie, socks off, legs in a tangle and pillows from the bedroom making a squishy nest. Maddie and I decide to let Mum choose the film and the pizza. So, extra pepperoni and *To Catch a Thief* it is.

I worried Maddie wouldn't be into an old Hitchcock, but Cary Grant captivates her from the very beginning up to about ten minutes in: longer than I thought. After a few minutes fidgeting, she wants to go up to her room and read, so I give her a piggy-back up the stairs and pop her in the shower. I come back down after she's all tucked up with her favourite book.

'Right, she's promised lights out after she's finished the next chapter.' I throw myself back down on the sofa next to Sarah.

'She's such a bookworm.'

Sarah smiles up at me, and it hits me: she looks worn out. Her once shining auburn hair is shot through with grey. Her face is lined, and she looks exhausted. It's not surprising, everything considered, but it's still a bit of a shock. She used to be one of the most magnificent people I'd ever met, and she still is in lots of ways, but her light is fading, and I'm here to bear witness. I kiss the top of her head.

'Glass of wine?'

Her eyes light up at the offer. Someone forgot to go to the supermarket, so we got a bottle from the pizza place. It wasn't cold, so I shoved it in the freezer. As I reach up into the cupboard to retrieve the glasses, I catch a glimpse of my reflection in the darkness of the kitchen window. A paunch has started to form round my middle, and my beard is looking scruffy. I hold my hand to my jowls and prop them up. I just need to smile more, that's my problem.

I return to the lounge with a determined grin on my face and hand Sarah her drink. I take a long draught of the cheap Pinot Grigio and wince at the vinegar taste.

'Ah well, the second glass is always better.'

A snort of laughter from Sarah, the light briefly illuminated.

'My dad used to put Canderel tablets in his crappy wine.'

'Course he did.' I chuckle and pull her in closer to me. Then I decide to dive in. We've ignored the elephant in the room long enough. 'So, how are you feeling?'

She sighs and snuggles into the nook of my arm. 'Hmmm . . . You know, been better, but at least we'll get some answers now. I really haven't been myself lately.'

'No, you haven't.'

'Yeah. Be honest with me, how have I been?'

'Just different. Less together, less sure. It's not just the forgetfulness; it's something else. You were the most dynamic and decisive person I knew. You seem a bit . . . lost.'

'I feel lost. It's not like I don't have a purpose. People need me: Maddie, Dad. But I've lost all my confidence. Why is that?'

'Well, from where I'm standing, you gave up your job to take care of everyone else, and that job was your life. It gave you confidence and drive, and now it's gone.'

She snuggles in tighter, and I grip her like a child. I have to say I feel pity for her, and it strikes me that pity is not an attractive emotion to feel for your partner. The road of dwindling respect ends in the cul-de-sac of pity.

'So, what are we going to do about it?'

'I don't know, Dan.'

'Well, I do. Professor Sarah Collier is not someone who gives up this easily. You need to get out there again and have a bloody adventure, love.'

She stiffens under my arm. 'Oh, here we go. This isn't about Geneva again, is it?'

'Look, just hear me out. I had another phone call from them this morning. Schiller are ready to bite your hand off for an endorsement.'

14

'Oh Dan, they just want to be able to use the word "Nobel" in a press release.'

'And who can blame them? I don't see what the problem is. A five-star, all-expenses-paid trip to Geneva to attend their conference and push forward some genuinely groundbreaking technology. What they're developing over there is going to change the world. It's the future, and we could be a part of that. And I'd love to show you the Schiller Institute; it blows me away every time I visit.'

'Why don't you go? Enjoy yourself. Go and do whatever it is you do over there.'

I pause. 'They want you, not me.' It's uncomfortable to admit that.

'Forget it, Daniel. I can't go waltzing off to Switzerland and leave Dad in the state he's in, can I?'

'It's not like he has a clue who you are when you visit anyway.'

Shit, I immediately wish I could retract that.

'Daniel, you really can be a complete cock sometimes, you know that?' She starts to get up to leave, but I grab her hand.

'Only sometimes? I'm doing better than I thought then. Sorry, love. It could be a really fun weekend, and God knows we need to let our hair down after the last few years. Mess around on the ski slopes and stuff our faces with cheese fondue, what's not to like?'

'It's a medical conference, Daniel. I think there's a limit to how much fun it would be.'

'I'm serious. It would be good for us. Good for me. It would be a great opportunity for me to network with the world's best.' In an instant, her eyes darken and her brow furrows, like a cloud has passed over her face.

'Oh right, I get it. This is your big moment, but you still somehow need me to make it happen for you?'

Wow. That comment stings like a whip.

'No, you're right. It's not my moment.'

'I'm tired.' She finishes my thoughts; we are so in sync. I nod and stroke a strand of hair from her face.

'Won't you even think about it?'

'Just leave it, Dan.' She puts her glass on the coffee table and creaks her body up off the sofa. 'I'm going to bed.'

I'm losing her. 'Don't be like this. I'm sorry. Look, I just wanted us to go away for a weekend and have a bit of fun, that's all. Come on, sit down—'

'No, Dan. I've had a shit day, and now you're making it worse. I'm knackered and I want to sleep, not listen to you going on and on like a spoilt kid who isn't getting his way.' Her voice is raised; the outburst is out of proportion. She sways a little from the wine and slumps back onto the couch.

'Here, come on. Let's get you up to bed.'

'I'm not an INVALID!' Her fury strikes me like a punch in the face. The word 'invalid' hangs in the air between us, and I feel like we're both thinking the same thing: 'Not yet.'

She heads for the stairs in silence. I watch her leave and then go back into the kitchen to rinse my glass. As I stand at the sink, head spinning, wondering what we're doing, I return to the reflection in the kitchen window. I look like shit. There's a painting that has always stuck in my mind: *Nebuchadnezzar* by William Blake. It depicts a great ruler who lost his sanity and was reduced to a kind of animal madness, crawling on his hands and knees, eyes bloodshot and haunted. It might be the drink and the stress of dealing with Sarah, but I see those same eyes staring right back at me now. I have the same look in my eyes, but I pray my destiny will be different. I am mid-descent, but whether I rise again or fall is yet to be seen.

CHAPTER 3
THE LANDAU REPORT

TEN MILLION FOLLOWERS –
WE COULDN'T HAVE DONE IT WITHOUT YOU

Wow! When I began writing for my local rag, *The Hamilton Gazette*, I would never have dreamed that one day I'd have such a massive audience of my own. Back then, I was a mom and housewife, regularly contributing to the paper about the progress of my darling daughter, who had been diagnosed with autism. I was determined to do everything I could to help her and find out answers from the medical community. A year later, after my marriage broke down, I felt like I had nowhere left to turn, and I started this blog to bring you the truth about the healthcare and pharmaceutical industry. I have always been so grateful for those early days; that's when this community became a family. For those of you who have stayed with me blogging away for the last couple of years, you will be excited to learn that this little Torontonian 'engine who could' has just hit ten million followers.

I have never hidden who I am, and at times, I've paid a high price for that. I don't write under a pseudonym. I am who I say I am. My head is well and truly above the parapet, ready to be lopped off by big pharmaceutical companies for what I have to say about them. I don't wrap my views in fancy talk or big words; I'm one of you. I say it how it is, in simple terms so we can all understand what's going on and what the medical community don't want you to know.

So, What the F . . . Is Going On?

You may remember from the last entry that I was looking into a well-known pharmaceutical company who had price-hiked one of their controversial products: Allergapen. It just so happens that this same pharma giant produces an oil-like cleaning fluid made from nuts, used to sterilize and clean hospital equipment, STILL IN USE in Canada. This cleaning fluid has been proven to cause extreme nut allergies in infants, and where better than a hospital to get access to a constant conveyor belt of newborns? The same company then goes on to sell us the Allergapen to counteract the anaphylactic immune response. Oh, and they have recently hiked the price by 400%. See anything nuts (sorry) about this conflict of interest? I sent my report to the Canadian government and am yet to receive a response, but just by speaking out, I am at risk of being sued for defamation. I'm a tiny fish in a huge ocean BUT I refuse to be crushed and am prepared to suffer the consequences. Bankrupt me, exile me, take away my family, but I will speak the truth.

Fan Girling

So, my all-time hero and woman of mystery Professor Sarah Collier is still proving hard to pin down, but my net might be closing in at long last. Through her pioneering work on the Ebola virus, Professor Collier has saved countless lives and was awarded the Nobel Prize in Physiology or Medicine in 2021. She famously shunned the ceremony, which only made her more appealing in my eyes. Anyone anti-establishment gets extra cool points from me, and those of you who follow my blog will know how much I admire this kick-ass woman. I have pestered, gushed and fawned rather too much for her to consider me legit. The chances of that are as likely as me regaining my revoked Canadian citizenship and being reunited with the daughter who was stolen from me. NOT HAPPENING ANY TIME SOON. But I'm just a girl who can't take no for an answer. I'm pushy. I'm like a dog with a bone, and this bone needs picking.

I have those feelers out to Professor Collier because I'm just desperate to get the inside scoop into such an incredible mind. And I may just be in luck because rumour has it, she's attending the much-publicized Schiller Conference in Geneva, a place where yours truly will be on the ground, giving you all the latest information from the titans of the Swiss medical community. Word is, the Schiller Institute are looking to announce something MIND-BLOWING (quite literally), and I intend to be on the front line, cutting through the crap and giving it to you straight. I am excited to see behind the curtain and investigate the inner workings of the Schiller Institute, and if I can snatch an interview with my press-shy idol, it would be the sweetest cherry on top. I promise I will not let my followers down. And you should know by now, I always keep my promises.

Check out *Landauleaks.com* in the coming days.

I'll keep you posted.

Terri Landau

CHAPTER 4

The road from Montreux into the canton of Vaud tapers from autobahn to narrow mountain road. The ascent makes the heart race; the thrilling climb into thinner, clearer air that will eventually come to a dead stop at the summit. The descent, by contrast, delivers that sinking feeling in the pit of the stomach. A literal comedown from an addictive high. Nestled halfway up the mountain road, about a mile before Château d'Oex, an un-signposted turn-off winds tight around the side of a sheer drop. Cut off from the world through a narrow tunnel carved into the mountain, the single-track road emerges and climbs towards two enormous grey pillars framing a solid steel gate. The Schiller Institute is a place of utmost secrecy. Behind the pristine steel, a snow-laden driveway leads down to a white structure half buried in the rock face. A seamless sweep of rendered outer wall encases a mirrored glass hexagon, which reflects the landscape, making it virtually disappear from all angles. A hidden crystal kingdom bursting with dreams and ideas and heralding the future.

Looking out across his frozen dominion, Professor Mauritz Schiller manoeuvres his Meyra Orbit wheelchair a little closer to the wall of glass so he can watch the black SUV pull into the driveway. He watches the car door open and sees the familiar figure of Helen Alder step out. Mauritz is fascinated by Helen. Her stride is confident, like an athlete at the top of their game. As she exits the vehicle, her eyes glance up at him over the fur collar of

her knee-length designer puffer coat, and he smiles in acknowledgement.

For the last few years, Helen's aggressive approach to public
relations has kept the Schiller Institute in the spotlight. Mauritz's
family business has overreached itself in recent times, funding too
many failed projects to count. Always attempting to be on the
cutting edge but often meandering down pathways that dropped
off a precipice. The result is that the deep pockets of the Schiller
Institute are slowly being emptied; and reaching the bottom is not
an option.

As Helen enters the foyer, she looks across to Mauritz through
the infinite panes of honeycomb glass. The Schiller Institute is
a place of absolute transparency: everyone on show, nothing to
hide. Helen has learned to take poker-faced phone calls and con-
verse like a ventriloquist. She is a solo player; she likes to keep her
cards close to her chest – tricky when there is always an observer
looking over your shoulder. It is new territory for Mauritz Schiller,
who is universally admired and obeyed, but not by Helen. Enter-
ing through the main door, Helen turns expressionless towards
Jan Pager, the security guard on the desk, knowing her image is
being recorded for posterity. Her face is scanned, and the bulletproof glass security door grants her entry.

'Well?' Mauritz asks from the doorway of his office, the general
requesting news from the front line.

'We almost have her.' She throws the words back over her
shoulder as she strides past him down the corridor towards her
office, shrugging off her coat as she goes. He accelerates in step
with her.

'Excellent. How can we secure it?'

'She's a tough nut to crack, but it will be worth all the effort. I'm
getting close, particularly now her husband's on board. Dangle

something shiny in front of Daniel Collier and he swoops like a magpie to grab it.'

'I need to know if we have *her*. I can't afford another humiliation. You know the logistics of getting all these high-profile people together; their diaries alone are planned years in advance.'

They reach Helen's office, a chaos of paperwork, Post-it notes and tech strewn across her glass desk. Helen falls back into a chair and removes her snow-encrusted Prada hiking boots. She ties her shoulder-length blonde hair into a ponytail, then pulls herself up to her desk and turns her attention to her computer screen.

'Mauritz, relax, I told you I will get her, but it's delicate.' Her tone is dismissive, and underneath his neatly trimmed beard, his chin juts forward in irritation.

'Sarah Collier was *your* idea, Helen; we have designed the whole event around the endorsement of a single celebrity of the science world and she's not even a neurologist. We could have had any number of high-profile scientists, but you wanted her. Why?'

'Because she can't be bought. True she's not a neurologist but she's the most famous scientist in the world right now and her endorsement of this new product will be bulletproof. It's exactly what we need. And tell me this: have I ever let you down before?' Helen raises her head from her screen, finally makes eye contact and flashes a confident smile. 'Let me deal with this my way, Mauritz.' She turns her back to him, reaching into her bag, but in the never-ending reflections of the faceted glass, he clocks her face, and on it is a look he rarely sees in the unshakeable Helen Alder. In this moment, she is unsure – he sees multiple faces of doubt.

'What is it? What's bothering you, Helen?'

She is losing patience and turns to reply, but then she pauses, her face softening as she sees the old man. In her first interactions with Mauritz, she had assumed this research was a personal quest for rehabilitation, but the more she learned about his world, the more she realised it was greater than that; he had no children, he wanted to leave something behind. He wanted the name Schiller to echo through time.

'I'll get her for you, don't worry, and she'll be as amazed by what you've achieved as we all are.'

Over the top of Mauritz's head, out of the corner of her eye, Helen sees something move. A quick flash in the corridor behind one of the pillars of concrete. She fixes her eyes on the spot, a couple of metres from her open office door. Her mind races.

'Just make sure you do, Helen. If this falls through, then the future of the Institute hangs in the balance.'

Her attention returns to the pillar, and her suspicions are confirmed. It is the white hair of someone hiding, someone listening. She knows exactly who it is. Someone she has not allowed herself to trust – and her instincts have been proven right. She decides to end the conversation before any sensitive information is shared.

'I am doing everything I can, Mauritz.' She picks up her phone and starts to scroll through texts. 'I have a few calls to make. May I?'

She smiles again and this time makes a special effort for it to reach her eyes.

'Helen, I'm trusting you with this. It's in your hands. Don't drop the ball.'

Mauritz is satisfied for the time being. He turns his chair on a dime, a silent pirouette, and sails towards his office to resume his position at the helm of the Institute. She watches him glide away down the corridor, and then her eyes snap back to the concrete pillar. The eavesdropper has gone. Helen looks down at her left hand. Blood is running down the side of her thumb where she has torn the skin with her forefinger. She puts it to her lips, tasting the iron tang and hardening her determination.

CHAPTER 5

SARAH

I enter Hartford Gardens through reception and give a friendly nod to Hassan manning the desk. He buzzes me in through the security door, and the smell of disinfectant smacks me in the face. I have a set of keys to Dad's door and let myself into apartment number six.

'Dad? It's me; it's Sarah.' There's no reply, but I can hear his beloved Classic FM playing in the other room. My entrance seems to have been timed perfectly to the Darth Vader death march from *Star Wars* – rude!

I got Dad an Alexa for Christmas and signed him up to a subscription service so he can just ask for whatever music he wants. The interesting thing is, I can log on to see what conversations he's been having with Alexa. He asks for the day and date a lot. 'Alexa play the Beach Boys' made me smile, and 'Lady in Red' goes without saying, but then 'Who's Sarah?' has popped up a few times. It's funny seeing it in writing, repeatedly. 'Alexa, who's Sarah?' Alexa has tried hard to answer that question for him. Various Sarahs have been suggested, but 'Time to Say Goodbye' by Sarah Brightman has scored highest: prophetic and slightly chilling. I decided a few weeks ago that answering the question 'Who's Sarah?' was my responsibility. Who Sarah is will be determined by me. I will remind my father of who I am, and if I can't pull up the old memories, then at least we can make some new ones.

'Dad? It's Sarah.' (I'll damn well keep saying my name.) Dropping my bag on the kitchen worktop, I put the goodies that I picked up at M&S into the fridge. 'I brought you some treats. Want a cup of tea?' Still no answer. I look out into the small patio garden. The afternoon is darkening, and the post-Bonfire-Night damp is already descending, leaving condensation on the glass. I can see the LED string lights that I set up around the fence, flickering in the dusk like tiny suspended fireflies. My dad is standing in the garden with a bamboo support cane from one of the plants in his hand. His arms glide elegantly up and down, side to side, his head and body moving in perfect synchronicity with the music. He's conducting the orchestra.

I stand and watch for a while, mesmerised. He seems to know every nuance of this score, and it's beautiful to watch. His wisp of grey hair and the beard he decided to grow have given him a God-like appearance. My dad was once a big man, a strong, reliable, sturdy father. He has shrunk, but watching him move his bamboo baton makes him look powerful, almost ethereal. Maybe he *does* have a glimmer of the Almighty. I leave him to his work with the orchestra, and I put the kettle on, eyeing him through the glass, the suspended solar fireflies like audience members with flickering torches in the distance. I change my mind, open the fridge and find a half-drunk bottle of Chablis: that's more like it. As the music comes to an end, I slide out into the garden and put a glass of wine into my dad's hand as I kiss his cheek. His crystal-blue eyes, always his most striking feature, gaze at me in the twilight.

'Alright, petal?'

We sip our wine and smile at each other. I put my arms around him and lay my head on his shoulder, and we sway together in a half embrace to the Brahms waltz that's now playing. He still smells like Dad. The smell of my parents' skin is a first memory for me. I can still smell Mum's peach-soft cheek: powder, bread and warm malted milk. Dad's cheek always smelt of leather car seats, cigarettes and toffee. I'm smelling a memory, triggered by his bristly face. It's Proustian in every possible way.

'There's a chill.'

I look down and see Dad has no trousers on and is barefoot. I didn't notice before, but he's only wearing a long shirt and his boxer shorts, and his feet are dirty, as if he's wandered through the flower bed.

'Come on, let's get you inside.'

I settle him into his chair and pop a blanket over his legs. Then I fetch a bowl of warm water from the kitchen to soak his muddy feet, and we finish our wine together. I can see his dinner plate on the side, half finished. Good: he's eaten.

'How's your week been then, love? You must be knackered, on your feet all day.'

'No, Dad, I'm not at the lab any more. I'm home with Maddie and Dan most of the time now.'

'What lab?'

'I'm not at the laboratory any more. I've retired from Oxford University.'

Dad stares at me, his electric eyes glistening and waterlogged. 'I meant at the shop. You work your arse off, you do. You should ask for a raise.'

That's when I realise: he thinks I'm Mum. It chokes me because his deep longing for her makes *me* miss her equally; grief is infectious like that. His eyes flick up to the kitchen door, half expecting Mum to pop her head around to ask if he wants a biscuit. Perhaps he really sees her; memories are powerful. I do look like her, and Mum really did work her arse off. She ended up having to retire early, forfeiting the pension but retaining some dignity and energy to relax a bit before the arthritis kicked in and crippled her. I hold his hand and smile.

'I miss her too, Dad, every day.'

'She's just popped to the shop. Will you wait for her to get back before you go? She'd love to see you.'

'Course I will.'

We sit there as the music takes a pause.

'How's Daniel, Sarah? You two doing OK? It's not easy, is it?'

BOOM. Just like that, as if someone walked in and switched on the overhead light, blinding and awakening. He's staring directly at me; he's focused and coherent. I'm grabbing this moment with both hands.

'He's OK, but I think he needs a break. He's been working hard recently, especially now he's the only one bringing money in. And I was really unkind to him yesterday; I think I'm pushing him away.' I shock myself with my honesty. I haven't allowed myself to admit it before. But it's true, I'm pushing him away from the hurt and the pain and the mess that my life is becoming.

'You know, I had a lot of stress in my job, which took its toll on me and your mum. She was a saint though, always knew how to calm me down, what to say, what to do.'

Dad looks at me with his kind eyes, the face creased and worn. A man whose life is truly etched into his skin like a map of his whole existence. 'Don't throw it away, all the years, all the memories. We behave like animals sometimes, but the loneliness isn't worth it.'

'Dad?'

'I wasn't the model husband, and your mum and me nearly didn't make it, but she had a spine of steel, that woman. She knew everything. Even at the end, she made sure it was all OK.'

I stare into my father's eyes; it's as if there is a whole universe in there. Then, a silent, imperceptible change, as if something just shifted with the effort of hauling up that heavy lucid memory of

Mum. A dark flood washes away the past; back now in the present. Only the present.

'Anyway, she'll be back soon. Don't mention what I just said, or she'll be all upset again.'

I hesitate for a second. And then I whisper, 'OK Dad, I won't say anything.'

I kneel to wash the mud from his feet. Then I dry them with a towel and put his slippers on. 'Want me to tuck you in?' I look up, and he's nodded off, so I recline the chair and pull the blanket over him. I tiptoe to the kitchen to get my bag, flick off the main light and look back at my dad, snoring. As I close the door to his flat, I glance down the hall. A 'lady in red' is standing there, looking back at me. Mum looks like she's just had her hair done the way Dad likes it. She smiles at me. I want to walk over to her and give her a hug, but I can't. I don't have time. I have to pick up Maddie from school.

As I exit through reception, Hassan asks me if Dad's OK, if he needs anything. I'm almost floating as I walk. 'No thanks, he's fine. He's asleep in the chair, but Mum will get him into bed.'

Hassan looks at me, confused. It takes me a moment to realise why he's looking at me like that, and then my words replay in my head. What did I just say? I laugh it off and make a swift exit to the car park. Dad's going to be fine, but I'm becoming less and less sure I will be.

CHAPTER 6

DANIEL

'So last time we were discussing the pioneering work of Alois Alzheimer and his discovery of microscopic brain changes in one of his patients.' The room of students in front of me stare at their screens; I have no idea if they are actually following my drift or watching dog videos on TikTok. 'Auguste Deter had been suffering from severe headaches, acute and distressing memory loss, unfounded suspicions about her family and other deteriorating psychological changes. She appeared to lose control of herself. Her short-term memory was most badly affected, and long-term memories from very early childhood took a front seat in her mind. Most distressing were her unpredictable behaviour, violent outbursts and abuse. Alzheimer saw a dramatic shrinkage of her brain and identified abnormal deposits around her nerve cells. As we still don't have a cure, or barely have a therapy other than drugs that can slow progression, understanding the brain is critical. Technology will provide the answer, and groundbreaking strides are being made to retrain the brain. But for now, what options do sufferers have?

'Contentious and controversial as the subject is, we're currently having a social awakening regarding assisted dying. Often in our field, we are faced with tough decisions. It's a terrible and fragile line we must tread because the fact is, we do have the power to end suffering, and when you see the agonising journey of some patients, the line can become blurred. But it's a complicated issue, where an abuse of power can have devastating consequences. So,

33

on that cheerful note, I'd like you all to research a list of the countries where assisted dying is either legal or is on the table for discussion. Let's have a look at the religious demographics and investigate the legal hurdles and loopholes. OK, that's it for today. Please don't just copy and paste from Google. I want your honest views and opinions . . . Let's open this up.'

There is a buzz of phones and a flurry of student energy as the mass exodus from the lecture theatre begins. Teaching this subject hasn't been all that fun recently, not that it ever was a laugh a minute. I seem to be living in a sort of maze of dementia at the moment, living it and breathing it, and whichever way I turn, all roads lead to nowhere. It's exhausting and I'm trying to keep it together, be calm and stay in control, but I have to admit, I'm struggling.

I remember the first time I saw Sarah. It was in a lecture theatre just like this. Our eyes met over a lecture on the biochemical analysis of cell structure in gene therapy. Sexy, huh? We were both students taking the same course, but out of a room of nearly two hundred, she just stood out. She always shone. Bright and brilliant. We were pulled together by some beautiful magnetic force. I wasn't stalking her, before you start throwing that one at me, but I found myself wanting to be where she was, sitting next to her in lectures, getting a drink afterwards to chew the fat. I think she felt the same. In recent years, though, it feels like trying to hold the wrong ends of two magnets together. As though the poles have reversed.

I flick off the light to the lecture theatre and realise I'm dreading going home. Last night's argument has left me feeling like shit, and I slipped out this morning without a kiss because I didn't want to upset her again.

This feeling of treading on eggshells around Sarah is familiar. It reminds me of the day she got the phone call from Nobel. She hid away in the bedroom to hear the news, but then she just didn't want to celebrate with me. My phone was exploding with messages of congratulations all through the next day, but she kept me at arm's length. I wanted to be part of her success because I felt that I was. You see, we were sounding boards for each other. I never understood why we didn't celebrate together. If I'm honest with myself, I did want to bathe in her glory a little. I'm good at what I do but not great. No matter how hard I work, I will never achieve the genius of my wife. But I have accepted that there are some people in the world that are naturally brilliant; I'm not one of them, and Sarah is. Maybe that was what I saw back then, maybe that was the magnet. But is love enough to keep a couple like us together when one flies high and the other is flapping like crazy to keep up?

The November chill wind whips my face as I step outside onto the street. I pull up my collar and cut through Queen Anne's Walk towards Russell Square Tube station. I hate the rush hour and suddenly miss my motorbike, which has been banished to the garage until the weather improves. As I push through the endless stream of commuters, I pass by the glowing thrum of the Friend at Hand, laughter spilling out from the open door. Half my department are crushed inside. I see Karima Falka at the bar; she catches my eye and waves, gesturing 'Fancy a pint?' I shouldn't really; I should get back to Sarah. But the 'friend at hand' gets the better of me. Go on then, just one. One for the road.

One turns into three, and when I get home the house is in darkness as I slide the key into the lock. A faint glow from a lamp in the kitchen and the silhouette sitting upright in the wing chair in the living room tell me she's lying in wait. I kick off my boots and sling my jacket on the banister, ready to face the music.

'Sorry I'm late. I had to . . . go to a meeting . . . Bit of an emergency. How was your day?' I speak in hushed tones, trying not to slur.

'It's late.' She's not sober either.

I must look like absolute crap, and I can't face Sarah when she's drunk. 'I'm going to jump in the shower and then . . . uh . . . head to bed.'

Her eyes are glazed and sad. I stop.

'You OK?' Her eyes come back into the room and focus on me.

'Not really. I'm losing control of everything. I can't find my dad any more, you're . . . wherever you are.'

'I'm right here, Sarah.'

'I don't want to be like this any more.'

'I know, love.' I come towards her and my eyes drift over to the coffee table. A pile of papers sits beside an empty bottle of wine and a lonely glass. The top sheet reads, 'The Schiller Institute: New Advancements in Neurology and Brain Disorder'. She's reading the material for the Geneva conference. Maybe there is a chance.

'Bit of late-night reading, anything good?' I know it's manipulative, but I have to try.

She looks at it. There is vacant confusion in her eyes, possibly the wine.

'Have you read this, Daniel?'

'Of course. I think this might be one breakthrough that changes everything. What do you think?'

'I think . . . in theory you may be right?'

'And?'

She rocks back in her chair and exhales.

'It's too late for Dad. I think somehow he's actually at peace in his oblivion, and Mum's there to keep him company.'

'Mum? Your mum?'

She sips her wine and swallows carefully.

'Yeah, he thinks she's there with him, which is fine by me.'

'What nature takes with one hand, it gives back with the other, I guess.' I don't really believe that, but I say it anyway because it sounds comforting.

'But science can intervene and perfect. We've always believed that, haven't we?' I smile; this is the Sarah I love. I know all she needs is a new story, a new focus of inspiration.

'It's different for you, love. You've already made your mark, but for me, I just want to be part of a success story, so I can look back on my life and be proud of something I did, know that I made a difference.'

'Oh sweetheart, you do make a difference, every single day, with your students, with Maddie . . .'

'We don't have to go to Geneva. I can figure out a way to politely decline.' I turn and walk towards the stairs. It's over. I'm deflated but that's how it has to be. My shoulders sag as I reach the bottom of the stairs.

'I would need to know more about the ethical implications and what Schiller intends to do with the patents and the marketing.'

I turn to her; a faint smile is forming across her lips.

'That's doable.' Dare I hope?

'From what I've read so far, this product could be a lifeline, but it could also be a terrifying Pandora's box if it fell into the wrong hands before it was fully trialled. We've seen that happen so many times before. Both of our reputations are at stake, Daniel.'

'Yes . . . but you're . . . seriously considering it?'

'I'll do this for you, Daniel.'

The blood leaves my head and my heart triples its beat.

'Really?

'Yes, really.'

I'm held in a moment of suspension. I can't believe it; this is happening. Oh my God. It's happening. We're doing this.

'You . . . are amazing.' I step towards her and kiss her on the lips. 'Thank you. You'll be so impressed with the Institute itself; I've never seen anything like it. The building alone is breathtaking.' I stop myself; I'm gushing.

'But babe, if I end up in all the boring conference lectures while you're skiing around the mountain having the time of your life . . . because I know you. I will *kill* you.'

'Listen to me, they will treat you like a queen, like a bloody movie star, and I will make sure of it.' My mind is racing now; I can hardly wait to pick up the phone and get the ball rolling. 'So, what do you want in your contract rider then? Iced grapes? Puppies and kittens to stroke?' She starts to laugh.

'Um . . . a hot Swiss masseur before breakfast?' I jump on the couch next to her.

'Oh, right, well in that case . . . a box of Cuban cigars and a bottle of Lagavulin in the hotel room.'

'Private jet?'

'Julie Andrews singing "doe a deer" on your balcony?'

She explodes into a belly laugh that ripples like a peal of bells. A sound that I haven't heard for a very long time.

'Shit for brains, that's Austria.'

We finish the bottle and head up to bed. My wife is amazing. There is something in her that can bend to the point of breaking, but it never does. I see her testing that strength every day.

I lie awake with Sarah nestled into my shoulder, stroking her hair and the skin on the back of her neck.

The wheels are in motion now and there is no turning back.

CHAPTER 7

THE LANDAU REPORT

GOTCHA!

OK. So, I know I'm persistent and annoying and sometimes underhand. Yes! I hold my hands up and admit I'll go to *any* lengths to get what I need. But I know you'll forgive me because this one is BIG.

The media have been speculating for months about what Schiller are launching at their conference in Geneva, but I have a person on the inside, so this information is first-hand. I haven't seen the research documents or the data to support this claim yet, but it's coming, and believe me when I say THIS IS RADICAL. This is the kind of technology that makes you look at the calendar to check you haven't woken up in a different century.

My loyal and faithful followers, you are going to need to sit down for this one. Isn't that what people say when there is a bereavement? Well, this is a kind of death. The death of our freedom, a complete immersion into data collection and control. And when I say 'control', I'm not joking. If medical passports to travel and proof of health documents to get into restaurants haven't shaken you awake, then this is going to be like a cattle prod in the ass.

Brain Implants

This is the most controversial piece of biotech ever invented, but it's here. Do you remember in the nineties when people said they would never get a cell phone? And now those same people have a PC, a tablet, a smartwatch, doorbell cameras and dog trackers. We succumbed without even realizing. We bought everything, we upgraded, and now we can't imagine even a single day without our technology. So maybe we deserve this. *This* is the thing you never thought would happen:

NEUROCELL

The Schiller Institute's neural implant.

Remember the word and look out for it. It will be all over the media soon, but remember you heard it here first and stay tuned to *Landauleaks.com* over the coming week as I report directly from the Schiller Conference.

THE FUTURE HAS ARRIVED.

Terri Landau

CHAPTER 8

The chipboard hoardings covering the broken windows along the Rue Gustave-Ador are long gone. Prada, Gucci, Louis Vuitton, all the luxury watchmakers, curated boutiques and private members' clubs are open for business. Geneva has undoubtably bounced back from the severe economic decline of the last two years. Seasonal skiers and summer hikers have kept the region on the map for tourism, but the affluence of the city has relied heavily on the pharmaceutical industry. Research and development institutes have been spreading out from the great cities of Bern and Zurich to Geneva, with biotech reshaping and redefining this once quaint *fin de siècle* town. And the cutting edge of Geneva's blade is sharpened by the Schiller Institute.

The icy water of Lake Geneva shimmers in the glare of the low sun as a lone figure strides over the Pont du Mont-Blanc towards the Cologny side of the lake. From across the water, the gleaming steel and glass structure of the Campus Biotech looms behind the Gothic church spires and neoclassical hotels, a lantern attracting students of science and the world's innovators like frenzied moths. This will be the hub of the forthcoming Schiller Conference.

The roads are largely empty at this time of day, except for the odd Porsche Cayenne hybrid and self-driving electric SUV gliding silently through the slush, carrying passengers out to their luxury lakeside villas. The sub-zero season has caused the lake to freeze, and ice sheets float on the water, cracking as they lap at the edge. Past the Ferris wheel of the Jardin anglais, the walker takes the embankment below the line of the road, staying out of sight. The snow-blanketed summer beaches of Geneva under the sparse shadows of bare trees are deserted, apart from a solitary dog walker. The figure stops momentarily, close to a children's playground. The wind picks up and catches a roundabout, pushing it into motion with an eerie whistle. Childless, the empty plastic seats spin like a phantom carousel. The swings seem to murmur in the wind, wanting to play. Echoes of warmer days, yet now their chains are restrained by the ice. Come spring, the ice will thaw and the children will return.

Onwards towards the Parc La Grange and through a small stone gate. Off the beaten track now and into a dense cluster of snow-laden evergreens. The ground rises towards a large neoclassical house, closed for the winter. The walker takes a sharp right towards a small inconspicuous black pine cabin at the side of the house, resembling a Swiss chalet, perfectly proportioned but in miniature. A faded sign painted into the woodwork reads 'La Guinguette', a beer garden and snack bar for summer tourists but now dilapidated and shuttered for the winter. A key opens a padlock; the weathered split stable door creaks open on rusty hinges. The walker checks over their shoulder to see if they are being watched, then enters, bolting the door behind them.

The gas canister of a portable heater is triggered and primed until it licks into a blue pilot flame and an orange radiant heat begins to glow. Removing gloves, the walker's fingertips are thawed. A small silver hip flask is pulled out and the burn of liquor slides down the throat, the tingle of almonds reviving and restoring. Switching on a lamp over a desk crammed with computers, cabling and a portable satellite receiver, the whole room flickers into life.

On a desktop, a large LED screen shows the multiple boxes of a surveillance program, a complex security system. But it's not for this place. Not for the quaint little Hansel-and-Gretel cabin in the woods, nothing to see here. The images on the screen are of corridors, an office, security gates and rooms made of glass. A red pack of Du Maurier Extra Lights on the desk proves too much of a temptation. A cigarette is withdrawn, lit and a single deep drag is taken.

Through a haze of exhaled tobacco smoke, a face emerges on the computer screen, a woman with shoulder-length auburn hair going grey at the roots. Her gaze is probing and direct, yet there is the slightest hint of pity in those tired eyes, as if she knows something profound but is biting back the temptation to tell. The headline above the face reads:

'Professor Sarah Collier: Genius, Pioneer, Recluse. The Woman Who Shunned Nobel.'

The realisation of what the next four days will have in store really starts to hit home. It's finally happening. It's everything they have worked for. A chance to change the course of their future.

CHAPTER 9

DANIEL

The empty carousel moves at a snail's pace, weaving its way around the airport arrivals hall, delivering the sum total of nothing to the frustrated passengers from flight BA116 from London Heathrow. My agitated fingers tap the handle of the luggage trolley, my patience is at boiling point. We should have demanded that private jet in the contract after all. We did insist on a point person to pick us up, and if they aren't waiting on the other side of the sliding doors when we finally emerge, I'm going to flip my lid. Listen to me, suddenly turning into a diva. But I'm nervous. This whole trip is because of me, and if it doesn't go to plan, then I'm . . . Well, I daren't think about that. I'm on the verge of climbing up onto the conveyor belt to search for the luggage myself when finally the first bag descends the ramp and everyone applauds.

Sarah strolls back from the toilet. She had a bit of a wobble on the plane; woke up disorientated and panicked because she didn't know where she was or who I was. I managed to calm her down and get her off the plane without too much fuss though. I suppose now this is our cross to bear. But she looks to be herself again as she bounces out of the bathroom and clocks my impatience with a comic roll of the eyes. I hate waiting.

'Alright there, Twitchy?'

I crack a smile. 'I'll be fine in a minute. Honestly though, where the hell are our bags? I mean, sod yours, but mine has all my ski gear in it.' She punches me in the arm.

'Relax, they'll come round soon. Fancy a coffee?' She glances over to a dancing robot next to a sign reading 'Montreux Jazz Café' and laughs. 'Actually, scratch that, I don't want to make you even more jittery.'

'THERE'S YOURS!' I'm embarrassed at my own loud out-burst. Who gets this excited about luggage? Sarah's black Tumi with a red and white striped elastic strap emerges from the hatch and is quickly followed by my black North Face holdall and boot bag. I haul our cases off, sling them onto the trolley and head for the exit doors.

'And . . . breathe.' Her tone is patronising, but I know I deserve it, so I let her off.

As we emerge from the tinted yellow glass doors of arrivals, there is a flutter of camera shutters and flashbulbs from a bank of photographers. I'm looking behind me to see who else is arriving, expecting Harry Styles or some K-pop star to be trailing in our wake. Then I realise, it's Sarah they are here for. Holy crap. For some reason, I dip my head and fall back behind her. As we follow the illuminated red line leading us across the shining faux-marble floor of airport arrivals, the hum of French and German voices builds around us and welcomes us to Geneva. I know she is hating this, but she smiles and tries to move forward, looking for an exit.

I spot a tall man with white hair standing dead still in a sea of frenetic travellers. He's about my age, smartly dressed in black, a polo neck and ski jacket, sunglasses and an expressionless mouth below his sharp crew cut. He holds an iPad displaying a white screen and the words 'S. Collier'. I guess they're not picking me up then, just her. Well, she is the guest of honour, I suppose.

I pull on Sarah's arm, guiding her towards the white-haired man. I nod an acknowledgement that we are indeed 'S. Collier', and he moves along the barrier to meet us. I've been to the Schiller Institute a few times in the past five years, but I've never seen this guy before. As I watch him come towards us, like the expressionless Terminator or some nightclub bouncer about to kick us off the premises, I instinctively try to make myself a bit taller and then immediately feel like an idiot. He has barely glanced at me and instead is totally focused on my wife.

'Professor Collier?' The Russian accent is soft but distinctive.

'Yes.' I feel Sarah straighten slightly.

Ignoring me, he gestures to the door. 'This way please, I have a car waiting.'

He takes Sarah and leaves me to push the luggage trolley in his wake. Sarah glances over her shoulder as she puts on her sunglasses with a wink to me, imitating his stern expression, playing the movie star. I grin and hurry alongside, enjoying the role play. We follow him through the terminal, away from the crowds and towards the door of a waiting black BMW. An elegant leg sporting a designer hiking boot steps down from the passenger door. As her body follows, I see her tailored puffer jacket and a warm smile framed by tousled blonde shoulder-length hair. A leather-gloved hand reaches towards Sarah.

'Professor Collier, so good to meet you after all this time. I'm Helen Alder. And you've already met Pavel Osinov, Schiller's head of security. He'll be looking after you during your time with us. We're thrilled to welcome you to Geneva.' Her eye contact doesn't break, and her voice is deep and soft, intelligent with a gently polished American lilt. Her shining eyes flick to mine, and I can't help but look away. 'And what a pleasure to see you again, Daniel. How've ya been?'

'Just . . . so thrilled we could make it?' I'm tongue-tied, like an incoherent schoolboy.

Sarah raises an eyebrow as she takes over; she's so much better at this than I am. 'Please call me Sarah . . . Shall we?' She indicates that we should get out of the cold and into the car. For someone who hates the limelight, she's very good at this when she has to be. She's taking control, calling the shots.

Helen Alder's eyes flick to mine. 'Throw those in the trunk, Daniel.'

I push the trolley to the rear as the automatic boot opens. I inhale a lungful of fumes as Pavel Osinov fires up the engine, clocking me in the mirror. As we drive out of the airport, Helen doesn't waste a minute and launches straight in.

'So, I've printed out a full itinerary for you, but I'll just run through it briefly now. There will be a little downtime to settle into your hotel this afternoon. The spa is wonderful; we'd be more than happy to book you a massage or any other treatments. Then there's the drinks reception at Schiller tonight, where we will give a presentation of the new technology to you and a few other selected guests. Black tie, of course.' Shit, that's me going shopping then. 'Pavel will pick you up at six. Tomorrow is a full day of press interviews and then the following day, the public announcement.'

'Sorry, Helen, let me just stop you there.' Sarah's voice is cool and firm; it's a tone I remember and admire. 'I am very happy to be here, but as Daniel has already explained to you, I can't go ahead and endorse this experimental technology until I have more information.'

Helen pauses for a beat. A broad smile showcasing expensive dental work spreads over her face.

'Yes, of course. Daniel did mention that, but once you have all the facts in hand, I have no doubt you'll—'

'It was a condition of me coming here. I just want to be clear. The research paper is impressive, but I have my doubts about

48

how ethical it is, and I want to see the trial data before we go any further.'

'I completely understand, Sarah.' Helen holds her gaze, her pupils widening at the challenge from my formidable wife. She then speaks, slowly and pedantically. 'Why don't you settle into the hotel and enjoy the city, and then this evening at the drinks reception, you'll learn everything you need to know, and Professor Schiller will be able to answer any questions you may have.'

'Great.' Sarah smiles back at her, but her hand is gripping mine a little too hard. She replaces her sunglasses and settles back into her seat.

We drive through endless concrete tunnels and snow-dusted building works, heading towards Lac Genève, travelling in steady traffic towards Chambésy as the lake opens up before us. The short drive along the north side of the lake offers a passing glimpse of the illuminated Campus Biotech's shining layers of glass. But it's the promise of a warm hotel room and a shot of schnapps that I'm holding out for. There's a crackle of nervous tension in the air; I can feel the excitement rising in me. I look up to the rear-view mirror. Pavel Osinov's eyes are shielded by his sunglasses, but I could swear he is staring right at me. I acknowledge him with a nod, but his head turns back to the road and I'm left with a feeling that we're going to be under a microscope for the next few days. I realise I'm gripping the car door handle, knuckles turning as white as the frozen landscape outside.

CHAPTER 10

SARAH

L'Hôtel du Lac Royal turns out to be a rather beautiful old-school affair. A turn-of-the-century building on the bank of the lake with a glass atrium at the front festooned with Christmas lights winking at us in welcome. They couldn't have picked a more prominent venue, with the back door to the Fairmont on one side and the Beau-Rivage on the other. I exhale as I see a gathering of journalists and photographers camped out front. Helen looks over her shoulder as both Daniel and I brace ourselves for the paparazzi. That indelible smile on her face looks painted on. I recognise that the currency of my presence here is measured in column inches and front-page photographs, but I'm not fully compliant yet. I haven't removed my sunglasses, so she can't see my fear. But I match Helen's expectant smile with a gentle shake of my head. No. I won't be facing the press today. Helen's smile tightens and she indicates to Pavel to pull down a side road. She makes a call. 'Hi, we're just arriving. We'll use the rear entrance . . . Yes, I realise that . . . Just have someone open the door.' She finishes the call and turns to me.

'You're getting the Grace Kelly treatment.'

The car pulls down a small alley to a loading bay next to a chocolate-box church of perfect dimensions, dressed for Christmas. Photographers and journalists follow from around the front; who do they think is in this car, Rihanna? Daniel hops out of the car and moves around to my side. He takes my arm and we move swiftly down a small flight of stairs to where a waiter is having a cigarette break. He jumps to attention and quickly opens the service door for us. Helen leads the way along the basement corridor, sweeping us past the recycling bins and a box of fish being delivered to the kitchen. I picture Princess Grace in a crown and huge white ballgown, trailing through sloppy fish scales and potato peelings as she steps daintily into the rusty hand-cranked service elevator. Welcome to Geneva. Five floors up and through a labyrinth of dark-green and mahogany-panelled corridors, Daniel and I are finally alone behind the closed door of room 515.

I stand by the window, watching the afternoon light skimming the lake. So, we're here. I wonder what the next few days will bring. The suite is rather dazzling. Classical with flourishes of restored original features – silk, onyx and marble. Lithograph prints and antique finishes. Mint green and beige striped wallpaper, striped curtains, striped bedding – thank God the carpet isn't striped. The wall behind the head of the bed is entirely mirrored, a window into a parallel universe; I wonder what's going on in there? Through a connecting door is a small sitting room, dark-green walls with a desk and shelves full of leather-bound books. Off the bedroom there is a gleaming monochrome marble bathroom, emitting an eerie blue neon light.

'Ooh, a welcome hamper!' Dan yells from the other room. I pretend not to hear. My head is pounding and my ears are ringing. The flight has taken it out of me. I breathe deeply, wishing the bed would swallow me whole, but I'm afraid to sleep. Come on, Sarah, perk up. I notice a bottle of champagne in an ice bucket on a tray at the foot of the bed and a fruit basket accompanied by a small envelope. Inside, a smart business card; on the back, a handwritten note.

Sarah, welcome to Geneva. Anything you need, call me.
Mauritz Schiller.

Daniel appears at the door, positively vibrating with expectation. 'Come on, love, come and explore with me.'

'In a minute. I've got a headache. Why don't you go and check out this spa we've heard so much about? Anyway, I want to call Daisy's mum, check Maddie's settling in OK.'

He makes his way over to his suitcase. 'Black tie . . . I need to figure that one out.'

'Break the rules, Dan, nobody cares about all that stuff.'

These outward shows of appearance are important to him. He moves around the room, creaking the floor of the old hotel. I sit on the bed and then lay my head on the pillow. I'm tempted to close my eyes, but I try to stay awake.

'She's impressive.'

'Helen?'

'Yeah, I like her. She reminds me of myself, when I was younger. Confident and self-assured.'

'It's the American way. Exceptionalism is educated into them from the second they are conscious.'

'I know. We pale in their shadow a bit, don't we?'

'Take it from me, accepting your limitations and letting go of that inherent belief that you can change the world is liberating . . .'

'What? You giving up your dreams over there, with your pants round your ankles?'

He nearly spits out the fancy Ladurée macaron he's been chewing.

'Sod off. We can't all win prizes.' He's sulking now.

I close my eyes, massaging my temples as I wish the weariness away. I shouldn't be this tired, but my body feels heavy as lead. My blackout on the plane scared me. I can't have it happen again here, in public. Dan starts banging around: hangers clanking in the wardrobe and shoes thrown against wood. Then he starts humming.

'Dan, please.'

'What?'

'Just be a bit quieter, I'm knackered.'

I close my eyes and settle back into the bed's embrace. I drift, I don't know for how long. The darkness and silence are broken with the gentlest movement on the crisp sheets. A slither of something moving across the bed towards me. Something is coming. I jump and my eyes snap open.

'It's OK, it's just me.' Daniel is lying on the bed next to me. He's holding something: 'Your pills.' His kind, apologetic face close to mine.

'Thanks.' He kisses my head, the doctor soothing my pain. I smile, reach out and take them, genuinely grateful. I take a sip of water and swallow two of the tablets. Daniel returns to his unpacking, humming gently to himself.

'So, I was thinking, we could hit the Leopard Bar for a cocktail? They make a great Old Fashioned here.'

He has no idea. No idea how I feel. How can someone so clever be so clueless?

'You go, I'm going to stay here.'

'But we're supposed to be having fun.'

'For God's sake, Dan, I just want to rest! You go and do whatever you like but I'm not—'

The bathroom door slams before I can finish my sentence. I don't understand where these outbursts in me are coming from. It feels like nothing, but I hear my raised voice and feel the angry aftermath and can't figure out how it happened. A few minutes later, the door opens.

'Sarah.' His voice is quiet, almost cautious.

'Yes?'

He's holding his phone. 'Karima's emailed. She's sent through the scan results.'

Now I'm wide awake. Daniel sits next to me on the bed, his hand reaching to grab hold of mine. I sit up, brushing the hair from my face. My stomach is turning itself inside out. News. My fate in a simple email.

'Right. Shit. OK.'

'We don't have to look at them now if you don't want to. We could wait until we're back at home?'

'No. No. I want to know.'

He squeezes my hand. 'If you're sure?'

'I'm sure.' I try to smile but I'm sure my eyes are betraying me.

'I'm right here with you.' He looks at his phone and scrolls, the brush of a fingertip and a life in the balance. I can't breathe. I watch him reading the screen and his face tells me everything I need to know.

'Tell me.'

'Babe . . . I'm sorry, I don't think . . . It's not good news.'

He raises his phone to show me. I stare at the screen for a second. The scan shows both a frontal and a side view of my brain. There are highlights in a number of areas, like clusters of tiny red beads. I know immediately what these show. Amyloid plaques. The hallmark of Alzheimer's disease. I close my eyes, the heat map of those tiny red dots burning into my retina.

Weeks of confusion and vague dread crystallise into a cold, brutal reality. I'm speechless. Numb. Daniel is speaking, explaining the results in technical terms, but I'm not really hearing him. Then he puts his phone down and holds me in a tight grip. I feel nothing. I'm shrinking inside my own body.

'We're in this together.' I hear his distant voice. Are we? I feel miles away, untethered and alone. But he keeps holding me and somehow the feel of his skin against mine gives me the strength to claw myself back from the depths.

'Well, let's face it, it's not a massive surprise,' I say eventually. I look in his eyes and clearly see the fear. 'It will be OK, Dan. We just have to make those memories I promised you.' His eyes widen. 'I mean it, love. We'll be OK. We just have to make the most of . . . what I have left, while I'm still me. Let's stay positive. It might be a slow decline, who knows?'

He shakes his head. Then, suddenly, he bursts into heaving sobs, his whole body shaking, expelling the pain. He cries into my shoulder as I stroke his head, running my fingers through tufts of dark hair.

'Daniel . . .' His sadness subsides but his grip on me tightens. And then I realise, I'm the one comforting him. I'm the one who is ill, I'm the one who is dying. There, I've said it: I'm dying. And yet it's him who needs holding up and supporting. Dan has always been weak. I knew this about him when I married him, and I still loved him. Flaws and all. Until death do us part. And now that time is coming, what does it matter anyway? We're all heading towards the inevitable; it's just that some of us may get there sooner. I'm stronger than I thought I would be. But now I have a choice to make. To give up or try to carry on living. I know which path to choose.

'Come on, Dan, dry your eyes, get dressed. Let's go and have that cocktail.'

CHAPTER 11

The Schiller Institute exudes a powerful identity all of its own. The precariously cantilevered glass hexagonal structure, with its roof of photovoltaic scales like the skin of an armadillo, has the architectural world scratching their heads. Anchored into the rock face, the substructure forms a basement of private quarters dedicated to Mauritz Schiller, where an entire wall span of glass gives a breathtaking panorama over the Rougemont valley towards Gstaad. The offices form the ground level around the circumference of the central spine of secure laboratories. Power for the building comes from the solar roof, and a deep shaft plunges into the mountain for ground-source heat. Due to the nature of the Institute's work, a satellite was launched about a decade ago to provide a secure intranet system. It is about the size of a microwave and is currently in orbit somewhere above Johannesburg. At this particular moment, it's struggling to process the billions of gigabytes of data required to make the Neurocell 'soft launch' a reality.

Helen moves through the Schiller Institute, ensuring all the arrangements are in place for that evening's event. Representatives from all the major biotech and pharmaceutical companies, along with selected guests from the Bilderberg Group and inner-circle power players who gather every year at Davos, will be in attendance. A handful of people with deep pockets who can turn a prototype into a mass-produced miracle. She has been planning this for months. Tonight's reception will be vital to the success of Neurocell.

The Schiller Institute is a working laboratory, but tonight Mauritz's quarters have been requisitioned to stage the event. The vast open space is tastefully furnished with mid-century pieces and a panelled wall displaying his treasured *Metamorphosis III* by his favourite artist and namesake, M. C. Escher. This vast complex graphic of tessellation was his inspiration for the design of the entire Schiller Institute. The art is reflected in the black polished concrete floor and expansive glass wall opposite. Everything is in place. The champagne is on ice, and Helen stands for a second and takes a breath.

A familiar squeeze of rubber on concrete disturbs her moment of reflection, as Mauritz Schiller arrives at her side. He smiles.

'How is everything coming together, Helen?'

'As you can see, it's perfect, Mauritz. We're nearly there. Just a few finishing touches and we'll be ready to launch Neurocell to the world.'

'Good. And Sarah Collier?'

'Like I said, we're nearly there. Pavel is going to collect them from the hotel later and bring them up to the reception. I've arranged special transportation to try and sweeten the deal.'

As if summoned by the sound of his name, Pavel Osinov appears in the doorway to Schiller's vast bunker. The sun is low in the sky, and the long shadows of Helen and Mauritz stretch across the polished concrete floor almost to his feet.

'Ah, speak of the devil.' Helen turns to Pavel and smiles. The Russian returns her gaze with calm authority. He nods. Mauritz continues but his eyes are now fixed on Osinov: he wants something.

'It sounds as if you have it all covered, Helen. Of course, I expected nothing less from you.' Helen raises an eyebrow at the compliment, remembering his doubts from only a few days before. 'Pavel,' Mauritz continues, 'I wanted to speak with you about Sarah Collier. It is absolutely vital that she is kept protected during her stay in Geneva. Her role in the launch of Neurocell is paramount, and I must ask you to stay with her at all times.

'Shall we?' Mauritz's chair moves towards Osinov, and the two men disappear down the hallway towards the glass elevator. That familiar boys'-club feeling of exclusion makes Helen's jaw tighten.

The elevator ascends and the men move towards Schiller's office door, closing it behind them. Helen emerges at the top of the stairs just in time to see the electric privacy glass snap white, obscuring her view into the suspended glass cube. Helen has been left standing in the corridor beside Pavel's office. The opportunity to look around while Pavel is occupied is a temptation too great. The door is locked but she knows the code to enter; she has made it her business to know. She enters the six-digit combination and opens the door. Slipping inside, she knows she only has a minute or two before the risk outweighs the potential gain. The top drawer to the desk offers up some stationery and personal belongings: cigarettes, interesting. She didn't know he smoked. The laptop and hard drive in the second drawer down look obsolete. Old spreadsheets and company security logs from the last decade that no one cares about. She's running out of time and closes the drawer with a reluctant shove, then reaches for the handle of the bottom drawer. Sliding it out, she sees the strap of a belt. She runs her fingers along the leather until they encounter something hard and cool. She traces its shape, realising the ugly truth before her eyes confirm it. She pulls it out. There, heavy in her hand, is a revolver. The grim implement glints, threatening the worst, its presence a warning. But Helen refuses to heed warnings of any kind. She's one step ahead, and that's where she intends to stay. She leaves the office, shutting the door firmly behind her, and walks away, composed and calm.

Her footsteps have long faded when the glass walls of Mauritz's office snap back into transparency and Pavel steps back into the corridor. As he nears his door, he pauses for a second and smells the air. Jasmine. He glances over towards Helen's office; she is deep in conversation with someone on a video call. He has a task, a mission that he must attend to without delay, but his senses are awake. Something is off.

CHAPTER 12
THE LANDAU REPORT

I'm Back!

Hi guys! Well, I've arrived in Geneva. You can follow my progress here on the blog and all my other social platforms, where I'll be posting videos so you can meet the world's top scientists in person. Don't worry, I always get their permission to film, well almost always, but sometimes someone slips through the net and let's face it, who doesn't like a secret leaked video or a surveillance-style gotcha?! After all, the undeniable truth is what I live for.

Anyway, I have landed and am en route to the Campus Biotech. I'll give you a quick tour and find out what's on the agenda in the coming days, while keeping my eyes peeled for VIPs to grab some hot mike interviews along the way. And speaking of VIPs, it looks as though the most important person of them all has been invited to be Schiller's guest of honour. That's right, Professor Sarah Collier, Nobel Prize winner and all-round badass, is tipped to be Schiller's guest speaker for the launch of Neurocell. It is yet to be confirmed but my source hasn't let me down yet, and on top of that, guess who has secured an interview with said badass? Ding ding, gold star for you! Tomorrow, little old me will be sat across from the one and only Professor Sarah M Collier. Breathing the same air as the woman who has saved millions of lives. Looking into the eyes of the woman whose revolutionary formula won her the Nobel Prize and asking her directly, 'Why have you decided to put your name to such a controversial piece of biotech?'

I'm not here to cause trouble, I'm here to work out what the hell's going on. I'm just asking for transparency. Before we know it, all the basic human privileges that we hold dear – our identity, our medical status and even our civic safety – could be GONE. They distracted you with 5G. We protested. It came to nothing. But what is getting swept under the carpet right now is the truth about how dangerous a device like this could be. Before we know it, access to certain areas of society will be divided between those who have it and those who don't, and I'm genuinely intrigued to find out why Sarah Collier is willing to back it. Sarah is not someone seeking fame or fortune. She has integrity and I respect her opinion, but from what I'm hearing Neurocell could mark the end of our freedoms as we know them. The stakes are really that high and Sarah Collier will have to answer as to why she thinks freedom is something we can afford to lose.

Stay still, don't move. I'm coming for you, Sarah.

Terri Landau

CHAPTER 13

DANIEL

Neither Sarah nor I are really in the mood for a party. We look the part, I suppose; I managed to get a bow tie and white shirt from the overpriced shop in the hotel lobby. I have a black suit, which I hope no one observes too closely. Sarah is wearing her favourite wrap dress. I can't pronounce the name of the designer but it cost a bomb and she looks wonderful. Our spirits don't match our appearance. I lied and told her we didn't have to go, but she insisted we get ready and pull ourselves together. I think she's welcoming the distraction, to be honest; I take courage from her resilience. This afternoon was really hard. I cried a lot. I knew the diagnosis was coming, we both did, but it hit me like a truck. The magnitude of the situation: what it really means. Where does it leave us? Where does it leave Maddie?

Sarah has been amazing, strong and composed. She really is an incredible woman. I haven't truly 'seen' her recently, I've been too wrapped up in my own world to notice, but she's been right here, all along. The green silk gripping her hips and waist complements her auburn hair, lifted up off the back of her long, elegant neck. She's sitting at the dressing table, smiling sadly at me in the mirror's reflection, before her eyes return to herself. She slowly applies her make-up, and I can tell what she's thinking: at some point she might not even recognise her own face any more. She's beautiful, but there is a lethargy in her as she stares at herself. Damage is coming. My body feels heavy and my mind is dark, but before I can sink much lower, there's a knock at the door. I cross the room to open it and am greeted by Pavel Osinov's miserable stare.

'Ready to go?' No pleasantries then. You can call him many things, but unpredictable isn't one of them.

'Yep, pretty much. Just give us five, we'll be out shortly.'

I close the door and Sarah is up from her seat, walking towards me. I reach out for her hands and pull her into me. 'You look incredible.'

'I don't feel it.' She tries a smile.

'Are you sure you're up to it, love?'

'We're in Geneva. Let's do what we came here for.'

I help her into her long coat and squeeze her shoulders, acknowledging the brave face she's putting on.

Pavel leads us into the lift, grim and silent, his Arnold Schwarzenegger impression wearing thinner every second. The lift doors open, and he hits the button for the top floor of the hotel. I raise an eyebrow at Sarah, who has also noticed and is frowning. This isn't the way out. My stomach in my throat, we rise through the levels to the top. This goon was mildly amusing a few seconds ago but now I'm worried. Where is he taking us? The elevator arrives and Pavel is out like a shot, down the corridor and through a door to the roof. We follow obediently. He opens a side door, and we are thrust back by an assault of noise and bright lights. Pavel leads the way outside onto a concrete platform, ducking low under the rotary blades of a helicopter, the down blast causing a cloud of freezing air and snow to obscure my vision. The deafening sound of the chopper drowns out Pavel's voice, but it seems this is how we are travelling to the Schiller Institute. My heart sinks. I'm not a great lover of this kind of aircraft; it's like riding on the back of a wasp, fragile and precarious.

Sarah grabs my hand and bellows in my ear, 'Well, we wanted a distraction; be careful what you wish for, I guess.'

Keeping our heads low, we move towards the door, climb in and buckle up. The worryingly thin glass door is slammed shut, and the helicopter engine gets faster and louder. We suddenly lurch up at a sweeping angle, caught under the thermal of a sudden gust, and my stomach feels like it's been left behind on the roof. Pavel leans over from the front and thrusts a headset at me; my shaking hands just about manage to pull it over my ears, and I lean my head against the glass. I watch Sarah in the reflection; she's calm and pensive. As we gain altitude, the blackness of the surrounding area opens up below, broken by lines of moving cars like strings of amber jewels, the small villages clusters of diamonds as the vastness of the Alps unfolds before us. Sarah holds my hand and I grip it, tracing her fingers in mine, not wanting to let go.

We fly low across the lake, a double moon floating in both water and sky. Then we follow the line of the autobahn until the terrain rises dramatically and the chopper ascends. Buffeting in higher winds up here, I breathe deeply through my nose, praying for this to be over.

Higher still through a narrow mountain pass, we bank left and dip towards a smaller cluster of villages, soaring over an ancient-looking château before circling broadly above a remote plateau. Hidden in a dense forest of pine trees I can see a floodlit circular platform come into view, and we hover towards it. The unpredictable winds force the pilot to make a number of attempts to land, finally coming in at a steep angle. The downdraught from the helicopter pelts the snow-laden trees, causing a small blizzard as we land bumpily. I exhale and the door is opened. Sarah takes my arm and we jump out, hunching as we move away from the deafening chopper blades, and follow Pavel across the snowy ground to a staircase that spirals down to a lower level. The wind is calmer here and we are led to a steel door, which swings open as we arrive. A warmly lit concrete corridor beckons us towards a hum of voices and clinking glasses.

The corridor opens out into a vast space, a curved wall of walnut panelling and a black polished concrete floor reflecting both the assembled crowd and the spectacular view through the window on the opposite wall. It's as if the entire side of the building is missing, revealing the moonlit Alps brushed blue, disappearing into an expanse of darkness. The room is filled with people in expensive tailoring and couture. I feel crumpled and suburban in comparison. As we enter the mass of bodies, a tray of coupé glasses hovers past and I swipe some champagne for us, thrusting one into Sarah's hand with a wink. Laughter and the hum of small talk trickle around us: the world's greatest minds and deepest pockets all together in one room. The adrenaline of the helicopter is clearly still pulsing through our veins as Sarah necks her champagne and reaches for a second. I take a small sip; I need to stay focused. She's looking a little overwhelmed.

'You OK?'

'I feel a bit odd.'

'It's the altitude. You'll be fine in a second, but take it steady?' I nod at her second half-drained glass. She smiles. I'm about to say something else when a voice from behind us interrupts.

'Professor Collier, I can't tell you how delighted I am to finally meet you. I'm so honoured to receive you here as our most distinguished guest.'

The clipped Austrian accent betrays the identity of the speaker before we turn to see Mauritz Schiller smiling up at us from his chair. He is striking, his slicked-back silver hair and neat beard accentuating his angular jaw and elongated nose. Dressed in black tie, his stillness and presence seem to create a space around him, an aura of respect that one does not step into. He holds out his hand to Sarah, who steps forward and squeezes it. His eyes remain fixed on her. As always, I'm left floundering like a spare part. I decide to pitch in for the hell of it.

'Mauritz, great to see you again. Quite the party!'

His eyes flash from Sarah to me, and the line of his mouth drops just fractionally.

'Dear boy, welcome. Both.'

The change in his expression was almost imperceptible, but it hits me in the stomach. I turn to Sarah. Mauritz's eyes are shining as she speaks to him. I cast my eyes around the room, taking in the luxury of the place and the elegance of the guests. Pavel is standing to attention at the side of the room, a few metres away, by the door. Ready to 'terminate' anyone not complying. Life and soul, he is. I scan for people I might know; the world of neurology shrinks the higher you climb, but there is no one I recognise. Still, the alcohol kicks in and I start to feel looser. I turn back to Mauritz, who is still entranced by my wife.

'I quite understand your concerns, Professor Collier. But the presentation should be experienced first before we discuss the details.' Sarah has a lot of questions, but I sense her pushing Mauritz too hard. I touch her arm and she breaks off her conversation with a smile. Then both their heads turn towards me. Except they're not looking at me, they're looking over my shoulder. A familiar voice like honey trickles into my ear.

'How was the flight? Did you enjoy my little surprise?'

I turn to see Helen wearing a velvet tuxedo, wide lapels plunging to the closely tailored waist with no shirt, loose-fitting trousers draping over stilt-like heels, making her taller than my six feet two. My eyes trace from her lips down to her sternum and miraculously contained breasts. I feel the heat of her stare, and not knowing where to look, my eyes flick back to Sarah. She is holding Helen's gaze with confidence as Mauritz placates her.

'Sarah, please be assured, I promise to speak to you again after the presentation. We're excited to hear your reaction.' He glances at Helen, who brushes a strand of hair behind her ear to reveal the pin-dot flashing light of an earpiece. Mauritz moves away to circulate with his guests. Helen spots my glass is empty and ushers a waiter over to refill it. Pavel has joined us almost by remote control, but then I realise that he too wears an earpiece. Helen's perfume is heavy and floral, and I can smell the powder on her cheek.

'So, tomorrow . . . I was thinking, while I manage Sarah's press interviews, perhaps you could go with Pavel out to the slopes? I know the interviews are dependent upon Sarah's decision to endorse Neurocell, but in theory, how does that sound?' Sarah gives me a withering look. I shrug, it's out of my hands.

'You boys go and have some fun while the ladies take care of business.' It's barbed but honest.

I smile and shrug at the Russian. His call.

'Whatever you want.' He sounds about as enthusiastic as I feel. This is going to be a barrel of laughs.

'Wonderful. That's sorted then. OK, now it's showtime. Please excuse me.' And with that, Helen strides powerfully through the crowd, leaving the three of us standing awkwardly.

A voice over a speaker cuts through the room, and the rumble of voices calms to a hush.

'Ladies and gentlemen, welcome to the Schiller Institute. We would like to invite you to our augmented reality presentation of Neurocell. Please take a headset, and a representative from Schiller will be on hand to assist you.'

Sarah and I exchange animated glances. She takes my arm and I lead her away. We both take a set of the AR glasses and fit them over our noses. There is a slight vibration to the ear, and then a tiny pin dot of light projects an image from the corner of the lens, through the iris deep onto the retina. I blink for a second, adjusting to the feeling as we stand on the brink of something exciting and unknown, about to be transported into the future.

The sudden brightness recedes and I feel for Sarah's hand. She squeezes mine. Hold tight, here we go.

CHAPTER 14

The room is still and silent as the lights are gently dimmed. The vibration of a tonal soundscape begins to rumble beneath the floor, a deep harmonic sound. The sheet glass wall of the Schiller Institute glows brighter, as if illuminated from within. The view of the valley intensifies; the dark peaks of La Pare and Wildhorn appear to slide closer together across the horizon, and in the far distance, behind the Matterhorn, a pink light breaks over the horizon. The music builds in perfect synchronicity with the rising sun; the light in the room turns to gold, then yellow, then blinding white. The glass wall begins to melt as though it is made of ice, rippling and collapsing until the entire structure itself has fallen away. The music builds to a crescendo of electronic orchestral sound. Then a voice speaks, calm and reassuring underneath the dreamy notes of a simple piano accompaniment.

'Neurocell has been in development at the Schiller Institute since 2004. Nearly twenty years in the making, it is the culmination of millions of man hours, billions of dollars and trillions of gigabytes of information painstakingly studied and trialled to produce a digital storage capability of one hundred thousand terabytes in a chip no larger than a grain of sand. This work has enabled us to create a new technology that has already changed the scientific world. And now it's ready for you.'

Mauritz Schiller glides silently to centre stage in front of the open window of this new dawn, and as he turns to face them, the assembled crowd takes a step forward to listen.

'My friends and distinguished guests, I want to show you a little glimpse of how far we have come. When I was a young man, I had dreams, I wanted to be an Olympian. A skier. That dream was in my grasp until I had an unfortunate accident while in training at the Hintertux Glacier. As I was airlifted off the mountain, they thought I was dead. They fought to save my life and I survived. Brain damage left me paralysed, with just my right hand to guide me through the world. I resigned myself to the reality that I would never walk again. But reality can be augmented. Science can defy limitations. We have brought ourselves to a new dawn.'

The assembly hold their collective breath as Mauritz places both hands on the arms of his chair, presses his weight onto them and, very slowly and deliberately, stands up from his chair.

There are audible gasps.

Schiller then walks forward towards them, tall and elegant, as he must have been in his youth, and spreads his arms wide, bending from the waist into a deep bow. The music rises again and the room erupts into applause. In that moment, the floor and walls shimmer and turn from the black polished concrete and walnut to glass. Beneath their feet, the standing crowd witness a maze of rooms, computers and work laboratories. The light from the sun moves across the floor as Mauritz continues to walk forward. The crowd parts to form a passageway through the room. The vast graphic tessellation of Escher's *Metamorphosis III* on the back wall begins to fragment and separate into a thousand pieces, like a puzzle unravelling. As Mauritz approaches the wall, a vertical line bisects the pattern and the two halves slide back to reveal another room.

'Please, come with me.'

The crowd takes a few steps with Mauritz, and the entire room shifts suddenly. The open space has now re-formed into the central laboratory of the Schiller Institute. Multicoloured low lights flicker from the processors, and the buzz and whirr of the enormous bank of hard drives appear to make the entire room vibrate. On one of the monitors, a magnified image of a crystal capsule appears. On screen, it is the size and shape of a rugby ball. Entirely made of glass with millions of tiny diamonds inside, pulsating with a blue light of electrical current, it begins to float above the heads of the crowd, who stare at the image, mesmerised, pulled towards its compelling beauty. Mauritz continues.

'Neurocell is an experimental implant. A microscopic Kevlar-coated chip that can be placed at the cranial root between the carotid artery and the vagus nerve. Less than a millimetre in size, it can be inserted with an injection through the mastoid bone behind the ear. The chip is powered by the heat of blood flowing from the artery, and information is passed magnetically into the nerve. We have been determined to find world-altering solutions to neurological diseases that will open the door to recovery for millions of people. Neurocell is the first of its kind. Our pledge is that this will be used exclusively for rebuilding damaged neural pathways and improving brain-related illnesses.

'As I stand here, a vision of what might be possible for my particular condition, I want you to consider every other neurological disorder: damaged or corrupted nerves, blockages, plaques of the brain in Alzheimer's patients. This technology can divert signals to unused, undamaged regions to give back life, movement, memory. This is no longer theory; we have the capacity to make this a reality. We at Schiller dedicate our findings to improving the human condition. With your help, we can bring this to every medical institution across the globe – who knows where this technology can take us. This is just the beginning.'

The crystal fractures overhead and rains down tiny diamonds across the polished black floor. Each fragment contains an exploding image: an old man hugging his daughter, his eyes bright; children laughing as they take halting first steps; members of the blind and deaf community seeing and hearing for the first time. The images accelerate in fast motion until there is a final burst of light. Across the sky, the word 'Neurocell' blazes over the valley and then slowly fades. The illuminated wall darkens, returning to its former solid state. The black concrete floor and glass wall, looking out across the valley, re-form. The lights dim to blackout, returning the audience to darkness. The AR presentation is over. There is no applause; the audience stands in awed silence.

'Ladies and gentlemen, please remove your headsets.'

Mauritz is seated by the window, back in his wheelchair, just as he was.

'My friends, what you have just witnessed is my vision. My legacy. My gift. This is what I am reaching out to you for, asking for your investment. I hope I have managed to convince you of its viability.'

A voice from the crowd interjects.

'Professor Schiller, are you concerned about the ethical implications of its use commercially rather than medically, which of course is inevitable?'

Mauritz nods, acknowledging the question.

'We have no interest in developing this for military purposes, or for information, social media, performance enhancement in athletics and sports, or – yes – pornography. Trust me, the financial offers have been tempting, but we have a patent, which ringfences Neurocell specifically for medical use only.

'Neurocell can act like a pacemaker for the brain, reconnecting and recultivating dying cells and making use of new ones to counteract the effects of early onset dementia and even, we hope, advanced cases. We have been offered a generous donation from a private benefactor this afternoon and have reached an agreement to begin the early trials in London as soon as we receive a green light.' The room erupts with applause and heads turn, seeking out the mystery benefactor. Another voice breaks through.

'How long do you hold the patent for?'

Mauritz's eyes narrow and he glances over to Helen; she blinks slightly and gives a tiny shake of the head.

'We will ensure that it is in perpetuity, but that, my friends, will be largely down to you all. Please enjoy the hospitality. I'm here to answer your questions.'

With that, Mauritz spins in his chair and heads towards the door; this is where the hard work begins. Helen strides across the floor after him and puts her hand on his shoulder, claiming him. The rest of the room is moving and buzzing with excitement as the distant beat of a techno soundtrack for the afterparty rumbles under the floor. It is only Pavel Osinov who stands completely still, galvanised. His eyes scan the room, then he breaks to leave in the opposite direction to Mauritz Schiller.

CHAPTER 15

SARAH

Sam Collier, my father, is standing in front of me, just as he always was, his deep-blue eyes kind and alert. He smiles and reaches out his hand to me. 'Sarah.' He remembered; he remembered my name. He does remember me after all. It's him, he's fully there, emotionally and physically. I take a little step towards him and raise my hand to take his; he's so close I can almost feel his touch. I smile back and an overwhelming feeling rises in me; I feel so full of love, almost bursting into laughter. All the anxiety, all the tension, of holding myself together for him, staying strong for him, propping him up, is gone. We're free from this illness, free to live again with hope. But then I blink, and he's gone. As I remove the headset, my eyes are clouded with emotion and I take a big breath, filling my lungs with a deep draught of hope and relief. Things are just the same as they were an hour ago, but somehow I've just witnessed a new world of endless possibilities. This has changed everything. There is hope.

I have to compose myself, but I'm trembling. The weight of the day on which a death sentence fell upon me suddenly feels lighter. The sense of excitement from the other people in the room confirms I'm not the only one blown away. Possibly by the presentation itself, but in my mind, the dazzling AR was nothing in comparison to the mind-blowing potential of Neurocell. I turn to Daniel, who is grinning at me and searching my face.

'You alright there?' He holds my arm, propping me up.

'I'm fine. I just saw my . . . I was just a bit overwhelmed.'

'So? What do you think?'

'Did you know?'

'Yes, but I hadn't realised it was this far advanced. We've been fighting a losing battle for so long now, slowing the progress of dementia with drugs, but this could offer a permanent answer.'

I'm speechless. He continues.

'Oh, love. I knew it. I knew it was the right thing to come here. We can be at the forefront of this.' His eyes are shining, he wants to be involved. His team in London have the most experienced and innovative surgeons, I can see he's already there. But am I? I have questions. In the room, everyone is in animated conversation, intoxicated with what they've just witnessed. They crowd around Mauritz, who is answering questions as best he can, but the voices seem distant.

Daniel smiles at me. He looks different, his face is smoother, and his eyes are clearer. He holds my arm as we intercept Mauritz and Helen, making a beeline for a group of investors.

'Professor Collier, I am curious to know what you think. Did the presentation satisfy your concerns?' He looks at me with proud eyes that ride on a wave of intense confidence. Helen is poised, scanning the room, and her eyes land on Daniel and then me. Am I in or out? It's time to decide.

'It's truly groundbreaking, I'm in awe of what you have achieved. This could be the technology of our lifetime . . . but I'm still—' Mauritz interrupts me.

'I know, I know, and I thank you for your due diligence. I expected nothing less. *Mais le mieux est l'ennemi du bien.*'

I smile back at him. 'Voltaire.'

'We mustn't allow "perfect to be the enemy of the good". It could be perfect if we allow this breakthrough to do good. And that may be down to you, my dear.'

Deep down, I know he's right. I think I have to help him. So many lives could be changed, including mine. Daniel hands me a glass of champagne and we toast. I guess I'm in?

Mauritz begins to talk me through the basic terms of my endorsement. I listen to what will be expected of me, but I don't seem to be able to make sense of what he's saying. I know what the words mean by themselves, but somehow they don't fit together. Syllables of disjointed consonants and vowels spilling together in a cacophony of nonsense. I recognise his voice but I can't piece anything together. I need air.

'I'm sorry, would you excuse me? I have to go to the bathroom.' I hand my glass to Daniel and move away, desperate to get some space. The hum of voices is deafening, and a flush of heat rises in my cheeks. I stagger through the crowd, trying to keep my balance and regain control of myself as I attempt to find an exit. Shoulders seem to barricade me in, but I break free from the maze of bodies, trying not to fall. I really do need some air. Finally, I find my way to the vast curved wall and follow it round, with my hand against the wood, to a door that is open just a crack. I step out and move unsteadily down the corridor towards a sign marked 'Ausgang'. I push the security bar and lean out into the dark, propping the door open with my foot as I'm hit with the chill of Alpine air. I stand, breathing deeply, resting my hand on the wall. The hot perspiration on my face and neck turns cold. That was scary. I feel like I'm losing my grip. Is it the AR technology that has knocked me sideways? I could hardly believe what I was seeing with my own eyes, but now I am left with the feeling that I can't tell the difference between fact and fantasy. I saw my dad. I don't know what to believe. A clicking interrupts the silence and I spin around, searching for the source of the sound. My foot slips from the door and it closes.

'Shit.' I try the handle, but it's locked.

'No worries, I have my key card.' I jump at the sound of a voice and turn to see who's here. An orange glow illuminates a face and a pair of troubled eyes. I've seen them before, but the darkness distorts the features, making his face appear ghoulish in the light of the flame. Pavel Osinov draws on a cigarette and exhales, looking straight at me.

'Oh, it's you. I just needed some air but now I'm locked out.'

'You smoke?' He offers the packet and I move in closer.

'Not since the early nineties. I quite enjoy having lungs that work.' I can't help myself. ·

Pavel fake coughs, then laughs. 'Smoking is compulsory where I come from.'

I can't help but smile. Maybe he's not so uptight after all. I lean against the concrete wall next to him, the cool air slapping me in the face and waking me from my stupor. 'Actually, sod it. Go on then.' I take a cigarette and let Pavel light me up. I inhale, but actually it's foul and makes my spinning head worse. I press my back into the wall next to him.

'So, you're Russian?' I'm a little intoxicated, I think, in more ways than one.

'Ah . . . They told me you were a genius.' A smirk crosses his lips. He dumps his half-finished smoke into the snow and pulls out his key card to leave. Then he pauses.

'I'm not really welcome there any more.' He stares out into the night.

'Faithful expat or rebellious defector?'

'Neither. I'm originally from Moscow. Special forces. Left the military, not by choice. I live in Berlin now, on a small island at the Wannsee.'

I've barely heard more than a grunt from this man, so I'm

surprised, not just because he's actually talking but because of how open he suddenly is.

'So, you were expelled? Do you miss home?'

'Of course. It's painful. But I have a good life, I can't complain.' He looks out across the dark trees, his white hair glowing in the moonlight.

'I must go back in. Please excuse me.' He swipes the keypad and opens the door, propping it ajar from the inside.

'Thanks for the cigarette.'

He smiles at me through the gap. His face looks different. It's no longer grim and threatening but sad. 'In or out?'

'Ha! Good question!'

I take one last drag of the cigarette and grab the door as he leaves. I shiver, cold sweat trickling in the small of my back, the flimsy silk dress sticking to my skin. I'll probably catch a chill. I make my way back through the door and close it behind me. Walking back down the corridor, returning to the throng, I see Daniel smiling and I think how handsome he looks in his crumpled suit. He looks relaxed and happy; I've missed that man. He's speaking to an attractive blonde woman in a suit. Her back is to me, but I catch a glimpse of her face as she turns around. It's a familiar face but I can't remember . . . Who is that? She tucks her hair behind her ear, revealing her neck to him, and says something, her head tilted. It makes Daniel's eyes light up, and he runs his fingers through his dark hair. It's a little tic he has. I think he saw Steve McQueen do it in a movie. It says, 'Look at my hair, look at my bicep.' He used to do that when I twinkled at him. A stab of jealousy digs into my gut, a reflex I can't help. My husband flirting with a beautiful stranger.

'Sarah, where have you been? We were worried.' Daniel's lips move, but the honey voice with the American accent is hers.

Shit, what's wrong with me? Of course, it's her. Helen . . . Uh . . . Helen . . . something? She's been in our faces all day; how could I forget? I'm losing my grip again. My face flushes in a wave of stifling heat. The taste of burned tobacco in the back of my throat makes a wave of nausea rise in me. The voices retreat and the faces distort. I reach for something to hold on to. My legs buckle beneath me, and I stagger forward. As I catch the edge of a table, I can hear the crash of its contents hitting the floor. 'Sarah?'

I go down hard, my head hitting the concrete floor, but I feel nothing, no pain. The distant voices retreat into the darkness.

'Sarah?'

Is that me? Is that my name?

CHAPTER 16

DANIEL

The snow chains grip the frozen surface of the tarmac as the vehicle ploughs down the mountain road with caution. The judder and grate of metal on ice clatter through my teeth as I squeeze the door handle and hold on tight to my wife, nestled under my arm like a poor broken bird. The heavy snowfall, illuminated in the headlights, obscures the windscreen as we descend the winding road from the Schiller Institute and head back to Geneva. Pavel takes the startling hairpin bends of the icy road with caution, hugging the side of the rocky cliff. The entire road is covered in snow and the visibility is about three feet ahead of us. Had I been driving, we would probably have gone over the edge by now.

Sarah's head is resting on my shoulder, and I hold her hands tightly in my lap.

'Nearly there now, love.'

I had to get her out of there urgently. The presentation at Schiller was a resounding success but Sarah had been hanging by a thread from the beginning. I knew she wasn't feeling herself before we left, she was unusually quiet. I thought maybe she had enough strength to get through the evening but the flight and the dizziness of the presentation, combined with the champagne, were more than she could cope with. I smelled cigarettes on her breath, so who knows what she'd been up to. I just needed to get her out before anyone noticed. Rumours, whispers and prying eyes are the last thing we need right now. Helen suggested calling an ambulance, but I didn't want to risk the truth about Sarah's condition being exposed. We're only just getting to grips with the diagnosis ourselves, and if it became public, particularly right now, then we would have a whole lot of explaining to do. I don't want anyone else involved. This is my problem. It's for me to deal with.

I stroke her head and lean back in the leather seat, trying to block out the swerving undulation of this damned car.

Pavel looks at me in the rear-view mirror.

'What is wrong with her?'

Oh God, I can't deal with an interrogation from him right now; I have enough on my plate.

'She's just a bit stressed, you know . . . wiped out. She doesn't normally go in for this kind of thing, not much of a party animal.'

'She's not well.' Was that a statement or a question?

'She'll be fine, just one glass too many.'

Sarah rouses at the sound of my voice.

'It's alright, love, go back to sleep, I've got you.' I pull her tighter into me and she exhales. Her hair is matted and stuck to her face, her make-up has smudged, her palms are clammy but they're cold in my hand.

Finally, we hit the yellow floodlit autobahn and I see signs for the city. The car accelerates and the slush from the road sprays out on either side. The road is empty. I eyeball Pavel in the mirror.

'We can't go in the front, not with her in this state.' He nods.

About an hour later, we're skirting the edge of the frozen lake, the city growing alongside. The snow has stopped, or perhaps it didn't creep this far down the mountain tonight. The stark light from a petrol station outside Chambésy is a reassuring sign that we're nearly there. I'm ready for this night to be over. Pavel pulls up around the side of the hotel and kills the ignition.

'Sarah, we're here, can you wake up?' She groans and lifts tired eyes up to meet mine.

'Where are we?'

'The hotel, love. It's time for bed.'

Pavel opens the car door and together we help her out. Retracing our steps from earlier in the day, we slip and slide down the short staircase to the basement level and find the door to the kitchen open. She takes my arm, and we walk slowly through the dark passageway towards the lift. She glances over her shoulder at Pavel and whispers to me, 'Being followed, Dan.'

Pavel and I make eye contact as the lift descends.

'I've got it from here. Cheers, mate.'

He looks confused and stern. His glance shifts between me and Sarah, who is leaning against the rail inside the lift. 'If you're sure?'

I nod and pull the concertina cage door across between us, barring his way.

'Until tomorrow.' His voice is monotone.

I crank the handle of the lift and we rise. He keeps his eyes on me until my feet are at his face and then he's gone. Sarah looks a mess, slouching against the rail.

'What happened?'

'You had a wobble, but you're OK now, nearly home.'

'Home?' Her eyes ignite and she smiles and appears to revive.

'Well, the hotel room, you know what I mean.'

'Hotel?' The tiniest collapse in her spine. I look into her weary face; she's looking at me but her eyes aren't really focusing. She's never been this bad before.

'Let's just get you into bed, shall we?'

I ease her gently along the corridor towards our room. We make our way to the bed in darkness. I flick on a lamp, casting a mellow glow across the floor. I lay her down on the soft mattress, pull off her shoes and sit beside her for a second. She looks up at me with frightened eyes.

'What's happening to me, Dan?'

'Don't worry, love, I'm right here with you. You've had a really tough day; we haven't stopped. It's understandable you're tired. It's my fault. The travelling and then the event, not to mention hearing all about Neurocell, it's pretty overwhelming. Sorry I put pressure on you.' I decide not to mention the diagnosis.

Her eyebrows crease and she turns her face into the pillow, seeking comfort. Her voice is muffled, and the words are swallowed, but they hit me like a slap in the face.

'What's Neurocell?'

I wasn't expecting her to be so confused so quickly. She's losing her grip. Things are unravelling faster than I thought they would. I need to hold on to her. I need her to be calm and clear. I need her focused.

'Nothing for you to worry about, Sarah. Just go to sleep.'

I roll the duvet into a cocoon around her and make my way to the bathroom, feeling grim. My stomach is twisting into knots and I'm starting to panic. What are we doing here?

Why did we agree to come? I should be looking after her, not making things worse. Breathe, Daniel. Losing your head now isn't going to help anything. I glance up to the mirror. Spanning the glass is something I hadn't noticed before. A large crack, running from one side to the other. It splits my face in two. Was that there before? I watch my eyes and then look down to my mouth and neck. My upper chest rises and falls, breathing heavily. My mouth is showing one face, my haunted eyes another. Two halves of the same person, split across the middle, divided. He knows . . . that man. He knows damn well what's coming. Coward.

I run the shower burning hot until clouds of steam obscure my vision. I undress and step in. The water sears my skin, cleansing me of the day's dirt. It's so hot, it turns my skin red. But I bear the pain; it's nothing less than I deserve. I've pushed and pushed and now things are at breaking point. What did I expect? Soon she'll be lost to me forever and there's nothing I can do to stop it now. I never deserved her anyway. I watch the water at my feet circling the drain, spinning around in a vortex. I wish I could release myself to its pull and drown in it. You are so out of your depth, Daniel.

I raise my head into the stream, gripping my face and letting the scalding water wash away my sins.

CHAPTER 17

The window of opportunity for Pavel's mission is narrow. The route back to Schiller is even more treacherous than the way down. Snow has compacted on the precarious mountain road and, despite the chains, the rear wheels of his BMW X5 skid and slide as he resists the temptation for speed. He watches the clock. Headlights on full beam blind him and he swerves off the road into an avalanche tunnel on the right. He switches the engine off and waits in the dark. More cars pass, their headlights casting shadows on the concrete walls; stragglers from the party being driven home. The throb of a helicopter overhead echoes into the distance. 1.30 a.m. He is about twenty minutes' drive away. He flicks on Leonard Cohen to pass the time and takes a sip of warming liquor from a hip flask. At 2.28, he heads back to Schiller. The gate is open when he arrives. A burned-out smoking flare guiding guests to the event is just an ember now that the party's over. He turns off his headlights and creeps forward to pull up just outside the main entrance, close to the cover of the woods. The wind is picking up again as he steps out of the vehicle, pulling his coat around him, and moves off through the pine forest surrounding the Institute. He stalks around the curved outer wall towards the south side of the building and checks his watch. 2.48 a.m. Perfect, Jan Pager will be starting his security round in the north wing, working clockwise. He'll need to move fast. The southern facet of the glass upper structure has a blind spot, just a metre in width, to the side of an emergency exit door buried into a concrete support panel. He pulls a phone from his pocket. Thumbing a code into a security app, he watches the surveillance system high up on the wall. Its red light stops blinking. Camera disabled, he proceeds to the door. His swipe card releases the locking mechanism and, cloaked in darkness, he enters the Schiller Institute. He then removes his coat and boots, leaving them on the floor, close to where he will make his exit.

Padding silently past his own office, he moves with the speed and silence of a cat, prowling towards Mauritz's inner sanctum. The darkness transforms the glass in this mirror-black labyrinth. A cloud passes the moon and consumes the last of the light. Mauritz's office has a higher-level entry system than the rest, but Pavel knows how to gain access. He climbs to the mezzanine level and reaches into his pocket to retrieve a square of acetate, which bears the imprint of Mauritz's finger. He touches it to the sensor and the whirr of a retracting bolt clunks loudly in the silence. The door opens and he slips inside. The room is quiet, except for the thrumming exhale of the forced air circulation. It's colder in here and the beads of sweat trickling from his neck wick into his base layer, sending a chill down his spine. He keeps his focus on the glass floor through to the level below, adjusting his eyes to the dark. Mauritz's desktop screensaver projects underwater images of jellyfish across the walls, long tentacles reaching out to sting and paralyse. He remains by the door for a second. 2.54 a.m. Then he moves towards Mauritz's desk.

Pulling a black nitrile glove onto his right hand, he tugs at the brass handle of a filing cabinet, the antique rosewood drawer scraping open. His gloved fingers walk through the metal filing bars, knowing exactly what they're looking for.

Down in the reception area, a single monitor on the bank of security screens is black. A second screen then flickers to black, and then a third. A sequence of security cameras malfunctioning. Jan Pager, standing with his back to the monitor in the small recess of his tiny office, doesn't notice. He places a pod of espresso into the machine and checks his watch. He's late for his round. Grabbing the cup and knocking back his caffeine shot, he checks he has his swipe card and torch and sets off on his patrol.

Pavel closes Mauritz's drawer, creeps out under the billowing tendrils wafting across the walls of glass and closes the door behind him. 2.59 a.m. He watches Jan across the diameter of the hexagon; he'll take the outer corridor first, tracking right, clockwise. Pavel descends the stairs and breaks left.

He slides along the corridor, in perfect synchronicity with Pager. He watches the torch disappear into the north stairwell, descending to patrol the lower level first. Without wasting a single second, Pavel heads towards Helen's office. A shaft of moonlight slices across the floor, casting a silver-blue shard, severing her domain in two. He codes the door open and enters. The Schiller Institute intranet has its own high-security private server, but he has known for a while that Helen is working outside of that system, something expressly forbidden to all employees at Schiller. It is safe to assume that what he needs will be found on her hard drive. He is about to make a move to her desk when he notices, in the darkness, the tiny bead of a red light, flashing. What the hell? All cameras in the north wing have been disabled sequentially, he has made sure his back is covered, but this is something else. A webcam? Shit. No time to consider. He needs to get in and out. He pins himself to the wall, hiding in the shadows. Crouching below the line of the red light, he gets down onto his hands and knees and scuttles across the floor, disappearing under the desk. Snaking himself across a carpet of cables, he slides up into Helen's seat without making a sound. His eyes remain glued to the red flashing light on the webcam. In his peripheral vision, a tiny movement causes his stomach to leap up into his mouth. He is not alone. He turns to stone, holding his breath as sweat beads his temples. He moves his eyes, trying to make out who or what is there in the room with him. Staring back are a pair of marble-black eyes and a halo of white. The black wall of glass reflects his own distorted face, caught in the act. You fool, you should have covered your head. Too late now. He exhales through his nose, punctuated by a thumping heart, and returns his focus to the desktop. Without waking the operating system, he slides a USB drive into the port with a click. A small box appears on screen with a command: 'Download to disk without startup.' Using his smartphone, he scrolls through Helen's hard drive until he comes to an encrypted file. He taps in a command.

'Unauthorised log-in, error code 976.' A warning box appears on the screen and then another one pops up in red and flashes. 'Error warning sent to user.'

Fuck. She's set up an alert. Pavel closes the app on his phone. 3.11 a.m. Suddenly, he hears the elevator descending to the lower level. Jan Pager is on his way back up. Time to go. He removes the thumb drive and eases himself across the floor. The clouded moon is breaking through with pockets of light, dappling the floor and walls, but he's already at the door. As he exits, his eyes flick to the webcam. The red light has turned green. It's recording. Shit. The heat rises to his face and his throat constricts. In the blurred mirror of the glass wall, he sees Jan Pager's torch on the move. Pavel makes a decision. He silently sprints down the corridor to his own office and taps in the code. He leaves the door open behind him; this will only take a second. He heads straight for his desk. Yanking open the bottom drawer, he reaches in. His hand scrabbles every inch of the space, groping for answers. His pistol has gone.

His heart is bursting out of his chest, triggered by a release of adrenaline, and the flight instinct takes hold. Pager's light is approaching his office. He looks up above his head to a small ventilation hatch in the roof. Like lightning, Pavel climbs onto his desk and punches the grille open. He hauls himself up with all the strength he can muster. His feet disappear through the hole just as the beam of a torch scans the room. His hands press fast against the steel walls of the shaft as he strains to reach the vent at the top. His fingers find the lip and he pulls himself up. Out on the roof, the winter blizzard is blowing at gale force, ice and snow stinging his face and limbs. Pavel tenses and leans into the wind. He carefully replaces the roof hatch and slowly makes his way across the ice-encrusted roof. Heading towards the south side, he sees the woods in the distance. Both his body and heart are now cold as stone as he scales down the building and sprints towards his concealed vehicle. Soaked through to the skin and frozen to the bone, he reaches his car, fumbling for the key with frozen fingers. Safely inside, he whacks the heater to full blast and smashes his hands against the steering wheel in frustration. Leaning his head into the wheel, he attempts to calm down and thaw out. He reaches into his pocket to pull out the hip flask of whisky and takes a sip of the reviving liquor. Shit, he left his boots and coat inside. It's too risky to go back now, the security cameras are operational, he'll have to deal with that in the morning. For now, he needs to get away unseen – at least this turbulent night will help there. He has really screwed up. Helen's computer may have alerted her of his attempted hack. And that webcam . . . This is messy, and Pavel is never messy.

But what really pierces him in the gut is that someone has been inside his office and stolen from him. They have diminished his power, but worse than that, they have exposed him. At the deepest level, Pavel Osinov's instinct for self-preservation is primal, in a way that should put the fear of God into whoever did it. But there are many ways to destroy a person; a bullet is just one of them.

CHAPTER 18

THE LANDAU REPORT

Is Altruism Dead?

Is anyone else tired of all the endless speculation and misinformation flying around on the internet? Anyone else tired of all the bad news? The politics, the self-obsession, all the doom-mongering and the complete and utter lack of altruism anywhere? I am. If you are someone who has one eye on real life and one ear tuned into social media, desperately listening to hear some good news but only being met with the breaking news of incessant negativity, then I'm here to throw you a lifeline.

The rumours are it's not all bad. That something transformative is on the horizon. So I for one am intrigued to learn exactly what was presented at the top-secret Schiller meeting last night. As expected, only a select group of potential investors were in attendance, so one thing I do know is that this biotech must be ready to bring to market, it's ready to move forward, so I feel we have a right to know exactly what this thing is and what it does. But like good children we will sit and wait patiently until it's our turn to be told, right? Um . . . I don't think so. If Mauritz Schiller truly has developed some earth-shattering tech that might change the face of medicine as we know it, we want to celebrate with him. For now, all I really have is the name: Neurocell. That and some tantalizing hints about what it might be able to do . . .

Let me start by asking you to consider this: how would you function without your smartphone? It's always there in your hand, that therapeutic ping or whoosh as an email drops, the vibration in the pocket that makes you feel wanted, the serotonin release more potent than the human touch. You know exactly what I'm talking about as you read this with your thumb working overtime. OK, so now imagine you can go hands-free. Yes, we've already done that . . . right, Siri? Now, imagine Siri is inside your head. You don't even have to speak, she'll just register your thoughts as requests, as you reach for something, read your messages or look at a menu. Got that? And what else? Glance to the left and a window appears in your peripheral vision: texts, photos, web pages and whatever else you need. Death of the pub quiz!

Anyway, we will have to wait and see what Neurocell is really all about. But I'm hoping it's worth the wait.

Today I will have exclusive access to Sarah Collier in a one-to-one interview. Professor Collier has been singled out to be our eyes and ears inside the Schiller Institute. In the next few weeks, Neurocell will be on everyone's lips. But I'm getting to Sarah right now. I always promised you I would keep you informed, and that's what I intend to do. We all want progress, we all want that miracle drug or piece of tech that will change everything. I want to find out what they have and why Sarah believes in it. Sarah is a notoriously private person, but I think if we are being asked to take her word as gospel with regards to Neurocell, then we need the truth, and that means asking some tough and personal questions. But don't worry, Sarah, I'm a pussy cat, I don't bite!

Check out *Landauleaks.com* for the full interview. Wish me luck.

Terri Landau

CHAPTER 19

DANIEL

'Daniel? Is it OK if I call you that?'

I'm riding shotgun with the Russian, my ski gear in the back. We're on the road to Gstaad; yes, the place where all the royals and Madonna go to take selfies in salopettes. I'm sure the two of us will fit right in. We've been driving in silence for about an hour; he's chewing and I'm pretending to write important emails on my phone.

'Can I ask something personal?'

I'm really not feeling chatty. 'Depends what it is?'

'Why did Sarah retire when she was at the peak of her career?' It's a bold opener.

'Yup, that is pretty personal, and my answer would be . . . probably best to ask her that question.' He steps on the accelerator as we start the climb into the hairpin bends of the Rougemont valley, winding our way up the mountain. The snow is banked up on the side of the narrow pass as we enter a concrete avalanche passage.

I feel relieved. Sarah was much better this morning, much more herself. I didn't want to leave her, but Helen has arranged to be there for the press interviews. She's in good hands. A few more minutes of uncomfortable tension and I break the silence.

'Why do you want to know?'

'Just curious how it must be in a relationship with someone so . . . impressive.' That's bait, I guess.

'Best keep your thoughts on the road.' The retort is loaded with 'stay in your lane' but I suspect it gets lost in translation.

Eventually, we pull up into a hotel car park on the outskirts of town. I get out of the car, unclip my Elan Wildcat rental skis from the roof rack and sit on the tailgate to pull on my Nordica Pro tech boots. Pavel emerges from the driver's side already booted up, with a face like a slapped arse.

'That was fast.'

He's not really dressed for the mountain, jeans and a puffer. His skis have seen better days. The knackered bindings, repaired with duct tape, look like an accident waiting to happen. Although I suppose he must look at me and think 'All the gear, no idea'.

'Come on, let's get up there. I need my fix of speed.' I throw my skis over one shoulder and trudge off.

We grab a half-day pass at the Rübeldorf lift office and take the cable car to a mid-station. Then a short traverse down to a chair lift, and onwards and upwards to the higher altitudes towards Les Diablerets. The mountain looks deserted, and my palms start to sweat despite the cold.

'There was a big storm last night. They haven't had time to blast. I think half the runs might be closed until they have cleared the bulk of it.' Pavel seems to be making excuses. Is he chickening out?

As we ride up in the chair lift, the view beneath our dangling feet is devoid of any skiers in the swirling snow below. Near the summit, the wind has picked up considerably and the visibility is virtually zero. Helmet on and goggles down, we are thankfully reduced to sign language. The chair suddenly stops in mid-air and we hang precariously from a cable encrusted with ice, which groans in the buffeting winds. A loud noise booms above us; the ice on the cable cracks and shatters above our heads, the shards raining down into the ravine below. I grip the safety bar, keeping my head low, and my gloves stick to the frozen metal. I peel them off, hunching further into a ball, protecting my face from the biting wind. Eventually, the chair lurches forward and we rise to the top. I indicate to Pavel that I will follow him and he speeds away, probably with the soundtrack to *Live and Let Die* playing in his head. My skis find the snow and I slowly move off on fairly shaky legs. The visibility is terrible; it's a total whiteout. I can't see the designated piste, or where the Russian has buggered off to. I slide forward cautiously, trying to remember all the technical details.

Suddenly, the ground beneath me seems to fall away and I am pelting down what feels like a wall of ice at a terrifying speed. I am out of control. I turn parallel to the right and dig in with my edges, slowing the fall, but the ice wall is unforgiving, and my skis are clattering, unable to grip the surface. I turn to the left, again no purchase. The sound of the wind is deafening.

The slope flattens and my acceleration slows as I feel the crunch and squeak of some packed powder beneath my skis. I shift into some more controlled turns. My thighs are burning like hell and my left ankle is agony, but I'm doing this. I have no choice; the only way is down. Through a pelting white veil of blizzard, I can vaguely see a figure waiting at the side. I think it's him. As I approach, he nods then smirks at me as I pull up next to him, lungs exploding. I'm desperate for a rest, but he launches himself off again, pointing to the right. Not waiting to catch my breath, I do the same and soon realise we are at the top of a very steep icy schuss. I yield to gravity and squat to increase the free slide down to God knows where. Pavel is just about visible in front of me. The vibration of hard ice under my feet ricochets through my legs, sending shock waves up into my teeth. And then suddenly I'm not skiing, I'm falling. My body is propelled through the air for several seconds and all I can see is white. I'm a dead man.

Out of nowhere, the orange flash of a net hits me in the face. It's the demarcation for the piste edge. My entire body flips and I'm thrown backwards as the tip of a ski catches a rock. The binding releases, spinning the ski at speed and hitting me in the face. I continue to pelt down an incline; the other ski plunges into a deep drift and yanks me around. I come to a jolting stop, my knee wrenching from the force. I bellow in pain, held in suspension over a deep ravine by the foot, like a hanged man. I flail, trying to find something to grip on to. The buried ski holds fast, but for how long? I feel the weight of my head and gravity pulling me down into the ravine.

Trying not to look down at the drop beneath me, I curl myself into a foetal position, fingers reaching until I feel something solid, a rock. Somehow, I haul myself to safety. I collapse onto my back, breathing hard. I stay there for what feels like minutes. Then a distant voice calls out to me.

'Hold on, I'm coming!' A few moments later and Pavel's face appears in my eyeline. 'Are you injured?'

I can just make out what he's saying above the howling wind.

'I don't think so,' I shout back. I remove my cracked goggles; thank goodness for the helmet. I'm seeing stars; the impact on my head was a close call, but I can move my neck, so I think I'm OK. I'll be black and blue in the morning but at least I'm alive.

'I need to get you down. You sure you're not injured?' Pavel yells over the blizzard.

'I think I'm OK, but I have no skis.'

'Don't worry, I know what to do.' Pavel grasps me around the waist, hauls me to my feet and leads me up the slope. We stagger over to where he has left his skis.

'One each, take your pick.'

I lock my right boot into the binding and Pavel takes the left.

My knee is throbbing but I don't think it's badly damaged. He holds me under his arm and around my waist, and like a pair of kids in a three-legged race, we slowly plough down to a slope-side restaurant about a hundred metres down the mountain.

Minutes later, I'm sitting at a small table, dripping onto the red check tablecloth as an open fire begins to thaw me out. I can't stop shaking. The place is empty except for one surly barman. Pavel sits down opposite me, placing two mugs of *vin chaud* in front of us. I sip my wine in silence. For a good few minutes, we don't exchange a word. I think we're both in shock. But the hot wine works its magic and I sit back in my chair.

'I think I need a bit more practice. Want to go round again?' I smile, despite myself.

'It was my fault. I knew the conditions were dangerous. We should not have gone.' Pavel is staring at me.

'Don't worry, you nearly got me. Next time, eh?'

I'm not sure I deserve a next time. In that split second when I thought I was dead, I saw Maddie's face and felt Sarah's arms tight around me – then she let me go.

'Sarah has Alzheimer's. Early onset.' Where did that suddenly come from? I can't look at him. 'That's why she retired. She wanted to spend her last few years with me and our daughter, Maddie. We don't know how fast she'll decline.'

'I'm sorry, I had no idea.'

'It's fine. It is what it is.'

'I didn't mean to pry.'

'Please don't tell her that you know. She wants to keep things private. Especially here, with all this attention.'

The words are spilling out of me before I can think them through. I don't tell him everything; some of this isn't for him to know.

I watch the flames of the open fire spit and crackle. A log falls on the hearthstone and smoulders. I don't move. I could happily burn here. At this moment, if I could change places with Sarah, I would.

I find my throat tightening into a sob. I try to swallow it back down and pretend the tears running down my face are drips from the thawing ice.

CHAPTER 20

SARAH

'I hope you are feeling better after last night. Are you sure you don't need a doctor?'

I'm still in my dressing gown, in an armchair. Helen has her back to me as she makes coffee. If I'm honest, I still feel nauseous and dizzy. It's like jet lag. I'm all cantankerous and on edge. But I lie and make my face look serene and in control.

'No. No doctors, thank you. I just fainted. I feel totally fine now.'

Helen turns, her face is expressionless for a second, like she's studying me; then she flashes her perfect white teeth. She's very good at this.

'Awesome. Then first up is *Landau Leaks*—'

'The conspiracy blogger? Really, isn't the woman who writes it a bit . . . unhinged?'

Helen pauses for a second, then slowly and deliberately hands me the steaming cup of coffee.

'This should "perk you up".' She didn't answer my question but continues.

'Then we have *New Scientist*, *The Lancet* and a couple of others this afternoon. You'll find all the talking points you need in the folder. Try not to go off script, but I'll be there to defer to. I've set up the interview room here at the hotel; I didn't think you'd want visitors in your private space.'

Helen is suddenly busy with her phone and doesn't look up.

'You OK with some of the junket being on camera?' Her eyes move from my feet, up my body to my face, with the subtlest wince. I glance at myself in the mirror; my matted hair and the deep sockets of smudged mascara shock me.

'I'll need time to . . .' To somehow put myself together. She smiles again.

'Sure. We start at nine.'

I cast my eyes over her notes, which list the key talking points of Neurocell. There are bullet points on things I should mention and other things that are marked DO NOT MENTION, in capital letters. As I turn the page, a shooting pain runs across my brow bone and I rub my temples.

'Are you OK?' Her sharp eyes are on me.

'Yes, just a bit wiped out. The coffee should kick in in a minute.'

'Good. Well, the interviews are in the Cigar Lounge; it's in the basement. I'll send a bell boy to escort you down if you like?'

'I'm sure I can find my own way down.' I get to my feet to start getting ready, but I sway slightly and sit back down. Helen watches and takes a step towards me. She touches my shoulder.

'See you at nine.' She picks up her bag and leaves the room.

It takes me about an hour to rouse myself and get in the shower, dry my hair, make my face look respectable and dress in something businesslike. I still look like a faded copy of myself. Every step is an effort; even lifting the brush to my hair feels as heavy as lead. At 9.15, I head down to the basement and follow the signs for the lounge. As I walk along the corridor, that familiar feeling of light-headedness creeps over me again, but my legs feel like I'm wading through concrete as I reach the door. I steady myself against the wall and it buckles under my palm, soft to the touch. The room has a cosy gentlemen's club feel: dark walls, with bookcases and an open fire. A leopard-skin rug and red and white candy-striped soft furnishings. The low light feels odd for this early hour but I'm grateful for the comfortable-looking armchairs. I sink into one of them and pour myself a glass of water from the carafe. My mouth feels parched. The heat from the fire is intense and I take a napkin to mop my brow, make-up running before we've even started. I guess Helen is wrangling the journalists in the lobby. I pull my notes out for a last look but the words on the page won't stay still, letters falling over one another, vying for my attention. I rest my head back into the cushion and press my lips together, breathing deeply, trying not to throw up. Maybe I'm not well enough to do this. I close my eyes for a second and swallow, trying to breathe. Grounding myself. I start to drift, down and down, into unconsciousness.

Through the silence, a timid female voice startles me awake. 'Professor Collier?'

I open my eyes, and black turns to grey, then watery orange. The disembodied voice orientates me to the silhouette of someone sitting opposite me. I try to focus my eyes but I can't quite make out a face. Who is this woman? How did she get in? Long dark hair falls around her shoulders; I fight to bring her features into focus. All I see is a blurred gash of red lipstick and heavy-rimmed tortoiseshell glasses.

'Hi.'

'Hi.'

'I'm sorry, I . . .'

'Terri Landau, I'm here for the interview?'

Landau? Yes, the blogger. I press my hands into the arms of the club chair to stand and shake her hand.

'Please don't get up . . . We'd already started, but you just . . . Shall we start again?' Her voice is soft and distant, with an accent I can't place. She remains still and focused. I glance down at the table to see a phone placed in front of me, recording. She must think I'm a total wreck.

'I'm so sorry . . . Um . . . I must have fallen asleep. It's been a crazy few days.'

'Oh, no worries. I'm feeling pretty overwhelmed myself. I've been wanting to meet you for a long time. I have to admit, I'm a bit starstruck.' Her hair falls across her face as she pushes the phone closer to me across the table and adjusts her glasses.

Her shyness is endearing. I'm surprised at my reaction, but I quite like her. She's an introvert, like me. I smile at her and sit up in the chair, running my hands through my hair and patting my face to wake myself up.

'You don't mind if I record? It'll help me with my copy.'

'Of course.' A cold sweat creeps around my neck and I feel clammy all over. I reach for the water but the glass and carafe have gone. Landau doesn't move.

'You've achieved something so awesome, and I want to celebrate that.'

I don't respond. Journalists always do this; they make statements that they want you to confirm. Putting their words into my mouth. I decide to wait for a question.

'The Nobel Prize, you broke through, big time.'

Another statement. 'Did I? I'm sure . . . I'm not the only one . . . responsible for that success.'

'I was surprised to get an interview with you after you stepped out of the limelight.'

Are we ever getting to a question in this interview? 'Well . . . I'm surprised this is all happening myself.'

'I'll try and make this as painless as possible. So, let's begin: Professor Sarah Collier, thank you for agreeing to this interview.'

I nod and attempt a smile. 'You're very welcome, Terri. I'm pleased to have the opportunity to speak to you.'

'Can I ask you a bit about your work, and then move on to Neurocell?'

'Yes.' Nothing more, no personal stuff, no gotcha questions. I check my watch and pinch the bridge of my nose with my finger and thumb, head pounding. She chews the end of her pen nervously.

'Why did you retire when you were at the top of your game?' Finally, a question I can answer. These words will be mine, not hers, and I will choose them carefully.

'It was time for a break. I wanted to take a step back, rest and enjoy family life for a bit.' That's it. I reach for the most generic answer possible.

'And I hear your father isn't well?'

'No, unfortunately he has Alzheimer's. Time is running out.' It's the truth, but I don't want to go there.

'I'm sorry to hear that.' I wait for the next question, my mouth tight and my hands squeezing themselves together. I turn my head to the door. Helen was supposed to be sitting in, fielding this probing interrogation. I try to sit up in the seat, but I seem to sink lower. Terri doesn't move.

'I'd rather not talk about that.'

'Of course.' She pauses, flicking through her pre-prepared notes. 'So, tell me: why would somebody who shuns the limelight agree to come forward and endorse something as controversial as Neurocell?'

Here we go. Possibly the most succinct question of all. I am asking myself the same thing right now, but she wants a definitive answer.

'Well, I was sceptical at first. The technology is truly ground-breaking and has the capacity to benefit millions of people. But it is true that this breakthrough carries a responsibility, and neural implants must be managed with exceptional care.'

My eyes shift to the page in front of me, to the dancing words. I try to somehow assemble them into a coherent answer.

'Mauritz Schiller . . . has dedicated his life to improving the human condition, and . . .' I glance down again.

'Under his management, Neurocell could bring . . . a new dawn to modern medicine . . . The possibilities are limitless.' Generic and clichéd. That's all they want: soundbites, nothing too complicated.

Terri remains still, but her image appears to waver in the distance. I puff my cheeks out from the heat of the fire. My face is burning, yet I'm cold. The discussion continues, a regurgitated cut and paste of other interviews, googled and rephrased. No follow-ups: each question just posed one after the other, like she's not even listening, just ticking boxes. Her silhouetted shape across the table moves in and out of focus, undulating like a snake. A distant voice, then two voices in conversation. Speaking simultaneously, overlapping, discordant and jumbled. Then her voice is suddenly loud and as clear as a bell.

'Is your diagnosis what caused you to black out last night at the Schiller drinks reception?'

My eyes snap open.

'I'm sorry?' I sit up in my seat.

'Are you OK?' Her voice is distant but soft.

I check my watch; it's 11.19 a.m.; we are way over the allocated time. Where the hell is Helen?

'We can leave things there if you're not feeling well?' She stops the tape.

I open my mouth to speak but no thoughts are in my head, no words form in my mouth. My mouth is open; I can feel saliva trickling onto my lower lip. She stands to leave, pausing at the door as she slides her phone into her bag.

'It really was an honour, thank you. You've given me everything I need.'

The room tilts slowly, the floor lurching up sideways to become a wall. Yet the crystal glasses on the table remain still. The pictures on the walls don't move. Terri stands in the doorway, frozen and unmoving. I need help but she doesn't move. She turns and walks slowly away, and I black out.

I feel carpet on my face and the taste of vomit in my mouth. I'm lifted up under my arms from both sides. My head lolls forward and I can't keep my eyes open. I watch my feet as they try to take baby steps forward. Then we are in the corridor, and then rising in the lift. I can see each level moving into vision through the concertina door as we move upwards floor by floor. My dad, then a lady in red, then Maddie waiting at the top. The lift opens and she runs away down the corridor, laughing. I try to follow, and my feet leave the ground for a second, swung forward, then back.

'Again, swing me again.'

'Nearly there, Sarah.' A whisper in my ear.

Yes, I *am* nearly there, I can feel it.

CHAPTER 21

THE LANDAU REPORT

World Exclusive: Professor Sarah Collier Terminally Ill

I did it. I finally achieved something I never thought would happen: an interview with my hero, Professor Sarah Collier. But this interview was bittersweet. This morning was a bucket-list moment and Sarah didn't disappoint; she was brave and candid, and I haven't stopped pinching myself since I left her hotel. Some of what Sarah had to say was hard to hear, I can't lie. You can read the full transcript on *Landauleaks.com* but here are some sections of audio clips from that precious interview. I have edited out some of the more personal moments in order to protect her, but here is my world exclusive interview with the one and only Sarah Collier.

Terri: Professor Sarah Collier, thank you for agreeing to this interview.

Sarah: You're welcome.

Terri (*shuffling papers*): You achieved something so awesome, and I want to celebrate that. But we're not here to talk about Ebola. We're here to talk about Neurocell, Schiller's controversial neural implant. I have grave concerns about the ethical nature of this technology, as do many of my followers.

Sarah: That's understandable. I was sceptical at first.

Terri: So why should we trust it?

Sarah: The technology is truly groundbreaking and has the capacity to benefit millions of people. But it is true that with

this breakthrough comes great responsibility, and brain
implants must be managed with exceptional care.

Terri: And what if the technology falls into the wrong hands?

Sarah: That's why I think it's important that Neurocell leads the
way in the development of neural implants. Mauritz Schiller
has dedicated his life to improving the human condition, and
under his management, the good that Neurocell could bring
to the world is limitless.

Terri: I hear Schiller are developing their neural implants with
a specific focus on tackling conditions like Alzheimer's
disease.

Sarah: Yes.

Terri: And is it true you have a special interest in that field?

Sarah: Yes, I have to admit . . . Unfortunately . . . I have . . .
Alzheimer's.

Terri: Sarah, I'm so sorry. When were you diagnosed?

Sarah: A few months ago.

Terri: And what will this mean for the future?

Sarah: It's sapped me of all my energy and I want to take a step
back and rest. Enjoy family life for a bit. Time is running out.

Terri: Thank you for being so honest, Sarah. I'm speechless,
and that doesn't happen very often. Perhaps we should
pause the interview for a moment? Let's take a break.

So there you have it, folks. It's with a heavy heart that I bring
you the breaking news that Professor Sarah Collier is terminally
ill. For the full interview, please follow the link below. I told
you it wasn't easy listening, but you heard it here first. Sadly,
her life is coming to an end, but her legacy will live on forever
through her pioneering work on Ebola and her endorsement of
Neurocell. I will be publishing a full write-up of Neurocell in the

coming days as the Schiller Conference continues, but for now, please join me in sending Professor Sarah Collier our thoughts and prayers.

Click on the link below or go to *Landauleaks.com* to hear Sarah's story in full in her own words.

Terri Landau

CHAPTER 22

SARAH

Hands press against my shoulders, pinning me down. I need to wake up but I can't shake this off. I push with my toes but there is nothing there. The smell of stale wine and cigarettes hits my nose. A face close to mine, breathing close on my cheek and in my ear. 'Relax, Sarah, just breathe, let go.' The hands on my shoulders tighten, fingers pressing into my skin, legs and feet wrapping around mine like tentacles paralysing me. My mouth is open to scream but nothing comes. Something tightens around my neck and enters my open mouth, reaching down into my throat. I gag and choke.

'It's OK, Sarah. It's me. It's Daniel.'

A blurred vision emerges into focus as the blinding sunlight from the open curtains prises my heavy eyelids open. I am back in my hotel suite. I ball the bed sheets into my fists and hold on for dear life, trying to stop this dizzying sense of falling.

'Can you sit up? That's right.' Daniel is on the bed next to me. He cradles me into a sitting position and then gathers up my legs and carries me into the bathroom. I flop like Maddie's broken Barbie doll into his arms.

The water of the shower spreads warmth through my head and shoulders, and the fragrant bubbles revive me. I step out and steady myself against the vanity and slowly pull on a bath robe. My face in the mirror is obscured by the steam. Who is she? Why can't I remember anything? Why can't I see? I begin to rifle through my wash bag. I need my pills. The heat of panic rises to my face. I need them.

Daniel is lying on the bed, reading the Neurocell notes from last night's launch. He looks up and smiles. I grip onto the door frame.

'How are you feeling?'

'Is that going to be the universal greeting now for the rest of my remaining days? . . . Have you seen my pills?'

'They were on the side table.' He doesn't shift from the bed as I hunt through the drawers.

'What's that on your knee?' He has a towel wrapped around it.

'Ice pack. I had a little Fred Astaire moment on the slopes.'

I'm drawing a blank.

'Bromancing the stone? Me and the Russian trying to bond? Never mind.'

'Oh right . . . yes . . . the skiing.' I'm still emerging from a brain fog. 'Hard work, was it?' He looks a bit worse for wear now I look at him. Red-eyed and a bit worn out. 'Is it painful?'

'Bit swollen but I'll be fine. I'm getting old, love, can't hack the fast lane any more.'

I look down into my hand; I'm holding my pills. I must have found them.

'You want one of these?' I hold out my painkillers to him.

'No . . . I'm good.' He wants to tough it out, I suppose. Men and their war wounds.

'How did the interviews go?'

The interviews? Oh God, did I even make it there? 'Why, what did Helen say?' I'm trying to rack my brain.

'No idea, I haven't spoken to her.'

'I . . . I can't really remember. She was here one minute, then deserted me. I had to figure it out for myself.' My brain moves to the dark basement corridor, the room with the fireplace.

'How many did you do?' Good question, the whole morning is a blur.

'No idea . . . a few.' How many journalists did I talk to? The cacophony of voices and the movement in the room, bodies crowded in – no, that was last night.

Daniel limps over to the minibar and nabs the giant Toblerone before hopping back to the bed.

'You know they charge twenty Swiss Francs for that . . . That's like three quid a mouthful.'

Daniel rips the packet and shoves a triangle into his mouth. 'I'm pretty sure Schiller aren't going bankrupt over chocolate.' He opens his laptop.

'What are you doing?'

'Looking for the press.' His mouth is full of chocolate.

'I can't understand a word you're saying. Which could either be your full gob or my mushy brain.'

He nearly spits out the chunk onto the bed, laughing.

'Come here.' I obey, but mainly because I want some of that gold-plated chocolate.

'Something has changed with you; you seem better.'

'It feels like there's hope today after last night.'

He looks at me and narrows his eyes. He stops chomping for a second and holds my arm.

'I don't want you to get your hopes up.'

'I'm just trying to be positive, that's all.'

He types into the search engine and pulls up various articles. A couple of local newspapers with bad paparazzi shots of us arriving at the airport. Then he scrolls down to *Landauleaks.com* and opens it. It's a stream of articles, inflammatory and under-researched clickbait.

'Babe, she's posted the audio of the interview. There is a headline that says "Professor Sarah Collier Terminally Ill". I thought you were being interviewed about Neurocell?' The blood drains

117

from his face as he clicks on the audio link.

A distorted and crackly interview plays. It's bad quality and has clearly been edited. I'm listening to the sound of a voice I don't recognise. And then, suddenly, we both hear it.

'Yes, I have to admit . . . Unfortunately . . . I have . . . Alzheimer's.'

'Sarah . . . what . . . the fuck?' Daniel is up from the bed and standing glaring at me, his injury miraculously improved.

'I didn't mean to . . . I was . . . I wasn't . . . Helen was supposed to be there to intercept a question like that.'

'WHAT QUESTION? I didn't hear a question, I just heard you VOLUNTEERING TO TELL THE WORLD that you have Alzheimer's. What were you thinking?'

'Daniel, I'm sorry, I wasn't feeling well. I was left alone while you were having the time of your life pissing around on skis. Shout at Helen, not me.'

He's limping around the bed now, his hand to his head. He pulls out his phone to make a call but hangs up. 'Shit. Shit. Shit!'

A feeling washes over me suddenly. Is he angry that our privacy has been violated or is there something else?

'You understand that your endorsement is now highly questionable?'

I open my mouth to speak but I have nothing to say.

'This is a massive conflict of interest.'

I go to grab my coat and boots.

'Where do you think you're going?'

'I need to get out for a while.' I can feel my face burning and tears starting to well up in my eyes. What have I done? I've betrayed myself. I never do this.

'You're not going anywhere. There are press and photographers downstairs. You . . . stay right here. I will deal with this.'

'How? What are you going to do?'

'I'm going to get her to retract the article. It doesn't even sound like you on the tape. We'll say you were drunk and you got confused about your father.'

'I'm not sure being drunk is a better explanation.'

I sit on the bed and watch him throw on boots and a jacket.

'I wasn't drunk. I'm not well and to be honest I really don't know why the hell I'm here.'

He's pacing around the bed, not acknowledging me. Why did I come? How on earth did I agree to this?

'I need some air.'

'Yeah? Well, open the fucking window then.' This is a different Daniel to two seconds ago. Are we sure I'm the one with dementia and the mood swings? He stops by the door and his shoulders sag; he turns back to me.

'I'm sorry, I didn't mean to be so angry. I just . . . I don't want the world's press scrutinising you, devouring your illness like vultures stripping a carcass. They'll hollow you out for all the tragic details. I don't want to deal with that.'

'Well, it's not you that will be dealing with it, is it, Daniel? It's me. I'm going to be dealing with this life sentence.'

'In private, not by hanging out the bunting for *Hello* magazine.'

I put my hands to my face because I don't want him to see me any more. I don't want anyone to see me any more.

CHAPTER 23

Mauritz Schiller's boiling anger is too much for him to bear. He slams his chair into reverse and hits the wall. Veins bulge in his neck and his face burns with rage. He hits the wall again and again. The force of his fury is so great that a hairline crack appears at the base of the glass wall of his office and starts to creep upwards. He inhales deeply through his nostrils, trying to compose himself, and then, tapping his finger against the arm of his wheelchair, on the electronic pad, he makes a call. An American voice answers.

'Hello?'

'The *Landau Leaks* article. Is it true? Does Sarah Collier have Alzheimer's?' His tight voice can barely contain his fury.

'I was just about to call you. It appears so. It's her voice on the recording. I'm just as shocked as you are. I know she hasn't been well during her stay in Geneva, but I had no idea it was that serious.'

'What happened yesterday?' He is angry. Demanding answers.

'Sarah was fine at our morning briefing but after her interview with Landau, she was very unwell. I had to cancel the other interviews. I didn't think—'

'How could we not know about this?'

'The Colliers have kept it to themselves.'

'And then she decides to announce it to the world's press without warning us? This is outrageous. A breach of trust.' Mauritz's voice rises with fury.

'It's unexpected and . . . unfortunate for us, yes.'

'How could you let this happen?'

'Mauritz, please try to calm down. I was managing a full press junket for the entire day. I am not in charge of what information Sarah chooses to disclose. I thought Pavel was supposed to stay with her at all times?'

This makes Mauritz pause. He looks out of the window as he gathers his thoughts.

Neither of them speaks for a second. There is just the sound of Mauritz's angry breathing down the line. Finally, Helen breaks the tension.

'Maybe we could turn this to our advantage.'

'We have made it clear one of Neurocell's primary uses could be for the treatment of Alzheimer's disease, and now the very person endorsing it is personally afflicted. It is biased. It is not sound.' Outrage has been replaced by despair as he realises the implication of Sarah's betrayal.

'Let's make it intentional. Let's reframe the narrative. The announcement of her diagnosis has been timed to coincide with the conference. She is invested in the technology both professionally and personally. She's putting herself forward as a trial candidate. That's the most powerful endorsement of all. We can make this work for us.'

Mauritz draws in a breath and closes his eyes, and the clouds start to clear from his mind. 'And what about the interviews that were cancelled? *The Lancet*? And the others? We need them on side. They won't be happy that we shut them out.'

'Quite to the contrary. The Landau exclusive will make them hungry for their own story. Collier's diagnosis and the groundbreaking technology *you* have developed will actually come together to make a much more colourful news piece. Forget the science-specific press, this could go viral, and that's exactly what we want.'

'Possibly.'

'Definitely, Mauritz. This is what I do. Let's use this to our advantage. Tomorrow's launch will be even more loaded. This is no longer theoretical, it's happening. Let's show the entire world what you have managed to achieve here at the Schiller Institute.'

He considers for a second the life raft Helen has thrown out to him. It could work, as long as nothing else goes wrong. 'Make it happen, Helen. The funding depends on it.'

'Have I ever let you down?'

He ends the call and takes a deep breath. He does trust her but they are not home and dry, not yet. There are billions of dollars on the table pending the successful launch of Neurocell, and they need to pull together. They need to work as one. They are only as strong as their weakest link, and Sarah Collier has buckled.

The architect of the whole security system at the Schiller Institute is Pavel Osinov – the surveillance cameras, entry systems and their digital log-in data. In his office, flicking between various screens of the surveillance video, he checks that last night hasn't left any digital footprints. He enters the system and erases his logged entry. He then scrolls through every camera covering the south side of the Institute and erases the twenty-minute window when three of the cameras went dark. He resets the time code, as simple as a cut and paste. He is in the clear, as far as he can see. But there is one camera he can't review, the one he doesn't have access to: Helen Alder's webcam. In the corner of his screen, he watches the live footage of the Schiller Institute: Jan Pager at the reception desk, the white bodies gliding around the research lab, everyone at their desks, everything calm. Something moving at speed down the corridor towards his office cuts through the stillness. He instinctively shuts down the surveillance images he is reviewing.

Mauritz Schiller enters the room with a face like thunder, the door closing behind him.

'I need answers, Pavel.' His tone usually reflects respect for his trusted ally and asset, but not today. Today there is a tremble in his voice, a fierce accusation. Pavel's mind races as he runs through the potential causes of the hostility; truth be told, there are many.

'Where were you?' Mauritz pins him to the wall with his gaze.

'I'm not sure what you are referring to?'

'Sarah Collier's press interviews. It seems like Helen Alder is doing your job for you. I tasked you with watching her while she was here. Why didn't you cut the interview short when she started going "off piste"?'

'What happened?'

'You mean you don't know?'

'I wasn't there, I was with Daniel.'

'And why was that, when I specifically instructed you to be glued to Sarah twenty-four-seven? Sleep in the fucking hotel lobby, if necessary, but don't let her out of your sight. Did I not say that?'

'Yes, you did, and I have been watching her like a hawk, trust me, but—'

'No "buts", Pavel, this is exactly the reason she needed to be monitored. This single stupid interview could have blown everything apart, the whole conference, the future of Neurocell.' Pavel takes a steadying breath and Mauritz slowly backs away from the desk, ready to ram him.

'It will not happen again.'

'Then why are you still here? Is Sarah hiding somewhere in this room?' Mauritz waits for Pavel to concede. His chair jerks forward an inch, threatening. His finger is twitchy.

'Well?'

'I'm on it.'

'I need people around me I can trust. You're standing on thin ice, Osinov.'

He spins his chair around and exits the room. Pavel exhales but confusion clouds his mind. He assumed Mauritz knew where he was earlier. Helen has scheduled everything and everyone to within an inch of their lives. She asked him to take Daniel skiing. Was it a coincidence or was it an orchestrated plan to remove him from Sarah's side? If so, why would she do that? Unless she had another agenda. Does she know what he is doing?

His attempt to hack her computer now feels even more pressing. More than an itch to scratch. He has to find out what she knows. Is it wise to poke the hornet's nest? Well, the hornet's nest is already stirring – he needs to pierce the queen.

A plan begins to formulate in his mind.

CHAPTER 24

DANIEL

I exit the hotel, my mind racing. I'm trying to contain my anger, but this spells trouble. I emerge from the warmth of the lobby and out into the assault of the biting wind. How could this happen? Sarah's condition is a private matter. It is not supposed to be the subject of gossip or clickbait for fame-hungry bloggers. I lose my footing on the freshly laid carpet of snow that covers the path and stumble in a frenzy of panic and rage. I know exactly who to blame. I am livid but I am also scared. Sarah's diagnosis is now out there in the world. People will be asking questions and expecting answers that I don't have. It makes it all so much more real. Something we have to have answers for. As yet, I have none.

I up my pace and limp over the bridge, my knee burning in pain, wrapping my coat tightly around my neck to block out the wind and cover my face. The frozen water of the lake looks fragile beneath me and I wonder if it would hold my weight. My heavy load. How long would it take me to drown if I dived in? I'd probably freeze to death first. Not helpful, Daniel. I have to find out what the hell happened. I press on, anger fuelling every footstep, past the Ferris wheel of the Jardin anglais until I reach the children's playground. Sparse barren trees reach their bony fingers towards me, threatening to grasp and strangle. I near the familiar ramshackle Alpine cabin in the centre of the park. A light is on inside. Good. The door is bolted from the inside and I hammer on the door, my fury infusing every strike. The rusty bolt grinds back and the door creaks open.

'Daniel! You startled me.' There's a chill in the room; the steam from my coat and the heat of my anger rise off me.

'Helen. What the hell is going on?'

She stares at me, a darkness descending over her eyes. 'I'm sorry?' Her voice remains steady and her cold expression makes me check myself and swallow. '*Landau Leaks*. The world exclusive about Sarah having Alzheimer's.' As the words come tumbling out, I move forward, looming over her. She holds my gaze, saying nothing.

'I thought you were sitting in on the interview.'

'Yes, it is unfortunate.' She turns and walks over to a side table behind the desk of computer screens.

'It's more than unfortunate, Helen. She's exposed now. This could ruin everything. I thought you were supposed to manage the press interviews?'

She pours something into a glass and turns towards me. She's unnervingly calm. 'I am not responsible for your wife's indiscretions, Daniel. You've heard the recording?'

'Excuse me?' I can't bear being spoken to like this.

'I asked . . . if you have heard the recording?'

'Of course I bloody heard it.'

She hands me the glass. Her face remains a mask of calm, making mine burn hotter.

'If Sarah has decided to tell her story, who are you to intervene? Her keeper?'

'Don't throw that "he's a misogynist" crap at me.'

Here's the thing about women like Helen. They throw their punches with words before my brain can engage. Her eyes move down to my suddenly clenched fists and she gives me a patronising smile.

'Daniel, stop. Have a drink with me.' I find myself taking the glass and knocking back the whisky. The amber liquor tingles and burns my throat.

'This situation is not ideal. But we move forward. I am handling it, unlike you . . . clearly.'

She is watching me, her eyes flickering with condescension.

'How was the mountain? Did you and Pavel get to know each other? He's fascinating, isn't he?'

There is sarcasm and mockery in her tone. She's deflecting.

'Never mind Pavel, what do we do about Landau?'

She sits back at the rickety wooden table with her back to me; multiple windows are open on her screen.

'Sit down, you're making me feel uncomfortable.'

What am I, a dog? My body, however, obeys, despite my ego, and I slump down on the threadbare corduroy armchair under the window. I feel as pitiful as the frozen dead flies on the sill. I remove my jacket and boots and feel the rough wooden floor through my damp socks.

'So?'

'So?' She still has her back to me.

'So, what now?' My face is reddening, and the veins in my neck are throbbing. She stands to face me and leans her body against the desk.

'We carry on as planned. This doesn't change anything.'

I want to believe her, but it all seems to be tumbling out of control. She moves closer to the rusty gas stove, which is emitting a withering heat. I look up at her, her blonde hair framing her exquisite face, her green eyes observing my discomfort.

'Daniel, you don't need me to remind you of the real value of what we're doing, do you?' She reaches for the packet of cigarettes on the desk. The gas canister in the fire peters out and dies as if she has power over that too. She puts a cigarette between her teeth and we look at one another in silence. I am transfixed. She continues to stare at me.

'Well?'

I wait, knowing what comes next. The silence that follows and her descending eyes, tracing down my body, command me, and I obey. Slowly and carefully, I begin to undress. It's automatic, without tease or effect. She watches nonchalantly, almost disinterested. I look down and see a livid black-red bruise across my belly, the skin welted with trauma from my fall. The bones of my shoulders are red and battered, my knee is swollen and my shins are torn and raw.

'Poor boy. You look like you lost a fight.'

I'm a mess. She stares at my wounds with both pity and delight. She approaches slowly. Her knee slides across my naked thigh and she brings her body close. A course of adrenaline rushes through me. I'm intoxicated. Then she bites into my lower lip. It feels dangerous. It is dangerous. It is always dangerous.

I taste blood as her teeth drag across my tongue. Her hand reaches for my throat. There is a lustful violence in her grasp, fingernails digging into my skin. It has never been like this before. Her grip tightens and I can't breathe. I grab her wrists; it's a reflex.

'Sorry . . . I'm just . . . I don't know what we're doing.' I feel embarrassed. 'I don't want to be this person.'

'But you *are* this person, Daniel.' It's a challenge. My heart is thumping in my chest.

'Dan. Listen to me. You have spent your entire adult life living in your wife's shadow. Too many people have walked over you too many times. When are you going to take control and change all that?'

I slouch under the weight of her words and she lifts my chin with her elegant fingers.

'I am here for you. Once this is all over, we are going to be together. Just the two of us. Just like we planned.'

And there we have it. We have plans, so now you know.

I shiver at the statement: words spoken out loud forming a commitment to the universe. Helen places a hand on the back of my head. Her kiss this time is soft and sensual. It's a promise, a true bond of trust.

I'm out of time and out of place. I don't expect you to understand what I'm doing. This is complicated. The anger in me is real; I'm angry at the hand life has dealt me. It's all a game, you see, a competition. Winners and losers. I've tried to play fairly. I've spent my life watching the sharks, the alphas, the assholes, fight and cheat their way to the top. Now it's my turn. It's time to do something for me. Time to make a new life for myself. A life after Sarah.

I get dressed and prepare to return to the hotel and lie to my wife. It isn't the first time, and it won't be the last.

CHAPTER 25

Across from the Parc La Grange, crawling through lanes of slow-moving traffic, Pavel heads back to the hotel to resume his babysitting duties. The damage has been done and now he must somehow pick up the pieces, but his mind is on other things. His hand grips the wheel, his fingers restless and flexing. He breathes deeply, steadying himself, thinking of the gun and of the thief who took it. He has important work to do here but he must focus, fall in line and play the game. He changes lanes across the static traffic and pulls into a side road opposite the park. A wooden cart by the entrance gates selling *vin chaud*, hotdogs and pretzels is shutting up shop for the evening. Pavel pulls a woollen beanie from his pocket, jumps out of his car and jogs to catch the vendor before he leaves. He follows a runner into the park and pauses to perch on the railing of a small bridge crossing a frozen stream. He looks up towards the silhouette of Villa La Grange looming in the dark, sipping wine from a paper cup and biting down into the mustard-smothered bratwurst and fried onions. His mind is heavy, the weight of the responsibility hanging over him, bearing down. Not the chaperoning – that he can do with his eyes closed. It's the bigger picture that's bothering him, how to do what needs to be done. He chews on the salt-crusted end of his bread roll and ponders.

In the middle of a small clump of trees, about two hundred yards away, he sees a small wooden cabin next to a children's playground. Maybe he'll perch on one of the swings and finish his snack. As he moves towards the dilapidated shack, the door opens. Pavel freezes for a second, mid-bite, as he notices a dark-haired, middle-aged man stepping out. There is something about his posture that is familiar. As he turns back to the doorway, he catches his face: it's Daniel Collier. Pavel doesn't move for a second, then steps inconspicuously towards the cover of a pine tree. What is Daniel doing down here? He assumed he would be back at the hotel, nursing his wounds – or looking after his wife. Daniel is speaking to someone in the doorway; the conversation appears intense. Pavel finishes his wine and sausage and disposes of the cup in a nearby waste bin. Then he moves closer to the cabin in the shadow of the trees, head down, trying to observe Daniel more closely.

Daniel is about to leave when a slender arm reaches out to clasp the back of his neck and pull him in for a kiss. The open door blocks Pavel's view and then the door is pulled closed as Daniel moves off. Damn. Pavel turns sharply away to face the park gates as Daniel heads quickly down the path and out onto the Rue Gustave-Ador. His instinct is to follow but he knows where he must be heading. On the other hand, what he doesn't know is who he was meeting in that cabin. Is it that important? To Sarah maybe, but not to him. Daniel's a dark horse, a deceiver, so what? In a way, there is now a sense of intrigue about the insipid Daniel. It perhaps makes him more interesting. Pavel makes the decision not to follow him but watches as he half jogs, half limps across the snow-encrusted grass, out of the gates and back towards his hotel. He smirks to himself and shakes his head. The man who sat weeping in front of him earlier in the day, distraught over his wife's condition, is a player. Funny old world.

Pavel decides to head back to his car. He considers driving after Daniel, offering him a lift just to see his face and hear his spluttered excuse. He needs to get back to the hotel to keep himself glued to Sarah Collier as Mauritz has instructed. He reaches the gate to the park and is nearly at his car when he happens to look back at the cabin. The light in the window extinguishes and the door opens. A figure emerges and begins to walk briskly back down the incline, directly towards him. He continues walking, head down. In his peripheral vision, he keeps track of the woman rushing to get out of the park before the gates are locked. His eyes flick to the rear window of each parked car as he passes, desperately trying to catch a reflection of who is following behind him, but the frost obscures his vision. Eventually, he reaches his vehicle. As he presses the fob to unlock, another car parked ahead is also triggered, its side lights flashing in sync. He opens his door and slides in quickly, leaning over to the passenger seat, turning his face away as the figure hurries past. He whips his head back to watch but isn't in time to see her face. He hears a door slam; then the engine of the other car fires up and a black SUV pulls out. Could it be? Pavel slides down into his seat as it pulls slowly alongside. He raises his eyebrows. It is. Drifting past his window, her blonde hair tied back, checking her lips in the rear-view mirror, is Helen Alder. He watches the familiar black car wait at the junction, then pull out and speed away.

So, Helen Alder is a player. He always assumed she was, but what exactly she is playing *at* with Daniel Collier is the bigger question. He always felt there was something duplicitous about her, something deceitful, but he wondered if his bias was just personal. He didn't like her, but then the feeling was reciprocated, she had made that quite clear. But he has learned something very valuable tonight. Now he knows something about her that he can use to his advantage. *Kompromat*. A tiny vibration echoes in the deep recesses of his mind. *Kompromat* is valuable, and he knows exactly how to use it. Now he has something to shame and expose her with if necessary – a bargaining chip. Helen has something that Pavel needs. She holds the key to locked doors, and now he has the leverage to break them open.

He presses the ignition; fire sparks fuel.

CHAPTER 26

SARAH

I can hear music playing. I am lying on my side, half of my body uncovered; half awake and half in a dream. Over the top of the music there is a conversation that I can't quite hear. I strain to understand what the voices are saying but can't make it out. Then there is a knock at the door. They're coming for me; I can feel it. I'm out of time, and my summons is long overdue. I try to get up but my body won't move; a suffocating paralysis has taken hold of me. The knock sounds on the door again; I have to answer it or else they'll break it down. It feels as if my body is glued to the bed. Eventually, I manage to wrench myself up, sweaty and trembling. The room is still and dark, my head is thrumming. Then I hear them again: the muffled voices. They're coming from inside the wall, a low murmur, interrupted by the laughter of a drunken reveller outside in the distance and a church bell tolling: two.

I'm now standing in the doorway between the bedroom and the sitting room, in the deep panelled gap between these thick old walls. I lean into the painted woodwork. The dark room is brushed by the slightest kiss of moonlight, and I see a figure sitting on a chair silhouetted in the window, hair covering their face. They are speaking but it's not directed at me. I can't understand the muffled conversation; it's indecipherable, submerged. There is someone else here; another voice. I can't see their face as their head is in their hands, but they seem upset. The whole atmosphere in the room is heavy with sadness.

My feet feel cold. I look down to see that I'm standing bare-foot on a marble surface. The chill penetrates the soles of my feet, creeping up my legs and hips into my belly, and I start to shiver. A light emanating from above me draws my head up and I see a face looking back at me. I should know this person, but I can't recall their name. Lank hair flopping across tired eyes. I grip the bathroom sink to keep me from falling and stare at the woman in the glass. Who are you? I reach out to touch her face, and her fingertips meet mine. We connect, we're alike in many ways. As I reach forward, I lose my balance and my knees slip and slide on the cold bathroom floor. I slump down, exhausted. I hate this. I am surrounded by strangers. I want to go home. I don't feel safe. The thoughts press down upon me and I start to sob, wet tears dripping down my face. I lie down and let the paralysis take hold once more.

A pair of warm hands wrap around my waist and caress my stomach, pulling me to my feet. I look back to the mirror. Two faces now, side by side. The same woman I saw before but now there is someone else beside her. A woman with sharp features, like mine. I look at her green eyes with heavy lids, and her lips part to reveal perfect white teeth. I compare our faces but the reflection is out of focus now, blurred behind a cloud of steam rising from the hot tap. Her head disappears behind mine, I can feel breath on my neck and a kiss. Our faces now wearing each other.

A hand reaches forward and draws a heart into the steam on the glass with familiar fingers. Then presses against my sternum and pulls me closer. Printing into me.

Standing in the bedroom, I'm now watching two people asleep under the covers. A man and a woman. They are so peaceful, entwined in a love knot, their limbs becoming one. There is no room for me in that tangle. I am left out in the cold, not welcome here. I am not welcome anywhere any more. Then the knock at the door booms loudly out of the silence. They're here. They're coming for me. It is time.

CHAPTER 27

DANIEL

It was a rough night; Sarah had another . . . episode, a nightmare I suppose you would call it. I found her on the bathroom floor in the early hours, sobbing and delirious. I got her back to bed and lay awake next to her for hours. I haven't been able to sleep at all. I have too many thoughts running through my head, too many worries on my mind. You probably don't have much sympathy for me, knowing what you know. But this whole situation is taking up so much of my energy. It's not just the deceit and the guilt, it's the sadness and the stress. It's every negative feeling you can imagine. The ugliness is coiled up inside me, ready to lash out and cause more destruction. I am using every last fibre of my strength to keep my shit together and I think the rope is starting to fray.

I'm hoping that after a few decent hours of sleep, Sarah will feel better. I just ordered room service for breakfast so I can get some nourishment inside of her; we have a big day ahead of us. Sarah is expected to stand up in front of hundreds of people at the Neurocell launch alongside Mauritz Schiller. This is the whole reason I convinced her to come here. Well, one of the reasons. Now you know my other reason for wanting to come back to Geneva: Helen Alder.

'Morning, Dan.' Sarah is awake. Her eyes are open.

'Hey you, how are you feeling?' I move to the bed and sit down next to her. 'Headache?'

'No, I'm feeling OK.' She rubs her eyes and sits up against the pillows I've packed around her. 'What's all this for?'

'You had a nightmare.'

'Sweet, my very own padded cell.' My sharp-witted wife is back, that's good.

'Hungry? I've ordered some breakfast.' I hop off the bed and start to pull some of her clothes out of the wardrobe. She doesn't answer. 'Sarah?'

'Yes, sorry . . .' She's looking out of the window at the bright Geneva morning, towards Mont Blanc. Sunlight illuminates her sad face.

'Big day today,' she answers me with a sigh, and continues to stare out of the window. 'How are you feeling about it all?' I lay her favourite dark-blue suit over the back of a chair.

Silence again. I pull her underwear from a drawer and return to sit on the edge of the bed.

'Sarah?'

'Yes, I heard you the first time, Daniel. How am I feeling about it? Well, you know me: I absolutely love public speaking in front of hundreds of people. And even more so when they all know my private business. When they all know that I'm dying.'

I'm not in the mood for being a punchbag this morning. I shoot up off the bed and head into the bathroom. I know I should be more sympathetic, but I can't help it. Sometimes she talks to me like I'm a total idiot. She's not the only one drowning under the weight of all this. I'm her carer now: dressing her, mopping up shit and vomit, and there is only so much I can take. I turn on the shower and stand under the water, letting the steam envelop me. I glance down and inspect my wounds. The water stings my grazed flesh but I revel in the pain. I return to the bedroom, towelling my hair. I pop a coffee pod in the machine.

'Only decaf left, I'm afraid.' I turn and smile. 'Want one?'

'Sorry I snapped.' Her eyes are seeking reconciliation. She's a mess. Her hair is matted and her eyes are hollow and haunted.

'It's OK, love.'

'Everything is getting on top of me. The last few days have been really hard. And now I have to talk about Alzheimer's to the world. I'm not sure I can. What will I even say?'

I wrap a robe around me and take a sip of the rubbish coffee.

'It's a lot to deal with, I know. But if anyone can do it, you can.' I need her to believe me. 'Mauritz Schiller could have asked any number of people to endorse Neurocell but he chose you. And that's because you're brilliant.' I kiss the top of her head and breathe in the smell of her hair. She smells of stale sweat. I recoil and smile sadly at her.

Her lips move to say something else but before she can utter the words, there's a knock on the hotel room door. She flinches, her eyes darting nervously to the door.

'It's OK, love. It's only breakfast!' I leap up from the sofa, open the door and let the waitress push a trolley full of pastry and real coffee, with real caffeine, into the small sitting room. '*Merci beaucoup*.' I cringe at my attempt at French.

'*Bitte schön*.' German. Of course, nice try, Daniel. I smile at her and hand her a few francs. I hear the door close as I lead Sarah from the bed and into our makeshift bistro in the other room.

'Madame, breakfast is served.'

She sits in her robe and nibbles the corner of a warm croissant as I lift the silver cloche and dig hungrily into scrambled eggs and wafer-thin bacon.

There's something faded about her, almost transparent. 'You'll smash it out of the park, love. You always do. And after today it will all be over. After the conference we can relax and then jump on an earlier flight home if you like. How does that sound? Get back and surprise Maddie.'

At the mention of our daughter, her eyes light up and I'm hit by another lurching wave of guilt.

'Oh shit, that reminds me, she wanted chocolate and a cowbell.' Sarah cracks a smile at me.

'What is she going to do with a cowbell?'

'I dunno, probably tie it around my neck so she can keep tabs on me?' That makes her laugh out loud, little flakes of croissant sticking to her bottom lip.

What I'm doing to my family must seem so cruel, but the train has already left the station. I didn't expect this all to happen so fast. I'm managing the situation as best I can, trying to reconcile myself with the fact that I have other needs. It's overwhelming and I'm in unfamiliar territory. Being a carer is tiring, it's draining me; and it definitely kills the spark of passion. But that's what I'm trying to explain. The intense pleasure; the irresistible, electrifying and forbidden encounters with Helen. That's *my* medicine, you see. That's what *I* need to remain sane.

'You're right, I just have to get through today and then we're done.'

I can't look her in the eyes. I grab my coffee, move to the bedroom and call through the door, 'OK, I just need to grab your passport so I can change the flight.'

'It's in my bag on the side.'

I find the bag and start to rummage. 'Why don't you jump in the shower, love? Freshen up a bit; you'll feel better.'

As I search through the contents of her bag, I feel two hands slide around my waist to my belly and I'm pulled into an embrace. I flinch slightly as fingers move over my bruises. Sarah's grip is tight and needy.

'Thank you.'

Her gratitude stops me cold. 'What for?'

'For always being there for me. For being my rock. For looking after me.'

I gulp down my last dregs of decency and turn into her. 'I'll always be there for you, for both of you.'

She lays her head into my chest. I don't believe I'm a bad person but I've somehow managed to separate my actions from my conscience. As if what I'm doing is not who I really am. I am damaging myself, not her, because what she doesn't know can't hurt her and her capacity to know is now diminished. My skin prickles as a charge of electricity passes between us: the magnets repelling. I gently push her away.

'How about that shower?'

She rolls her eyes at me and smiles. 'Well, if I smell that bad!'

I laugh it off and return to her bag. I lay my hand on her passport and flick through the pages. Opening the page with the photo, I see a woman I have long forgotten. My wife, but back then, not as she is now. A younger version looking out at me, that enigmatic stare, like she knows something magical. She did. She knew. I close it, shutting out that penetrating stare and my doubts. I pocket the passport.

Now it's time to do what we came here for.

CHAPTER 28

SARAH

Mauritz Schiller sits across from me in the gaudy orange and gold dining room of L'Atelier Robuchon along the Quai de Mont-Blanc. His eyes scrutinise me over the rim of his coffee cup. Pavel Osinov is standing by the door, fiddling with his earpiece and checking his watch. Daniel has gone on ahead to get things ready with Helen and now I'm being briefed ahead of the launch.

'I am so sorry to hear of your condition and I realise this must be a very difficult time for you. But really, I must insist: no more surprises please, Professor Collier.' Schiller's tone is like a rap on the knuckles from a disappointed teacher and I note we're no longer on first-name terms. I glance over again at Pavel, whose eyes are glued to the door.

I decide to give him what he asks for. 'No more surprises,' I agree, as I push my cup away; any more caffeine and I will be hovering off the floor. I take a deep breath and turn back to my briefing notes.

'Good.' He looks down at his own set of papers and we sit, waiting for the appointed time.

Pavel checks his watch again and nods to Mauritz, who leans towards me.

'Ready?' I look up from the papers.

'As I'll ever be.' My stomach leaps as the clock ticks down to the whole reason we came here. I'm nervous as hell, but I'll rise to the occasion. I always do.

'Well then, let's go.' Mauritz manoeuvres his chair towards the

147

door and out onto the pavement, where his dedicated driver is waiting. Pavel ushers me towards the rear door of another car and we move off.

We make the five-minute drive towards the famous Campus Biotech, a place I have seen countless times in brochures and medical literature. The huge gleaming cathedral of science looms over us, a towering glass and steel façade. The evergreen trees encapsulated within the transparent structure give the impression that the Campus is somehow capable of harnessing nature. It is exactly as I expected: high-tech and flawless. As we round the corner, I look through the tinted glass window of the SUV and my heart punches up into my mouth. I can't believe what I'm seeing. Cast onto the enormous glass façade and wrapping round the building opposite is the projection of a face: my face. I remember that photo being taken after the Nobel Prize nomination. I was exhausted but we had won. That woman is now staring back at me, but she looks different. This improved version of Sarah Collier has an unlined face and sparkling eyes that are sharper and greener than mine. Her perfect hair is gently blowing in a digital breeze as my name, 'PROFESSOR SARAH M. COLLIER', fades up from beneath. Like the screens of a stadium rock concert, she appears to the gathering crowd like the Beyoncé of biotech. The animated Sarah seems to look straight at me, and I stare back at her. What have they done to me? How do I live up to that? As we pull into the terrace out front, a gaggle of journalists and photographers spot us and rush over to the entrance. The car slides past the crowd and onto a ramp at the rear, which descends into an underground car park. Pavel opens my door and a small group of assistants flock around me, guiding me across to a holding area where Mauritz is waiting, reading notes. A make-up artist powders my face and someone is smoothing out the wrinkles in the back of my jacket. I smirk to myself; it really should be the other way round: powder the backside and de-wrinkle the face, love.

A sound guy threads a cable through my shirt and down my trouser leg and wraps a mic pack around my ankle. I'm preened and poked from all angles, as I continue to look through the prepared statement and try to steady my nerves. The topic of my diagnosis has been neatly woven into the speech Mauritz is about to make, which will take the pressure off me considerably. It feels as though all I will be expected to do is stand there with a smile and tell the world that I endorse Neurocell.

'Sarah, I must say, aside from the shock of learning about your diagnosis, I felt . . . I feel very sorry for you.' I look up from my notes and see Mauritz watching me.

'Thank you. It hasn't been easy.' An image of Dad asleep in his chair, the last time I saw him, mouth wide open snoring, passes through my mind.

'It is a terrible disease. Truly. You are coping?' His voice cracks with concern.

'I'm getting there.' The look on his face touches me. I wonder what my dad is doing right now, and my eyes fill with tears. The tissue in my face from one of the panicked assistants reminds me that smudged mascara is not a good look for a Nobel Prize winner and I swallow my emotions back down.

The doors at the end of the corridor open and Daniel and Helen come through, deep in conversation. They are surrounded by several chaperones and 'hangers-on' tapping on phones and talking into 'walkies'. I mean, what do all these people do?

'Everything's in place. Are we ready?' Helen's authority pierces through the buzzing agitation of the room.

'Yes.' Mauritz is looking at me. 'Professor Collier?'

'Absolutely,' I lie, forcing a confident smile.

Daniel detaches himself from Helen and pulls me into a hug. Hands wrap around me and he whispers in my ear, 'You've got this.' I catch Helen looking at me. Her face is passive but her green eyes seem black. She tucks a strand of hair behind her ear and tilts her jaw towards me, then mutters something into her radio.

Mauritz glides away towards a side door and I begin to follow, but Helen blocks the way. 'No. This way.' Pavel leads me through a door and into a corridor. I can hear the buzz of expectation coming from the auditorium. He gently opens the door that leads to the stage. The sound of the audience flips my stomach. This is it.

The lights dim and the rumble of the crowd subdues. An orchestral soundscape worthy of a Spielberg movie begins to play. A beam of light shoots from the ceiling of the domed amphitheatre, cutting across the stage as a rumble of bass shakes the whole auditorium. The space is plunged into darkness, and a calm, commanding female voice announces:

Ladies and gentlemen, introducing a world exclusive.
Neurocell.

A chorus of sound and a burst of light ripples around the hall as something begins to emerge through the floor, centre stage. A seated figure, in black silhouette; Mauritz Schiller rises slowly into view.

A world without sickness, a world without doubt. A doorway to the far reaches of the untapped mind. Neurocell.
    Ladies and Gentlemen, please welcome to the stage,
Mauritz Schiller.

On a huge wraparound screen enveloping the amphitheatre, multiple high-definition images of Neurocell against a backdrop of some utopian scientific future play on a loop.

Mauritz remains perfectly still in the spotlight, receiving his rapturous applause. The claps and cheers fade and he holds the silence with his signature commanding confidence.

'Esteemed colleagues, respected reporters, welcome guests: my name is Mauritz Schiller, and today I present to you a new future. A future many thought would never be possible but a future that has arrived.'

Mauritz continues his speech as I stand waiting. I swallow, trying to moisten my dry mouth. What if nothing comes out when I try to speak? Why did I ever agree to do this? Too late now. Bright sharp graphics celebrating the wonders of Neurocell play out across the auditorium, buying me a little more time. As the screen cuts to darkness and the applause subsides, I brace my knees as I hear Mauritz introduce me. The time has come, there is nowhere to hide.

'Widely regarded as one of the greatest scientists of her generation. My friends, I present: Professor Sarah M. Collier.'

A spotlight hits the door where I'm standing and the sudden thud of entrance music makes me jump with a start. I feel the gentle push of a hand in the small of my back as my legs begin to walk forward against the instincts of everything else in my body. As I step onto the stage, that same doctored image of me emerges on the screen. Neurocell everywhere, Sarah Collier everywhere, all at once. It's dazzling. This is it, the moment I must face everyone. I stride out and take my place next to Mauritz. The glass screen of an autocue has materialised alongside a microphone, and something, long forgotten in me, kicks in. That part of my brain that is totally capable and totally in control. As I step out of the shadows, the crowd cheer and I can't help but smile: *they are with me.* The spotlight follows me over to a lectern and I gather myself. The applause dies down and Mauritz continues.

'Neurocell presents solutions to problems that have troubled humanity for centuries. I have faced many obstacles in my own life, as this chair will tell you.' He smacks the arm of his wheelchair and pauses, holding the crowd's attention. 'I have used my personal experiences to create tailor-made solutions to specific problems. That is why I am exceptionally proud that Neurocell has won the confidence of Professor Sarah Collier. Yesterday, Professor Collier announced the sad news that she is suffering from Alzheimer's disease. Her bravery and courage are an inspiration to us all, and her involvement in Neurocell is invaluable.'

The crowd erupts into a burst of applause. It's unnerving. As the noise dies down, there is a pause. I look over at Mauritz. It's time to tell the truth. I turn slowly and find the microphone. The autocue rolls but I'm speaking from the heart. No one gets to put words in my mouth. Not today. I look out into the crowd, take a deep breath and begin. My voice is clear but quiet.

'When I heard about brain implants, I was . . . scared. It struck me as Orwellian, you know, the thought police. Let's be honest, it's like Putin had a wet dream.' There is a smattering of laughter from the audience and I see Mauritz scowling at me. I'm going off script; too right I am. 'But the more I read, the more I realised that Neurocell could be the key to unlocking so many answers. As you heard, I was recently diagnosed with Alzheimer's. It is a cruel disease, a death sentence for many people. It is a lot to come to terms with, but Neurocell gives me hope. Some of you may be sceptical of my involvement. And yes, it's true I have a very personal stake in Neurocell's success. I am now a patient, but from that perspective, I can tell you, science and medicine are personal. Tell the woman who dies of breast cancer for want of better screening that it is not personal. Tell the man with motor neurone disease who loses increasing control of his body each day that it is not personal. Tell the parents who look on helplessly as their three-year-old dies of leukaemia that it is not personal.' My voice cracks under the weight of my words but I swallow and breathe in the silence of the crowd. I look into the lights and continue. 'From my perspective as a scientist, I depend on facts and data to get to the truth. Well, here are three important facts. One: I have Alzheimer's disease. Two: I don't know how much longer I have left to live. Three: if Neurocell is a success, then . . . maybe hundreds of lives could be saved from this dreadful disease. I'm prepared to take a leap of faith for the sake of others. I believe Neurocell is the future. We just have to use it wisely. Thank you.'

The combined roar of hundreds of voices raises the roof as the audience erupts. The stamping of feet shakes the floor and the ovation continues for what feels like minutes. Mauritz Schiller is grinning from ear to ear with a look of gratitude. I smile back at him. The sound from the crowd seems to travel into the distance and I shrink inside my own body.

I've done what they wanted. It's in their hands now. I turn, searching for a way out. As I scan the room looking for Daniel, a sea of faces glazed in smiling adoration surges towards the stage. I back away, eyeballing the exit door, passing beneath the enormous projected image of Sarah Collier, 'The Face of Neurocell'.

I've delivered Schiller's future and now I can go home.

CHAPTER 29

'Mauritz, that was outstanding.' Helen intercepts him as he arrives at the entrance to the vast forum full of medical trade booths and licensing stands. The post-launch party is in full swing and Mauritz is ready to take his victory lap, before heading to a more intimate gathering of investors and financiers who will take Neurocell from prototype to the marketplace within a few months.

'It was magnificent, Helen. You certainly know how to put on a show. I couldn't have done it without you.' Mauritz smiles. 'I'm grateful to you. For your professionalism but more importantly for your loyalty.'

'Mauritz . . .' Helen smiles knowingly at him. She did this, she'll take the compliment and own it. The room is filling with excited delegates pouring out of the auditorium, all eager to discuss marketing strategy and celebrity endorsement and no mention of 'the cautious restraint of ethics'. Helen places her hand on Mauritz's shoulder as they continue to move through the crowd. 'I just had a very interesting conversation with one of the Chinese investors. They want to get ahead of the game. Their very generous advance will be in the company account by midnight tonight.'

Mauritz slows and turns to look at Helen. For a second, a flicker of doubt crosses his face: is this the Pandora's box that he feared it might be? He buries those thoughts with a thin smile.

'This is your legacy, Mauritz.' She's right. The future of the Institute is secure and the name Schiller will live on long after he takes his last breath. She leans in and Mauritz plants a kiss on her cheek.

From the corner of the room, hovering in the shadow of the doorway, Pavel Osinov scans the room. Out of the corner of his eye he watches Mauritz Schiller in deep conversation with Helen Alder. For months he has been gathering the information he needs but now it's time to apply some moderate pressure. Nothing too obvious, but he must step up his game. He sees Helen leave the atrium and watches her weave her way through the melee, her blonde hair towering above the crowd. He lets a few seconds pass and then he follows her out, striding behind, keeping her in his sights. As he turns the corner, he sees her slip through the entrance to the stage. He sprints forward and catches the door before it closes behind her. Silently, he slides through. There is no one here. He waits for a second in silence, then moves into the first row of seats. The whole place is in darkness.

'Following me, Osinov?'

Her voice makes him turn on his heel. His heart stops for a second. Helen has stepped onto the stage and is watching him in a pool of half-light.

'Just tying up some loose ends.'

'Hmm. I have a few of those to sort out myself.' She watches him, her mouth and chin brushed with light, her eyes in darkness.

'Yes, I know all about them.'

'And what exactly do you think you know?'

Helen has chosen to take centre stage. It's time for Pavel to find out more about the performance he's been watching for some time now. Remaining in the darkness, he begins to move silently around the perimeter of the amphitheatre.

'I know something that is worth a lot to you. Something that you would rather keep secret.'

Helen laughs. 'How fantastically vague. I really don't have time for this.'

'I know about you and Daniel Collier.'

She spins, following the direction of his voice, her face now blinded by a stark spotlight.

'I will tell his wife everything, unless you do as I say.'

Helen raises her hand to her eyes, against the glare, and holds her ground. 'How clever of you. Now listen to me.' The fury is rising within her as her fingernails dig into her palms.

'I'm all ears.' Pavel's voice is now suddenly close behind her. She feels his breath on her neck.

She raises a hand to strike but Pavel catches it by the wrist before it lands. 'Be careful.' He holds her and feels her body strain against his grasp. She moves her body closer to his and they come eye to eye.

She speaks slowly. 'If you want to tell Sarah Collier that I'm fucking her husband, then be my guest.' She leans in, her mouth close enough to bite his ear off. 'But if you ever threaten me again, I will take you down.' Closer still, her tongue almost burrowing into his ear canal like a serpent. 'I know all about you. I know what you have done. I know who you are. And I know why you are here. So stay the fuck out of my business, and I will grant you the same courtesy.'

Pavel holds Helen's gaze as she backs away and bathes in his discomfort. There is a flicker of admiration between them; the recognition that you are only as good as your opponent.

Finally, with a satisfied smile, she walks away. As she reaches the door, she turns to study him. Now it's his turn in the spotlight. It's a shame. Maybe he could have been an ally, two like-minded souls. Two damaged people. Too late for that. She pushes the door. Light from the corridor casts a long ominous shadow across the stage as she makes her exit.

The dance is over. For now.

CHAPTER 30

SARAH

It's over. It's done. Now we can go home, back to Maddie and Dad and our quiet, uneventful lives. I want our garden, our kitchen, the peace and quiet. I can hear the echo of the post-launch party, reverberating around that enormous cavern of glass. The music is still pumping, that image of me is still plastered everywhere. I feel like I have done something worthwhile here, but I can't take the scrutiny any more. The pitiful looks, the kindly smiles and taps on the shoulder. I pull my hands away from my face as I perch in a silent cubicle of the bathroom, grateful for a moment of solitude. As I reach into my bag for my pills, I hear the bathroom door open. Heels click across the tiles, slowly and intentionally. I pause for a second in silence. The person on the other side of the door is waiting. I remain still and inaudible, trying to pretend I'm not here. I open the cubicle door and find Helen Alder, leaning against the sink, smiling, with two glasses of champagne in her hands.

'I thought I might find you in here. You were amazing out there.' She offers one of the glasses to me. 'Neurocell has been given the green light by the investors, thanks to you.'

The glass hovers between us but I'm not taking it.

I smile politely and move to the sink to wash my hands.

'Oh, I didn't do anything.'

She steps to my side and places the glass down next me. She looks at herself in the mirror and adjusts her hair. I watch her manicured nails and glance down to her waist and the curve of her hips. 'Well, your endorsement was all we needed. And now that's done, we can celebrate . . . right?' Her eyes shine at me through the mirror and her glass is lifted in a friendly toast.

'I'm just glad it's all over, to be honest.' I pick up the glass and take a sip of the champagne.

'Ten million pounds isn't too shoddy for an afternoon's work, is it?' She is staring at me intently. I nearly choke on my drink.

'Ten . . . million?'

She smiles. 'The endorsement fee, Sarah.' She takes another sip of her champagne, her eyes glued to mine over the rim of the glass. 'Daniel didn't mention it?'

'No, Daniel didn't mention it.' I set the drink down next to the basin, wondering what the hell is going on. A fee for my endorsement? Have I been bought without knowing it? That's not who I am, that's not what this is, surely? Red-hot fury rises to my cheeks. Helen is watching me, smiling with her teeth and probing with her eyes. Then she laughs.

'That's so strange.' She breaks her stare and looks back at her reflection. 'I wonder what else he hasn't told you.'

Her statement hangs in the air; I realise she is waiting for an answer. I watch her through the mirror. Her face changes and she smiles with a subtle nod. Then that slight flinch of pity at the corners of her eyes, and the curl of her lip. In that moment, a rush of confirmation hits me. Everything I have feared is there in that single look. She breaks eye contact, turns away and walks out of the bathroom without saying another word. He's sleeping with her. Daniel is having an affair with Helen Alder. It has been right in front of me all along: his awkwardness when we met her outside the airport, the body language at the drinks reception, her strange scrutiny of me from the moment I arrived. Everything suddenly clicks into place. I feel sick. My stomach pulses and bile surges up into my mouth. I run over to the toilet and vomit. The acid taste of champagne and metal in my mouth. I vomit again, sinking to my knees.

Trembling, I wash my face in the basin. This can't be happening. It can't be real. I have to leave. I have to get out of here. I down the rest of the champagne to get rid of the taste of bile in my mouth, push myself up from the marble sink and leave the bathroom, my hands holding on to the walls to steady myself as I make for the exit. Fuck you, Daniel. Fuck these people. I want to go home. I take the corridor away from the noise of the crowd. I'm almost at a run when I turn a corner and slam straight into a mountain of unmoving muscle.

'Oh God, I'm so sorry.'

Pavel Osinov's expressionless face looms down at me. 'Easy there. Everything OK?'

'I'm fine.' I barge past, head down, trying to get to the door. Then I stop and turn back, his face watching me intently. 'Actually, can you take me back to the hotel?'

He gazes down the corridor towards the party and squints with uncertainty.

'I think they would like to congratulate you in there?'

'Don't bother, I'll get a taxi.' I turn to leave the way I was going.

'No, wait, I'll help you.'

He draws closer. I let him pass and he leads me towards the exit and down the stairs into the car park. We climb into the vehicle, Pavel starts the engine and we pull away. I try to remain calm but my mind is a cacophony of questions. A dot-to-dot of irrational connections. Helen Alder? Surely I'm mistaken? Am I jumping to conclusions? My judgement is just so unreliable. Is this paranoia or am I being taken for a fool? But there's something about it that makes sense. Daniel has been to the Schiller Institute for work numerous times in the last year, so the opportunity was there.

And things have started to become strained between us recently. I thought it was the stress of his work and the burden of my dad. But the way Helen spoke to me just now was so intentional and loaded. She didn't say the words but she wanted me to know. She was flaunting it. And what the hell was she talking about, ten million pounds? Pavel turns to me.

'Are you OK?'

'No,' I say without thinking.

'What happened?'

I feel my eyes well up with tears but I force them back down. I hadn't bargained for the sudden flash of images from a future that was now dissolving into nothing. Nothing ahead: no plans, no life with Daniel. Does it have to be like this? Is betrayal really the end of everything? But without trust, what is there?

'I don't have anyone I can trust any more.'

'I only ever trust my own instincts. I have had to learn that the hard way.'

He's right, and those instincts just reared their heads and bellowed a warning in my face.

I am truly on my own now.

CHAPTER 31

THE LANDAU REPORT

The future is here. The future is Neurocell. Well folks, I did it. I made it all the way to Geneva, interviewed my hero Sarah Collier and was in the room for the spectacular press launch of Neurocell.

So, it seems my source was right about pretty much everything. Professor Mauritz Schiller has developed a technology that will provide an electrical support mechanism for the brain. An implant. It's everything we feared but it has the potential to be so much worse. In the wrong hands, this technology could be very dangerous. But it has already been invented, it is already here, and it has been endorsed by one of the world's leading scientists. The fact that Neurocell was received with such unanimous approval from the scientific community means that the plans are already in motion, whether we like it or not. But the pledge from the Schiller Institute is to only permit the use of Neurocell for medical purposes and to help eliminate neurological disorders. If this promise is upheld, then it has my full support. Anything that can save lives or relieve suffering gets a big thumbs up from me; that is what the pharmaceutical industry is there for after all, right? But how many governments across the globe would like to get their hands on this technology? And what would happen if they did? In a world where resources are becoming limited and the global population is accelerating, the future is very uncertain. Now consider this: can you think of a better way to control populations than with brain implants? It's a serious issue and the threat is already knocking at the door. I kid you not. My most trusted source has revealed another exclusive to me. You'd better sit down for this one.

The Wrong Hands

I have heard reports that Schiller has been targeted by Russia. According to my source, an agent has been discovered inside the Institute tasked with stealing the Neurocell prototype. Sounds like a conspiracy theory but we've seen this happen so many times before. Turn out the pockets of any government minister and I guarantee you'll find a wad of roubles. The financial incentives are clear but I don't believe that's why this dam has been breached. Ex-FSB spy Pavel Osinov, a cyber terrorist who is best known for running Russian troll farms and misinformation hubs, has infiltrated the Schiller Institute. He is a sleeper, a Kremlin asset and a very dangerous individual. At this point it is unclear exactly how this has been possible but as their head of cyber security, it doesn't take a genius to work it out.

I am putting myself at risk by revealing this to you, but I am not afraid. The truth will set us free, and as far as I'm concerned, the truth is worth fighting for.

I have no doubt that my name will be destroyed by the media and I will be on the receiving end of Russian misinformation, but things could also get much worse. Russia is notorious for carrying out assassinations on prominent journalists who speak out against their regime. I fear for my safety but Pavel Osinov must be exposed and Mauritz Schiller needs to take action. It is a bold accusation for me to make but if you don't believe me, I have evidence. My source has sent me proof of Osinov in action, literally caught in the act on a webcam. His identity in the video is undeniable. See for yourself; click on the Vimeo link below to access the footage.

I will continue to report the truth to you for as long as I can, but for now I have to go to ground to protect myself. Please trust me when I say your safety and that of future generations is my priority.

Wish me luck.

Over and out.

Terri Landau

CHAPTER 32

SARAH

Pavel speeds through the town, avoiding the traffic on the lakeside. The snow is falling lightly now, the glittering powder dusting the roads and dropping a veil over the windscreen. Maddie would love this. The festive glow of coloured lights and decorations makes my heart ache for her. Daniel can stay here with Helen. I don't want to see him. I don't want to hear his excuses or face what he's done, especially while we're still here in her city. I want to be home with Maddie and Dad, and then maybe I can face Daniel: on my terms. We head into a long tunnel, one that I remember from our arrival at the airport. Pavel's heading to the French border. This isn't the way to the hotel. I look over to him.

'Where are we going?'

'I'm taking a back route.' His eyes remain glued to the road. I hear the click of a lock as my fingers touch the handle of the door and my mind races.

'It's not too friendly round here at night.' Pavel indicates a huddle of figures crouched under the bridge, warming their hands around a brazier.

'Where are you taking me?' He doesn't answer and flicks on the radio. We are speeding along roads that are unknown to me. I just want this nightmare to be over.

'Please stop the car and let me out.' There is rising panic in my voice but he doesn't hear it and races around a corner.

'Don't worry, this is a shortcut.'

I cover my face with my hands. I rock forward in the seat and put my head onto the dashboard, not knowing whether to scream or to weep. We are going fast and I don't know where we are. Out of nowhere, a voice that doesn't belong to me spills out of my mouth.

'JUST LET ME OUT!'

The car pulls up to the kerb and he kills the engine. Oh God, what is he planning to do to me?

'There . . . Sarah . . . See, we're here.' I raise my head to see the little church behind the hotel. The faint music of a choir hovers out through the open door and a warm glow emanates through the stained-glass window. The side door to the hotel, decorated with wreaths and holly, is within sprinting distance. I decide to stay calm and act like everything is perfectly normal.

'Thank you, I just need to pick up my bag, then . . . if you could take me to the airport . . .'

He turns to me with a look of surprise on his face. 'The airport?'

My breathing is shallow and high in my chest. My head feels light. Not now, please. I close my eyes and grip the door handle, readying myself. Then I open the door and stumble as I get out. Pavel follows.

'You are not well, please let me help you.' Pavel offers me his arm. I recover my balance, keeping my eyes focused on the hotel entrance.

'I'm fine, I won't be long, wait here.' I approach the sliding door and the porter nods and smiles. I take the small flight of stairs up to the old elevator; the concertina doors creak open and I step inside. Just as they close, I see Pavel mounting the stairs after me. Why is he following me? The lift stops and the doors open. He's standing there, looking at me, waiting.

'What do you want?' He doesn't reply. Why is he here with me, escorting me to my room like I'm under arrest? I don't want him here.

The dark corridors are narrow and endless; they all look the same. Waves of confusion wash over me as I lurch forward. I glance back over my shoulder and Osinov is there behind me. I turn the next corner, then the next. Looking back, he's still there, always a few feet behind. Get away from me. I feel for the room key in my bag, then I turn and stand in the centre of the corridor, my feet sinking into the carpet as I sway, trying to hold my ground. He rounds the corner.

'I'll be fine from here.' I stare him down. 'Thank you.' My voice feels weak and breathless. He stops a few feet away.

'You are sure? Let me see you to your room. I'm worried about you.' My grogginess distorts his voice and his face is a blur.

I think I'm about to vomit again. This isn't the same as the other episodes I've become familiar with, this feels much more physical. Like I'm being stabbed in the stomach. I turn and stagger towards my hotel room door. I can hear him approaching behind me. I slide the key into its slot and the green light flashes. I open the door and slam it closed behind me, leaning my back into the wood, perspiration beading on my forehead. I can see the shadow of his feet under the door.

'Sarah? I'll wait in the lobby.'

I don't reply. What's he waiting for? The blue night light from the bathroom casts a sickly hue over the room. The striped walls and drapes meld and bend, pointing me towards the open window. The room is freezing. A curtain floats in the breeze coming off the lake and a scattering of snow rests on the sill. Who opened the window? Who's been in here? The bed has been made, everything is straight and organised. The room is somehow the same but different; reversed. I throw my bag onto the bedside table and open a bottle of mineral water that's sitting there. I shrug off my jacket and remove my shoes. I pitch forward, putting my head between my knees, trying to steady the rocking motion in my head. This pain is deep in my head and the images flashing behind my closed eyes are bright and vivid. Eventually, I lie back on the crisp, perfect sheets. The water quenches my dry throat and eases the sharp metallic taste. I must have been sick but I don't remember when. Why am I here by myself, where is Daniel?

'Daniel?' I call through to the other room but there's no response. I turn my head to see his North Face bag on the floor, packed and ready to go. Did Daniel go skiing with Pavel after all? My thoughts are interrupted by the buzz of my phone. A text from Daniel:

Where are you? Wondering where you've gone. You OK?

Where am I? Where should I be? I swallow, my throat feels dry and swollen. Then a memory of the prickle of bubbles on my tongue sends a wave of nausea through me again. Helen staring at me through the mirror in the bathroom, offering me her champagne. That look in her eyes. Then I remember; she's fucking my husband.

I turn into the bed and bury my face in the crisp white sheet, biting into the cotton, stifling a scream. My heart begins to slow and my breathing becomes steadier. I try to lie still, listening to the creaking floors of the hotel. Someone moves in a connecting room. I'm suddenly aware of a presence. I lift my head and my eyes focus on something – some*one* – standing in the door to the bathroom. It's her, it's Helen. Fury bites into my chest. I kneel on the bed and launch myself at the door. I grab at her, punching and dragging at her hair, ripping her apart. The towel wrenches the hook from the bathroom door, pulling out the screws. It comes off in my hands, along with the heavy robe hanging underneath it.

'Fuck you, Daniel.' I swing the towel across the table, knocking a lamp to the floor. I grab it and hurl it at the mirrored wall behind the head of the bed. The lamp breaks and the bulb shatters into tiny pieces but the mirror remains intact. I stand panting and swallowing back sobs. A woman is watching me from the other side. She's bedraggled and feral. She slowly begins to move around the room, throwing clothes into a case and grabbing toiletries from the bathroom. She's leaving, going somewhere. I watch her looking through the side pockets of her bag. That's what I should be doing. Planning my escape, not sitting here feeling sorry for myself. I begin my search too. I find my house keys, a wad of euros, but there's no passport. I turn my bag inside out, it's not there. I root through my suitcase, in all the drawers, in all the rooms. I search my coat pockets and my bag again. Where the hell is it? Then I remember: Daniel took it this morning. I pull open Daniel's North Face bag and start to tear his stuff apart, searching every possible crack and crevice, but my passport is gone. So now what? My phone vibrates again, making me jump. Another message from Daniel:

Where are you? I'm worried.

Where am I? I'm in no man's land right now, staring into the void. And yeah, I bet you're worried, Dan. Worried that I've worked out your seedy affair. Nervous I've figured out the lies you've told. Something darker is nudging my gut instinct. Why did he lie to me about the endorsement fee? Why did he want me to come here so badly? Something else is going on here. That's not some little white lie to cover your back. Unease fills me. I hold my phone, trying to work out my next move. I need more time. I need to think about my own safety first. For now, he has to think that everything is completely normal, so I reply as if nothing is wrong. Playing the Sarah he knows, the compliant wife and ally.

Not feeling great. Gone to bed. Enjoy the party x

He instantly replies.

Hope you're OK. See you later ♥ x

He's bought it. Then my phone rings: it's Pavel.
'Hello? Will you be long?'
'I'm on my way down. Just looking for . . . something. Two minutes.' I hang up and continue the search for my passport. Then I notice Daniel's laptop sitting on the side. This is my chance. I want answers. I want to know everything that my husband has been doing. I've never been one of those people who snoops, we trust each other. I'm always on Dan's laptop, buying him clothes or ordering the weekly shop. But I'm spying on him now. I feel a pang of sadness as I enter his password; I feel like the betrayer. I scroll through emails, junk and deleted files, nothing interesting. I click on his search engines, Safari and Google, all history has been cleared. Oh Dan, you can't even pick up your pants from the bedroom floor but here you are ensuring your searches are clean. Then I notice another app: Firefox, buried in his launchpad. Bingo: his full search history. *SBB.ch*: a website for a Swiss train line. IC 175 Geneva to Zurich. What's in Zurich? The next search item is for the hotel breakfast, then the cocktail menu in the hotel bar. But below that is a link to *The Landau Report*. My disastrous interview. I click on it and notice that a new post has been published. I open it. My phone rings again. Pavel. I cancel the call as I skim-read the blog post about the Neurocell launch.

As I begin to read, my stomach sinks. I scan the text, trying to comprehend what I'm reading. I feel the rug being pulled from under my feet. 'Osinov . . . Kremlin asset.' It's right there in black and white. He's a Russian agent. Daniel, who the hell have you got yourself involved with? You are way out of your depth. You're going to get burned and you're taking me down with you. So, what's my plan? How am I going to get out of here? I turn to the woman in the mirror, who looks back at me none the wiser. I glance at the open window of the hotel and a shudder ripples through me; I'm on the fifth floor, not a chance. My phone rings again. It's Pavel and I'm out of time. I cancel the call for a second time. Then a text message.

I'm coming up.

Fuck. My heart punches against my ribcage, I have to get out now. I stuff my remaining belongings into my bag and dart out of the room. I take the corners of the corridors at speed, arriving at the elevator to see it rising to my floor. There is the shadow of a man behind the glass; it's him. I turn and sprint back towards my room and the service elevator. I slam my hand into the button, praying for it to come. I hear the main lift arrive and footsteps in the distance; he's coming. The door to the service elevator draws back, just in time. I turn and look over my shoulder as the shadow of the Russian stretches into the light. I step into the lift and the door cranks closed. Come on, come on. The reaching shadow at the corner turns into a man and for a second he stands eye to eye with me, as the door finally squeezes shut. In the last millimetre of the gap, I see Pavel dart back the way he came. I hit minus one and the lift drops fast towards the basement. The doors open onto the dark corridor and I sprint past the busy kitchen, barge through the emergency exit and come face to face with a sous-chef on a crafty cigarette break. I give him the fright of his life, but I have no time to lose. I step onto one of the waste bins and haul myself up and over the wall, into the small courtyard and through the side door of the church. Gulping huge mouthfuls of air and holding my side from the stitch that is stabbing at my ribcage, I walk quietly through the silent nave, my footsteps echoing across the floor. I could stay here for a while with the candles and the calm. But he'll find me, I have to disappear entirely. At the main entrance, several people are arriving for mass. I push my way through the throng and out onto the street. I take a left towards the lake and run for my life, not looking behind me. I run and run, stumbling on into the night like a fugitive. A footbridge and a narrow path lead me to a small island, isolated and away from the busy streets. Finally, I come to a stop, holding the stitch in my side. I drop my bag and slump down on a plinth beneath a huge bronze statue, hiding myself from the road. I'm dizzy and breathing hard. I can normally hold my drink but I'm pretty sure that champagne was spiked, this feeling is so wrong. As I catch my breath, I remember a time, not so long ago. I got a call from the care home: Dad had gone missing. They found him sitting at a bus stop, soaking wet and as vicious as a startled animal. Everyone around him was gently coaxing him to safety, afraid he would lash out and bite them. But I knew where he was going. He wanted to go back home to Mum. Is that me right now? Am I the patient needing to be tamed? My head and my world are spinning out of control. I'm lost on an island, in a city of strangers. I slump down against the plinth and lean my head into the stone. My face finds the indent of an engraving, some useless words of wisdom: 'Man was born free and he is everywhere in chains.' Jean Jacques Rousseau looms above me, staring out across the lake. I look down at my wrists, a shadow cast across my hands appearing like iron chains, gripping and restraining me. Then, from somewhere above, huge snowflakes start to drift gently down from the trees, resting on my fingers. An angel sending a message to me. We always run out into the garden when snow falls. I'm coming home, Maddie.

CHAPTER 33

DANIEL

Sarah's OK, thank God. I was worried when she suddenly disappeared from the party. I thought maybe she had wandered off disorientated, but she's safe at the hotel. Which means we have the night to ourselves. I look over at Helen, sitting next to me in the back seat of the taxi, scrolling through her phone. I move my trembling hand through the golden curtain of her hair and stroke the back of her neck. She turns her face to me and smiles, but her eyes don't leave the phone.

'What are you reading that's so important?'

'Neurocell is trending, as is #SchillerInstitute and #SarahCollier. Look.' She holds out her phone to show me but I don't want to look. I don't want to think about my wife right now. I lean in to kiss Helen's cheek; her flawless skin smells like orange zest and jasmine.

'Come on, put your work away, it's done.'

Helen pulls away and continues scrolling through social media, replaying Instagram stories of the launch.

'There are no photos of Sarah at the afterparty.' She chews her lip. 'That's not good.'

I don't care. I shift closer but she glances up to the rear-view mirror at the driver and tenses. 'At least we know she's back at the hotel, all tucked up in bed. Asleep and safe.'

Helen doesn't reply. This situation is not easy. Despite what you may think, I do have a conscience, I just don't feel its weight. Or rather I can bear its weight, but the more I do, the more resilient I become. It's the stamina of deceit, I guess. The taxi pulls up at the side entrance to the Parc La Grange. I have to confess, I'm a bit drunk. Helen exits and I thrust some euros at the driver. I don't wait for the change and fall out of the car after Helen. The snow has started to fall heavily and a fresh blanket has covered the path. Helen is fiddling around in the boot of her parked BMW. She grabs a bag and changes her shoes. I look down at my suede loafers and shrug. We approach the locked gate and she steps onto a low wall, hauling herself over the broken railing. I follow, tumbling over the other side as Helen turns and hushes me, my shoes slipping and sliding in the ankle-deep drift. I move in her wake, two feet behind, following in her footsteps: the story of my life. We walk up the incline towards the cabin. Just a black silhouette, it appears smaller in the dark, almost invisible. She unlocks the door and it creaks open on its rusty hinges. We enter and Helen bolts it behind us. I sway over to a lamp by the small table and fumble for the switch, while Helen triggers the pilot light on the gas heater. It's colder inside but the intoxication in my body is keeping my face hot and my mind soft. Something is on her mind; I can feel it.

She moves across the room, pulling her long tailored puffer coat tight around her. I stand and watch as she takes two glasses and pours whisky for us both. I feel like I may already have had one too many to perform in a satisfactory way tonight but it's hard to say no to Helen at the best of times. I have delivered and obeyed, and we've arrived at this point because of me. We are no longer master and servant but equals. I like this feeling; it gives me courage to ask for what I want.

'You're drunk.' She hands me a glass.

'You don't say.'

'I could take advantage of you.'

'So what's new?'

She smiles at me, puts her cool hands on my flushed face and pulls me in for a kiss. We clink glasses.

'To us, darling.' Her green eyes are penetrating. 'To the obstacles we've overcome and the ones we have yet to face.'

I am mesmerised by her beauty. I want to do everything in my power to make her happy, to make myself worthy of her.

'You have the passport?'

'Yes.' I reach into my inside coat pocket. Shit, it's not there. Her eyes bore into me. A look on her face like I have never seen. Fierce and threatening. 'Wait.' I feel inside my back pockets, patting myself down, hunting for the damned thing. Then, reaching into the other inside pocket, my fingers find the leather cover of Sarah's passport. Thank God. 'Ha . . . Just kidding.' I smile and lean in to hand it over. Her eyes move to the identity page and she exhales.

'So, what next?' I am hoping that the neck-to-ankle puffer coat she's wearing might find its way to the floor, but she is all business tonight.

'Next, we return to the Institute. I have to take care of things there, wipe the hard drive. Mauritz will be heading back after the party, so we need to manage that situation carefully. Then to the hotel, to pick up . . . our patient. And then on to Zurich.'

'And after Zurich?' I say it quietly but my voice betrays a knowing doubt. She pauses, her eyes fixed on me.

'You know what happens after Zurich, Daniel.' She passes a hand through her hair and stares at me like I'm an alien being. I do know what happens after Zurich, but I wish I didn't. I'm hoping for a different answer, almost praying that maybe that bit was imagined or just hypothetical. I inhale, raise my glass and take a big gulp of Dutch courage.

'It's all arranged. As we planned. Don't you trust me?' Her voice is steady and calm.

'Of course I trust you.'

She slides forward and presses herself against my body. The scent of whisky and jasmine, blending into a heady cocktail. Man . . . They should bottle that. I can't help myself, I am power-less to her touch. Slowly she unzips her puffer coat. I can't hold back, I don't want to. My marriage is dying. Let's face it, it's already dead and buried. And now I have the opportunity for happiness. A fresh start. I'm in love with an exceptional woman and she loves me back. I can't look away.

Keeping me fixed in her gaze, she unbuttons my flimsy shirt. It's cold and clammy, stuck to my skin. I tremble at her touch. Her hands move down my torso to find the button of my trousers; I flinch as her fingers pass over bruises and the deep graze above my hip bone. I am totally at her command. She lets my trousers fall to the floor and studies my injuries. She moves her fingers and nails over the damaged skin. She then presses, digging her nails in deep, opening the wound. The pain courses through me.

'You're everything to me. But if we are going to be together, you must be prepared for the pain of what comes next. It won't be easy, but you must be strong.'

I clench my jaw as her fingers press deeper. I lean forward to kiss her on the mouth but she pulls away.

'No, no, no, be strong for me. Bear it, Daniel. Tell me what you want.'

'I want you, Helen. I want to be with you. I'll be strong.' The pain is unbearable, but then, like other pain, like guilt, all of a sudden, before you know it, it is bearable.

Her eyes light up with a beautiful ferocity and her grip tightens. 'Call me Sarah.'

I tense up and look into her face, questioning what she's just said.

'Call me Sarah.'

I look down, suddenly feeling hot in the face, embarrassed and stupid. This just feels so wrong. She lifts my chin up.

'I need to know . . . you are all in. Call me Sarah.'

I am all in. This woman is my future.

'Sarah.' The sound escapes my mouth, no louder than a gasp, as easy as breathing.

The heart beats in a different way when you know what you are doing is wrong. It's a punch, not a flutter. There is a primeval call deep within me now that I have to answer. I know it's uncomfortable for you to hear this, but I need you to understand the hold she has on me. I am in her grip, I have no choice.

It's beyond my control.

CHAPTER 34

Sprinting along the hotel corridors, Pavel barrels down the spiral staircase towards the lobby. He reaches the reception and scans the room for where Sarah will emerge. He glares at the concierge.

'Service elevator?' he snaps in frustration.

'*Sous-sol, Monsieur.*' He smiles with a shrug and returns to tapping on his computer.

Damn, she's heading for the basement. He careens out through the side entrance towards Rue de Monthoux and takes a left towards the side alley where they entered the day before. A large sweaty man adjusting his kitchen cap and stubbing out a cigarette looks up at him. He smiles, rolling his eyes, indicating the church behind him. Pavel heads up the alley towards the street, sees the open door to the church and darts inside. The sound of an organ and the beginning of evening mass stop him in his tracks, and he stands at the side of the vestry looking out into the small, scattered congregation. His eyes scan the pews for Sarah, she's not here. He turns on his heel and runs back to his car, parked up at the end of the street. Firing the ignition, he spins the wheels on the packed snow and swerves out, no time to waste. He pulls out into the traffic, weaving his way through oncoming cars. Horns honk and arms are flung up as he speeds up to the bridge, scanning the pavement on both sides. He hangs a right at the bridge by the statue of Rousseau and crawls along the taxi line in front of the Four Seasons Hotel. There's no sign of her. She was heading to the airport. He U-turns back on to the road and accelerates, foot to the floor, along the lake towards Chambésy. His phone rings: here we go. He punches the hands-free button on the steering wheel.

'Sarah?'

'No, Pavel. This is Mauritz Schiller.' The tone is hard and cold.

'Mauritz? I'm just—'

'Do not say another word! I am calling to inform you that your contract with the Schiller Institute has been terminated and I am severing all contact with you. Your cover is blown. Traitor.'

'What are you talking about?' His heart is racing. He braces himself for what Mauritz has to say next.

'Your affiliation with the Kremlin.' The words are spat down the phone.

'Who told you this?' Pavel's face is now burning red hot with rage.

'Let's just say it has been brought to my attention and now I have brought it to the attention of the *Kantonspolizei*.'

'Mauritz, please. There's been some mistake. Who has told you this? Helen Alder?'

'It has been published online and the whole of Geneva and our entire industry are talking about it. We've gone viral, but you, my friend, are the virus. I will not allow you to sabotage my life's work, to single-handedly destroy Neurocell and the future of the Schiller Institute. You will not succeed. Do you hear me?!'

'Mauritz, wait. This is not true. You must believe me!'

'You are now under criminal investigation and have no place here in Geneva. This is the last time we will ever speak. Goodbye.'

As Schiller hangs up, his hand is shaking. Devastated at what he just had to do. He looks to his driver and then clicks a button, raising the partition between them. He doesn't want to be observed right now. This humiliation and shame at such a betrayal stir up a delirium in him that he has rarely felt. How could he have been so blind? How could Pavel have taken advantage of him after all the trust he had afforded him? The car ascends the mountain road towards the place he has founded, imagined and built from the ground up. The Schiller family name, just like the building precariously perched in the rock, now hangs in the balance. Everything is at stake. The launch of Neurocell was a great success but his celebrations were cut short when talk at the party turned to rumours of a Russian conspiracy. Helen had pulled him aside and they had read the *Landau Leaks* article together, both of them stunned. Helen had tried to defend Osinov, suggesting they bring him in to let him explain himself, but Mauritz's reaction was like a guillotine falling. Absolute severance, he wanted Pavel cut out like a cancer. Helen told him she would handle it and had left the party with Daniel Collier. He suspected there was something going on between them but his employees' personal affairs were none of his business and with Osinov terminated, Helen was his only ally. But for now, he was alone with his thoughts and his fears. He tapped on the touchpad of his chair, bringing up the screen in the headrest, and read the *Landau Leaks* article again. He needed to torture himself just one more time, chastise himself for his blind trust in Osinov.

At the bottom of the blog post was a Vimeo link. He clicked on it, to watch it again, just to be sure. On the time log, at 3.11 a.m. yesterday morning, a blurred image of a figure moving around Helen's office. It could have been anyone, except the white hair and broad shoulders were unmistakable and that final turn of the head at the door confirmed Pavel Osinov's identity beyond any doubt. Mauritz's mind was in turmoil, he imagined every possible scenario, every hacker and every foreign agent dipping their filthy fingers into his secrets, rifling through his files. He put in a call to

Jan Pager, who was on duty at the Schiller Institute, and instructed him to activate an immediate security lockdown. Assessing the
nature of the breach and the scale of the damage would take days,
if not weeks. Mauritz will do it alone; he will take whatever steps
necessary to protect his legacy.

A message buzzes on his phone. He looks at the screen and recognises the sender.

Can we speak. Urgent. Where are you?

Mauritz pauses for a second, his heart quivering with stress.
He draws in a lungful of air and holds a hand to his chest. Can
he deal with this right now? He gathers his composure and sends
a location pin. No message. Something has changed in him. His
trust has been broken and a sadness grows inside him. He will
lock the doors and keep all of them out. No more trust. Shut them
out. Shut them all out.

'Mauritz, the only way to find out if you can trust someone is
to trust them.' His father's words had served him well through-
out his life. But now that trust has been damaged beyond repair.
He stares out of the window, watching the snow fall as the car
approaches the impenetrable gates of the now dark and silent
Institute. As the gates retract, he mutters to himself.

'*Sie sind ein Narr*, Mauritz. You are a fool.'

CHAPTER 35

SARAH

I clasp the door handle of the taxi that's winding its way up the treacherous mountain roads, forging a path that will bring me closer to the truth. My grip on sanity is loosening as the separation between reality and this living nightmare rips down the middle; but I'm still holding on. I need an ally and a way out. The road disappears under a covering of settled snow, the salt grit on the tarmac crunching under the tyres. Chinks of light in the windows of the small villages we pass flicker as the vast dark walls of the mountains rise on either side of us. The car reeks of pine air freshener and with the heater on full blast, the atmosphere is nauseating. I drop the window and gulp lungfuls of the freezing air. Who this woman is, sitting alone in a car, staring out into the black night, gasping for breath, is anyone's guess. My whole life has changed since I came here. The Alzheimer's diagnosis confirming my worst fears. But Daniel lying to me and cheating on me at a time when I need him most is more than I can bear. He said he would be there for us, for me and Maddie. He lied. It's as simple as that. So now who can I trust? It's time to take control. I need answers.

The taxi slows as the headlights shine a beam against a high, unwelcoming steel gate.

'*Est-ce l'endroit?*' The taxi driver pulls to a stop. The snow is so deep he can't go any further.

'*Oui, merci.* This is it.'

I pay the fare and step out into the cold, dark evening. The taxi reverses slowly back up the deep snowy ravine, then turns and pulls away, leaving me alone on the mountain road. Walking over to the floodlit intercom, I'm just about to press the button when an electric buzz breaks through the silence of the night and the gate starts to slide back slowly, steel grating against ice. I wait for a gap and slide in.

I descend the winding approach to the building below. The glittering honeycomb of illuminated glass that I remember from the last time is dead. Now it's just a black hollow void, no light, no sign of life. The tracks from a car in the deep snow cut a path for me to follow. I slip and skid, nearly losing my balance as I descend towards the main glass door of the reception. The wind has picked up and a flurry of snowfall turns to stinging ice as the wind drives sideways. I shield my face, pulling my flimsy jacket up around my neck.

'Hello . . . Hello?' My voice is swallowed by the wind as it howls against the glass of the Institute. I pull out my phone to call Mauritz Schiller. There is no signal. Shit. What the hell am I going to do? There is no way back, I'm stranded now. I'm about to move around to the side of the building when I notice something on the other side of the glass door. I step closer and see a figure seated in the dark, in the centre of the reception area.

Mauritz is sitting in his wheelchair, watching me, out here in the wind and the cold. I step towards the glass and hold up my hand against my reflection. He doesn't move. His face is in shadow. I tap my hand on the glass, until the tap becomes a loud bang. Slowly his chair begins to creep forward, his face appearing in a sliver of moonlight.

'Can't you let me in? Please?' My voice is absorbed by the wind and Mauritz watches me carefully.

'Mauritz. Please LET ME IN!'

He withdraws from the window and turns away. I hear a beep and swish of the glass door sliding open. I rush forward and step inside the pod. The door slides closed behind me and I step forward to gain entry but the second door remains closed. I'm trapped, in a prison of glass. Why is he toying with me?

From a speaker inside the pod, Mauritz's voice echoes.

'I was surprised . . . and a little offended that you left the party so quickly.' He remains at a distance in the dark. His voice is soft and calm but there is the edge of a threat.

'I'm sorry, I had . . . forgotten my medication.'

'It was also a breach of contract.' He removes his scarf and cleans his glasses.

'Shall we return to the conference then?' I'm at the end of my tether.

Mauritz remains silent. The corners of his mouth tighten.

'I did what was asked of me. Neurocell received its ovation, that's all the press will be talking about.

'Please can we talk . . . properly? I can't speak to you like this.' My hands are pressed against the glass. I'm close to tears but I will not break. There isn't time for that.

The glass shifts against my palms as if the sheer force of my will has moved it aside. I stumble forward out of the pod and fall to my knees on the floor, damp and trembling.

'Come with me.' He reverses and heads for the central elevator. I follow. Every light in the Institute is off, every computer terminal black, not a single sound. We enter the lift, he taps a code on his touchpad and we descend in silence.

The lift stops and we move into Mauritz's private quarters. The room where the party was held, with the wall of walnut with the tessellation artwork. I steady my legs as the graphic wall begins to dance and slide. I really need to sit down. I reach into my bag and retrieve my pills. Mauritz moves over to a side table and returns with some water.

'Thank you.' I take my medication and relax into an armchair. We are now face to face. It's time to face facts.

'I want to ask you about Helen Alder. She has been . . . liaising with my husband.'

Mauritz places his glasses on the bridge of his nose and peers at me. 'My dear, I have suspected Helen and Daniel's . . . connection but I try not to concern myself with affairs . . .' He coughs with embarrassment and corrects himself. '. . . business that my employees choose to engage in outside of the Schiller Institute.'

My face reddens, that's all the confirmation I need. I can't bear this humiliation, so I lie. 'I know that Daniel is having an affair with—' He holds up his hand.

'Please, your private life is none of my business. What do you want, Sarah?'

'I need to get home, urgently.' I look down into my frozen hands; the palms are red raw.

'I believe there were a few other obligations in your contract – a breakfast meeting with the press tomorrow, and a photo call – but under the circumstances I think we can waive these. Look after yourself. I'm sure Daniel will be right behind you, ready to . . . explain himself.' He smiles kindly and inclines his head.

'He has my passport, I need your help to get home.' I shift uncomfortably in my seat.

Mauritz waits for a second; his eyes narrow into a frown of curiosity.

'The embassy can help you with that, I will ask my driver to—'

'Professor Schiller. When Daniel first came to the Schiller Institute, what was the purpose of his visit?—'

'His visit?' Mauritz's head inclines in curiosity.

'All the trips he made to Geneva on behalf of his department, the affiliation with Schiller . . .'

'I'm not sure I follow you, my dear?'

'The meetings here at the Institute. How did he seem?'

'I'm sorry but Daniel has never been here before.' I stare at Mauritz as a tidal wave of dread rises to my throat, drowning me.

'But he always came back buzzing with stories and enthusiasm about what you were developing here.'

'He may well have been in Geneva, but he was never here at Schiller.'

'No, he told me all about . . .' Had he told me anything, though? What exactly *had* Daniel said about all those weekends away? My hands start to tingle as the blood rushes to my thumping heart. 'Ah!' A sharp exhale of breath as I try to contain my urge to cry out.

'I'm sorry, my dear, but last night, at the launch, was the first time your husband had ever set foot inside the Schiller Institute.'

The black polished floor starts to move like liquid tar. I want to sink into it and let it swallow me whole. I'm drowning in shame. My husband is a liar.

Daniel was never at Schiller.

So where was he? And what was he doing?

CHAPTER 36

The blast of a siren and flashing blue lights startle Pavel as he sinks deeper into the seat of his SUV. He opens his phone to watch the footage from *Landau Leaks* again. The grainy clip of his face from Helen's webcam. She is the source. She has been feeding Terri Landau all manner of information and yet he has taken the blame, his whole life exposed for all to read. There was a grain of truth in her shit-stirring. His father had worked for the FSB and Pavel had been tarred with the same brush; it lingered on him like a bad smell. For Helen to have discovered this, she must have been snooping around too. What else did she know? What else did she take? His gun. Tonight, he will make sure his weapon is returned to its rightful owner.

He pulls a black beanie over his white hair; he won't be caught out like the last time. The amber pools of light from the street-lamps and the festive glow from the grand houses that line the edge of the Parc La Grange are the only signs of life on this quiet side street. A second siren shrieks in the distance and a flurry of *Kantonspolizei* speed down the Rue Gustave-Ador towards the centre of town. His nerves are steady because he knows: that's not how they come. The people he is truly afraid of don't come with sirens and warnings, they come with Novichok and stiletto blades in the dark. He exits the car and takes up a steady jog along the treeline through the darkness, just an ordinary man out for a run. He reaches the locked gate, mounts the wall and the railings and thumps down into a deep drift of snow on the other side. A third flurry of blue lights speed past, flashing neon all around him. He remains crouched low on his haunches until they have passed. His heart steady, his destination certain.

Pavel moves uphill towards the grand house at the centre of the park, keeping close to the line of the wall. He reaches a steep incline and sees the small black wooden cabin in the distance. It's in darkness, with not a flicker of life. Maybe there is no one here, perhaps this will be an easy smash and grab. Tonight, he intends to find out what Helen Alder really knows; but there is something else she has in her possession that he needs, something other than his gun. Something even more important, and this is where he'll find it, he is sure of that. He has nothing to lose now.

Despite the lifeless appearance of the cabin, the two sets of footprints in the fresh snow leading to the door tell him all he needs to know. He leaves the path and moves quietly to the side of the building, knee-deep in frozen brambles, keeping close to the wall. He treads carefully, moving slowly around to the rear, staying low and out of sight. Then he barrels over a broken section of the stone wall and crouches with his back to it.

He peers around through the gap and notices a faint glow from the small, cracked window at the back of the cabin; he can hear voices. He creeps closer to the wall, the soft squeak of compressed snow deadening any sound from the undergrowth. At the back of the cabin is a stack of discarded wood, some plastic recycling bins and a pile of old planks and scaffold poles. Nimble like a midnight fox, he picks his way through the rubbish without making a sound and stops below the windowsill. He remains crouched for a few seconds, trying to make out what the voices are saying. Then he steps onto a pile of planks and hauls himself up. Placing his fingers on the window frame, he slowly rises. The glass is filthy, but he can just about make out Daniel and Helen, deep in conversation. Daniel is sitting in a chair with his head in his hands slumped forward, Helen sits on the arm with hers folded, her head tilted back. He can't make out their muffled conversation, so he stretches himself taller, his ear leaning in towards the crack in the glass.

'What on earth did you imagine, Daniel? The endorsement fee is ours, but the transaction can only happen if we carry out the rest of the plan. It's a lot of money, it was never going to be easy!'

Helen turns her head, looking directly towards the cracked window. Pavel ducks down and freezes, trying not to move a muscle. He's desperate to hear the response but he can't risk being seen. He hears movement and his eyes return to the filthy glass. Daniel remains slumped, Helen towers over him. Pavel strains to hear more but their voices are soft and indecipherable, and the wind has picked up. Pavel casts his eyes around the rest of the room, surveying the space. A single door at the front and two serving hatches bolted closed, probably used in the summer when the cabin became a snack bar. Then he notices a second door to a possible outhouse; it gives him an idea. He carefully steps down from the window and around the corner of the building; the broken glass and bits of old wood buried in the snow crunch under his feet. There is a small extension built onto the uphill side of the cabin wall. A possible way in, but the lock is bolted and rusty, and snow has drifted high against the door. He could break it down, but not without making a noise. The wooden walls of the cabin rest on a brick foundation, the render covering the bricks is broken and decayed. He pulls at the mortar, which comes away like powder in his hands. The stones behind are loose and crumbling, and within a few seconds he has removed a small section, just large enough for him to twist and squeeze his shoulders through. He worms his way under the wooden floor of the cabin, like a snake penetrating a nest. Thin shafts of light leak down from the room above, as Pavel shuffles on his belly along the dank earth. Twisting onto his side, he moves towards a wooden pillar propping up a section of the rotten floor. He moves slowly until his eye finds a small gap. He can see the soles of Daniel's shoes and the outline of the chair he's sitting in. He can hear Helen's footsteps pacing the cabin and their voices are clear as a bell. Something scratches in the dark near him, a disturbed rodent perhaps. Pavel lies still and silent.

'We discussed this, Daniel. I can't believe you are getting cold feet, I knew this would happen.'

'I just think we can do what we need to do without . . .'

'Without what? Hey?' She kicks his foot, hard. 'Without what?'

Pavel shuffles deeper towards the centre of the room; he needs to hear this. What are they planning? He finds a corner of a board that is rotten, pushes his fingers into the powdery wood, prising a large piece away. Now he can see both their faces. Daniel's expression is agony, Helen's a mask of rage.

'It's just so . . . inhumane, Helen.'

A sudden flurry of movement and a slippery tail and hairy body surges across Pavel's face. The prick of tiny claws and sharp teeth scratch his cheeks and neck as a rat evacuates its hiding place. A yelp of shock escapes from Pavel's mouth. He jumps, grabbing at the creature, pulling it off him. It scuttles away and he puts his hand to his mouth as he lies there for a few seconds, listening. There is no sound in the room except the hiss of the gas fire. They have stopped talking. He strains his eye through the gap. He waits, ears pricked for any noise from the floor inches above his face. Not a sound, not even the creak of a floorboard. The back of his neck prickles, he's in danger. He needs to get out now. Very slowly he begins to inch his way back, his eye fixed to the crack in the boards. Then a shadow slowly passes across the gap, then blonde hair, and then an eye so close he can see the pupil dilate.

He starts to struggle backwards but it's hard in this confined space. A floorboard is wrenched up and he blinks in the stark light. Then there is a sudden rush of air as a blunt object slams down into his face. Something heavy and metallic smacks into his forehead and the bridge of his nose. The crack of bone and a blinding, searing pain runs through his skull and down to his teeth and jaw. He jerks his head to the side and a second strike hits the back of his head. Then he feels nothing except a soft slow-motion submergence into dark water. The cold, damp earth under his cheekbone and the taste of blood warming his mouth make it seem as if he's drowning. The crack of a floorboard being wrenched up and a pair of heavy winter boots blur into his fading vision. The last thing he feels before he loses consciousness is the sting of zip ties being wrenched around his ankles and wrists. He is tied fast to something holding him down. Caught in a trap, tethered by the neck. He's a dead man.

CHAPTER 37

SARAH

Mauritz Schiller sits across from me, observing my turmoil with detachment. My head feels light as I try to make sense of what I've just heard.

'I'm sorry, you must be mistaken. Daniel has been visiting Schiller almost every other weekend for the past year, for his work with the London College of Neurology.'

'No, my dear. I believe we brushed shoulders once, in Frankfurt, if I recall. But Daniel and I have never met here in Geneva until last night. You seem to be confused.'

All those trips, all the gifts he brought back, the kisses for Maddie, all the stories he told me, the tales of the technology he had witnessed, the people he said he had met. His ecstasy and exhaustion. All of it was a lie. There is something else I need to confirm.

'Were there any . . . financial incentives for my attendance at the conference?' My head is swimming and I feel sick.

'Didn't you read the contract?' I look up with exhausted embarrassment and shake my head.

'I didn't have a chance, I trusted Daniel to make the arrangements.'

Mauritz doesn't move, his eyes fixed on me. 'Ten million. It felt to me like a lot of money, but Helen Alder assured me that an endorsement from you would be worth its weight in gold.'

'Oh God.' I drop my head down into my hands. Blood leaves my head to feed my broken heart, and the sound in the room grows distant. I mumble to him, 'Please, Mauritz, help me get home.' I suppose I am hoping he'll just magically summon his helicopter for me again.

'What's the matter, Sarah? You don't seem well. Let me see if I can get Daniel to bring your passport—' He pulls out his phone and starts to make a call.

'Wait. Stop. Who are you calling? Please don't, just . . .' I place my hand on his, urging him to stop. He stares at me.

'Helen? It's Mauritz. Is Daniel with you? I have Sarah here . . . Yes, don't worry, she's safe. She's not going anywhere.' He stares at me. It's a warning.

I push my hands into the arms of the chair and haul myself to my feet. My whole body feels heavy, like it's filled with mercury, my muscles buckle under every step, and I can't seem to control my spine.

'You'll have to excuse me, Professor Schiller . . . I have to leave . . .'

The floor has turned to black tar and is now sticky under my feet, but I work my way to the door and out into the corridor. It stretches out before me, a mile long. My hands press into the undulating glass walls as I stagger forward. I hear the squeeze of rubber wheels on the floor as Mauritz follows.

'Wait here and we can help you, Sarah.' He's close behind me.

I lurch forward, staggering towards the elevator, pressing through the thick air around me. I reach the lift and step inside, turning as the glass door slides closed, melting like rendered fat.

The eyes of Schiller drill into mine.

'Where are you going?'

'I can take care of myself.'

The floor begins to rise but I remain where I am. It travels up my legs, past my hips and swallows my torso until the gelatinous floor consumes me right up to my neck; I'm going under. I need to move quickly. I reach my hand up for the button on the elevator and slam it hard. Everything stops. Then I begin to descend, leaving Schiller behind, watching me fall. The elevator stops and the doors open. I crawl on my hands and knees out into the corridor, then I stagger to my feet.

The sound of a door banging in the distance is like a bolt of electricity through me. I have to go now. Wrenching myself out of this languid stupor, with every ounce of energy I can muster, I force myself to sprint. Door after door, emergency bars on double doors swing open and an alarm sounds way off in the distance. Automatic lights flick on and off as I pass through dark corridors. I can't feel my legs but I can hear the sound of my feet pounding the hard floor. I have to find an exit. Finally, I see the sign, a way out. I push through and come face to face with a concrete wall. Bolted to the wall is a steel ladder, offering a vertical escape from this underground tomb. I place my foot on the first rung and haul myself up. My breath is quick and sharp as I climb, pulling with my arms and pushing with my legs, through the dark. The panic tightens my chest, making my heart race, but I keep moving towards the surface.

Finally, the ladder emerges into a small service area of machinery, air conditioning and electrical processing equipment. I stop and crouch, listening. I can hear banging below; Mauritz's security guards have been alerted to my flight. They sound distant, but they won't be for long. They are coming, this is my last chance. I run over to the emergency exit, illuminated in green: it is chained and padlocked. I slam my body against the release bar and the door opens a crack, but the chain catches tight. The opening is too small for me to squeeze through. I search for something to jam into the gap. A small step ladder is propped behind one of the processing units. In a frenzy of panic, I drag it out and pull it towards the exit.

Then there is the metallic ring of footsteps on the ladder behind me. Shouldering the door open until the chains catch, I force the ladder into the gap and twist hard. The aluminium cuts into my arms as I wrench and force. I strain and twist, the ladder buckling as it wedges the opening. The freezing air rushes in through the gap. I push through, scraping my shoulders against the sides, and pull the ladder through after me. I'm free. I look back at the building behind me; I'm standing on a metal walkway on the cantilevered side of the Schiller Institute, hovering over the valley below. I need to get back into the cover of the woods. I can hear the door banging behind me and raised voices. I carefully follow the walkway around the building, until it reaches the cliff. I swing my leg over the handrail and jump down into a drift of snow, which catches my fall. I press on through the waist-deep snow, staggering out into the woods, my legs buckling beneath me.

Then a powerful feeling starts to rise in my chest. It is a volcano of erupting anger and rage. I want to rip and tear at my own flesh and scream. What has happened to me? What has my life become? With what little energy I have left, I summon the thought of my little girl. The thought of Maddie rouses a furnace within me, I push harder into the night, and I run like hell for my life and hers. Suddenly, there in the distance, I see the moving lights of the road. Like a frenzied animal I dart through the trees, and I stagger and stumble out into the open. I launch myself into the path of headlights moving fast towards me. They blind me and I turn away from their glare. I hear a screech of brakes and the scream of a car horn as I go down, throwing my hands up to protect my face. The impact slams into my side, my body crumples to the frozen surface of the road, but I feel nothing as I slide like a hockey puck across the ice.

The wail of the car horn fades into the distance.

I lie there still, out on the ice. Broken and alone.

CHAPTER 38

DANIEL

'Search his pockets, take his phone.'

Helen's voice is calm. She kicks the bloody scaffold pole to the side of the room as I finish binding his neck to the joist under the floorboards. I can see the deep-red blood pooling behind his head and through a tear in his black beanie. It looks to me like a serious head wound. As I tighten the zip ties around his neck, I check to see if he's breathing. I can see his chest rising and falling, but it's shallow.

'I think he needs an ambulance, Helen.'

'Good idea, let's invite the cops round too, we can all have beers and a cosy chat.' Helen is working fast. 'We need to move.' She is sorting through a leather holdall, gathering her belongings, making sure she has everything she needs.

'What are we going to do with him? We can't just leave him here.' I am pacing the room, trying to get my head around what's happening, as reality spirals out of control.

'We don't have time for this, Daniel. Pull yourself together.'

I lean down over Pavel's body and stuff a cushion under his head to at least stem the bleeding.

Helen throws her bag at me; it hits me in the face. 'Get in the car. Now.'

I head for the door. As I turn back, I see her disconnecting the hose from the gas canister. She drags it behind her, trailing the hose to the floor and lodging it in a board close to where Osinov is lying. She turns the tap on the canister to full and the gas starts to hiss into the unconscious Russian's face. I look down at the man tied up beneath the floor, already resembling a corpse in a grave. More and more I'm starting to feel like I'm living someone else's life. I'm beginning to wonder who the hell I am. When did I become someone capable of this?

She looks up at me and smiles.

'Helen . . .' She stands and looks down into the wooden grave.

'He's a traitor and a spy, it's no less than he deserves . . . Now move.'

We retrace our steps out of the park, trudging through the snow back to the perimeter wall and the gate. She throws her bag over and looks back at me. I offer my hand, taking her foot and launching her over the top. We stand either side of the railing, like prison bars between us. I've always known Helen was trouble. From the first moment I set eyes on her, I knew this would be volatile and dangerous. It was at a conference in Frankfurt, I was playing pool and noticed her at the bar with a line of martinis. I wasn't looking for anything, but the connection was instant. She understood me on a different level. She saw me, I was flattered and dazzled. She even laughed at my jokes. Helen began opening doors for me emotionally and professionally and there was no going back. It was a frenzy of alcohol-fuelled late nights, pillow talk and tangled limbs. But now, as I look at her through these bars, it feels messy. Our shared vision has become distorted somewhere along the line. Suddenly, the mundane cycle of school runs and care homes, pizza nights and laundry days feels like a cool oasis in a scorching desert.

We climb into Helen's BMW and she pulls away, hanging an angry U-turn and out into fast-moving traffic. We take the south side of the lake towards Thonon-les-Bains. Aside from the rush of wind and the roaring engine, the silence in the car is deafening. We sit in this tension for an hour or so, driving towards Montreux and then turning east up into the Rhône valley. The amber lights of the highway pulse past in monotonous succession and a light flurry of snow triggers the automatic wipers. The dark-blue yawn of the early-morning sky emerges from the low peaks of the Alps as I stare out of the window.

'Helen, are you sure there's no other way?'

She reaches over me into the glove box, grabs a pack of cigarettes, pulls one out with her teeth and slams her hand into the lighter.

'Don't try to worm your way out of this, Daniel, you need to face reality and get on board.' The lighter pops, she drops the window and takes a drag. 'You're in denial and it's a really, *really* big turn-off.'

The stale smoke swirling from her mouth to my nostrils isn't exactly doing it for me either, but I bite my tongue. Her hands grip the wheel tight and the car lurches into a hairpin. My hand shoots out to the dashboard. 'Helen, take it easy.' She defiantly rams her foot to the floor and the rear wheels spin and skid against the incline.

The road begins to narrow and twist as we approach Ormont-Dessous, the steep bends turning my stomach as I hang on to the door handle for dear life. A granite wall suddenly appears in front of us and she swerves right.

'Helen, for God's sake . . . Slow down!'

Then I remember: shit, Pavel's phone . . . I forgot to take it as Helen had instructed. I was too focused on making sure he was still breathing. Too late now.

Her foot is now fully to the floor and the engine is screaming. The noise from the open window forces her to shout. Her voice is deep and threatening. She turns to face me. 'Did you think we were playing some kind of game . . . for kicks?'

I stare into her brilliant green eyes, withering under the glare of that fierce gaze. 'I thought it was just about the money.'

She takes a final drag. 'Daniel, I'm getting very bored of this.' She spits the cigarette butt out of the open window.

We climb higher and higher, the altitude sucking the air from my ears and lungs. She's right. I did plan this with her, but here we are, ascending to a summit so far above my stratosphere that I daren't look back. I reach my hand around her neck and she nudges it with her jawbone.

'I needed the passport to make the bank transfer.' Her voice is steady and calm but she is speaking to me like I'm twelve years old. I am going to do what she's asking. And I will do so willingly. We both know it.

'And then?' I'm not going to say it, I'm going to make her say it.

'Well, we can't stay where we are, can we?' She's playing with me. I want to stop this game but I can't.

'No.' I am saying what she wants to hear.

'So, where do we go?'

'We have to leave.'

'And you know my circumstances, don't you, Daniel? How am I supposed to leave when those circumstances still exist?' She is coaching me, teaching me.

'You can't leave.'

'Unless . . .?' Her head turns towards me and holds my gaze. I return her look, mesmerised by the power she has over me.

'Unless . . . you take her place.' There, I have said it.

'I need you to trust me. How else are we going to be together?' The question is rhetorical. These games are not safe for a rational human. And I still count myself as rational, despite the deep shit I'm standing in. There is a pause. It's that moment when I'm suddenly aware that I may look back at this point in my life and wish that I had followed a different path. Made a different choice. Helen eases off the accelerator and takes control.

'Are you ready for this?'

'I am ready.' And I mean it.

She turns towards me, holding my gaze. In a sudden flurry of movement, something darts out from the side of the road, straight into the beam of the headlights.

'HELEN, LOOK OUT!'

A figure is standing in the centre of the road. The headlamps dazzle and blind them, and their hands shoot up to protect a screaming face. The horn blasts and Helen's foot stamps on the brake too hard and too late. The rear wheels lock and the back end spins out of control on the frozen road. I'm jolted forward into the choking throttle of the taut seat belt. The car slides sideways at full speed, hitting the kerb and flipping onto its side. My door buckles as it makes contact with the crash barrier and my head is punched by the full impact of the airbag. Something slams into my face. And then the world goes black.

CHAPTER 39

Pavel Osinov's eyes open. There is a quiet hiss close to his ear. He turns his head and groans as he slowly regains consciousness, his eyes scanning the darkness. Something tight around his neck cuts deep into his Adam's apple. His whole body is aching in pain. Earth and dried blood stick to his face and plastic zip ties cut deep into his wrists behind his back and his ankles. He is losing the feeling in his fingers. Lying on his side on the floor, Pavel attempts to right himself and sit up, but a cable tie has been pulled tight around his neck and is anchored to a joist. He strains his neck and feels the plastic contract tighter. He stays still, moving his eyes around in the darkness, surrounded by dead rats.

And then he smells the gas. This is bad, he needs to get out, fast.

He casts his eyes to the floor joist; it's jammed in tight but not secure. As he moves his head, the cable tie cuts into his neck, nearly choking him, but he twists and pulls until the prop begins to shift. His eyes bulge red; he is nearly unconscious when suddenly the rotten wood gives way and the post dislodges itself from the floor above. His neck is free but the weight of the armchair buckles the floor and with a sudden crack it collapses into the void, inches from his face. He curls tight into a ball, holding his breath. He rolls onto his back and through the collapsed section of floorboards he wriggles his way up into the room. He looks around, and inches himself on his side towards an old wood stove with iron feet. The raw edge of the iron foot is sharp and he starts to work the plastic ties binding his wrists. The pain in his shoulders and arms is excruciating but eventually the ties snap apart and his hands are free. There's a large trunk in the centre of the room with an empty whisky bottle and two glass tumblers on top. He reaches over for the bottle and dashes it against the floor. He then uses the broken shard of glass to cut through the remaining ties binding his ankles. Up and onto his feet, he moves quickly to the door and kicks it open, shoulders the window hatches and leaps back to turn off the tap of the gas canister. He steps outside, coughing and retching in the freezing night air. After a short recovery he re-enters the room, now ventilated against the noxious air. He really hasn't been paying enough attention to Helen Alder. First the private server that she set up at Schiller, then her liaison with Daniel Collier. But tonight he has learned what she is truly capable of. He smiles to himself with a snort. They are not so different, maybe that is their problem. She has his gun, but he is finally about to find out all her secrets. Touché.

Pavel moves across the cabin floor, pulls out his phone and illuminates the screen. He will tear this place apart until he has found exactly what he came here for. He opens the lid of the trunk and the tumblers crash to the floor. He rifles through her clothing and coats until his hand falls on hair. He snatches his hand back in shock . . . Surely not. He slowly shines his phone into the trunk and peels back cloth, his heart beating in expectation of finding the scalp to which the hair belongs, but as he pulls, the hair comes away in his hand. It's just a wig. Long and dark. Maybe she likes to play dress-up with Daniel, kinky. Well, each to their own. Pavel shines his phone over to the desk, strewn with paperwork and notes. He boots up her computer and waits for it to load. He rifles through the papers, documents, bank statements and other files. But what he's looking for won't be on paper. The computer powers up and the box appears; enter password. Pavel is no stranger to a hack. Crouching down, his eye in line with the keyboard, he turns the phone light to blue and casts it over the surface. He studies the worn letters of her keystrokes and the greasy fingerprints. About eight or nine are frequently used. No numbers. That narrows it down. He considers who Helen really is, what are her weaknesses, where are her pressure points. It's just a word that he needs. A word that no one else would ever know. What might she do in secret? He looks at the label of the shattered bottle of whisky on the floor. Knob Creek. He snorts. No. Not quite Helen's style. Then he glances at an ashtray on the side, with several whole crumpled cigarettes, barely smoked. Helen's little guilty secret? His favourite Russian smokes were always in his right-hand drawer for those moments of stress. He reaches for the handle of Helen's right-hand drawer and pulls it open. There, stuffed in a corner, is a crumpled packet of Du Maurier Extra Light. Nine letters. He taps in the letters carefully, observing the capitals. He watches the spinning wheel turn and turn until . . . Bingo. He's in.

He taps the keyboard immediately, finding her server. Schiller's files are all labelled with coded numbers. He clicks through each one, desperate to locate the one he needs. Useless invoices and receipts. Not what he has been sent here to retrieve. He continues, file after file, document after document. Still nothing of interest. Maybe she's clean after all. Then he clicks on a file named 'Josephine', buried in a chain of other documents. As he checks through the codes and numbers, his heart starts to race: this is it. This is the one he suspected she had, the deep-encrypted file he has been searching for. The Neurocell prototype data. So, he was right about Helen Alder all along. How the hell did she get this out of Schiller under everyone's nose? The private server, bypassing Schiller's intranet logs. He smirks to himself. With his phone, he photographs the evidence.

Just as he is about to close down the system and remove the hard drive, he sees another file. 'S. COLLIER.' He opens it. The first file is an article from *The Lancet*. He clicks on the next; a screen grab from an email: 'Sarah Collier; value as a celebrity endorser.' The next is a series of family photos of Daniel, Sarah and their little girl. Pictures of them on holiday, with grandparents, playing in the garden, screen-grabbed from social media. The intrusion seems strange and obsessive. These private and personal images of the Colliers have no place on Helen Alder's computer. What's the connection? Why so personal? He opens a final document and leans in to read. There is a PDF attached to a covering letter. The attachment contains medical forms in French and German. Written on the final page is an official declaration of intent. He blinks, and rubs his eyes; there in print is something he could never have predicted. As he reads, the blood leaves his face and he places a hand to his bloodied head. Dry throat swallowing in disgust. His life has been a catalogue of damage and deception but the plan unfolding before his eyes makes him feel sick to his stomach. This is on another level. Who could possibly dream up something so cruel? She has to be stopped.

Helen Alder is now in his crosshairs.

CHAPTER 40

DANIEL

I open my eyes, vision blurred. It feels like I've been asleep but I'm not in my bed. My head is throbbing. The sound of wind whipping through trees is all around me and there is the creaking and cracking of snow and glass. The freezing wind makes me want to pull the covers up tight; I feel so tired, I think I'll just lie here a while longer.

I feel a searing pain in my back, like a hot knife in my spine, and suddenly I'm wide awake. The seat belt has wrenched itself around my neck, restricting my breathing. As I lift my hand to pull myself free, I realise it's thick with blood. I put my hand to my head and lift myself away from the airbag pinning me into the seat. The car seems to be seesawing like a rocking horse, and freezing air is rushing through a broken window. I reach down and unclasp the seat belt.

'Helen?' I try to turn my head towards her but my neck has locked in a spasm.

'Helen, are you OK?' I turn my shoulder towards the driver's seat but it's empty, the door is wide open. Outside, I can see the navy dawn sky still peppered with stars. Then, beneath the car, I see a sheer dark drop, falling into a chasm below. The vehicle is swaying precariously over the void.

'HELEN!!!' I yell, but my hoarse strangled voice is swallowed up by the howling wind and the deep ravine below. I have to get out, NOW. My right hand is badly cut and bleeding. The impact of the airbag must have thrown me sideways into the passenger-side window. I crunch down on glass in my mouth and my palm stings as I slide it into the door release and pull at the catch. The mangled door doesn't budge, jammed shut from the impact. The car continues to rock in the wind. It's as if every breath I take in and out is moving the vehicle. I press my feet into the well, sliding myself under the airbag and stretching higher up across the headrest. The car lurches sideways as my weight shifts. I catch myself and try to steady the movement, leaning my head back, bracing my feet against the shattered dashboard. A gust of wind outside lifts the front end and the car steadies itself. Barely daring to breathe, I inch my way backwards through the passenger-side window. The fragments of glass left in the frame drag across my back, tearing into my shirt. I fall out of the car and land on the rock. I push against it with my feet and shuffle back away from the creaking wreck as it hangs off the precipice. I lie there for a second, breathing heavily, trying to rouse myself and get my bearings. *Helen, where are you?*

I turn my head; pieces of buckled and torn metal from the crash barrier wrap like ribbons around the bonnet of the car. The driver's-side wheels are hanging off the edge. Helen must have been thrown free or managed to get out before the impact. Maybe she's on the road, injured.

A cracking sound shudders in the silence of the dawn. The hard-packed snowdrift that cushioned my fall starts to loosen from the rock beneath me. The car groans and begins to edge, inch by inch, further towards the drop. I nudge myself back slowly until I'm nearly at the road when the car suddenly lurches over the side of the ravine with an almighty metallic heave, pulling rock and snow with it. The ground beneath me begins to slide. I turn onto my front and scramble, with every ounce of energy that I have. Arms and legs, hands, fingers and feet grip and push for my life, escaping the collapsing avalanche.

I hear the slamming and tumbling of the car. Glass breaking and the metallic wrench of the vehicle hitting the rock face. Then silence, before a final distant smash as it plummets to the valley floor. The smell of petrol fills my nostrils and the shock of the impact adds to the pain in my head and my back. I turn into the snow and vomit violently, and then lie still, flat on my face. Slowly I lift my head, pull myself onto my knees and try to stand. Eventually, I manage to find my feet and stagger slowly along the road. In the distance, about fifty yards away, I can see a small quivering heap on the ground. *Helen.*

My adrenaline soars. She is hurt, lying in the road. I limp into a jog and push through the pain to get to her side. 'Helen! Are you OK?'

I reach the splayed body and kneel down to help. As the woman on the ground turns her head, a bolt of terror shoots through my body, lancing my heart.

'Sarah?' My wife turns and stares back at me. What the hell is she doing here? I've fallen into a nightmare of my own making. I stare at her in disbelief. Her haunted eyes stare back at me in shock. She's trembling violently and her broken voice is pitiful.

'Please. Help me.'

CHAPTER 41

SARAH

'Sarah?' The deep voice with a German lilt wakes me. I can hear the beep of a heart monitor and I'm hit with a strong smell of amber. I drag my eyes open and turn my heavy head towards a warm glow emanating from the corner of the room. There is a figure seated there, watching and guarding me. Making sure I don't escape again.

'Where am I?' My voice sounds high and tinny, like I've had tubes thrust into my throat. My head is bandaged.

'You're safe.' He didn't answer the question. He doesn't need to. I know where I am; I am back in the Schiller Institute. Mauritz's chair whirrs in the silence as it moves slowly across the floor towards me.

'There was an accident, Sarah. You were unconscious when you came in and I decided to perform a scan to ensure there was no internal bleeding to your brain. Everything seems fine but I'd like a second opinion. For now, you just need to rest.'

'I can't stay here, Mauritz. I need to be with my daughter. I must get back to London.' I push myself up in the bed. I have to shake myself out of this. I need to clear my head and regain my strength.

As I shift, a sudden flash of blinding lights and the scream of a car horn catch me and I clasp my hands to my face for a second, trying to steady myself.

'Oh God! The car . . . It hit me . . .' Another jolting stab from my memory courses through me and I swallow a sob. 'Were other people injured?' My hip bone throbs as I remember the impact and I wince in pain, lying back on the pillow. As I feel the agony in my bones and bruised muscles, another kind of pain lances into my chest. Daniel was in the car, I saw his face. Then, as the picture becomes clearer, my hands move to cover my mouth, stifling the cry that is about to burst out. She was driving, she looked right at me. Helen was driving the car that hit me. I'm shaking and my breathing is shallow.

'I have to get out of here.'

Mauritz places a cool hand on my burning face. 'Sarah, you need to take this seriously. You are in shock and your body must have the rest it requires. Once I have the results of the scan, we can talk about getting you back to London.'

I shift in the bed, about to protest again, ready to get up and get moving. Mauritz puts his hand on my arm to stop me.

'There is someone here who is desperate to see you.'

'Daniel?'

Mauritz smiles and nods. I don't know if I can do this, I don't want to see him. I hate being cornered like this. I know him, I know what he'll do. He'll hold my hand and tell me how scared he was, he'll tell me how much he loves me.

Mauritz leaves the room and a few seconds later Daniel cautiously enters. I push myself up, propping the pillow behind my back, and stare at this man. His face is one I have looked at every day for so many years. The lines around his eyes and his pinched smile. The mole above his left eye, the greying temples. The man I trusted, the man I loved. Yet looking at him now, he's a stranger, I don't know him at all. He feels like an echo from the past, like the scratchy sound of an old gramophone playing in another room. But then I see his face, full of remorse. I see walks to the pub on long summer evenings, and lazy Sunday mornings, and pizza and movie nights. The father of my daughter, my husband. I told you.

'Hey you, been in the wars?' His hunched shoulders and pock-
eted hands send a ripple of comfort through me. I fight against it.
He inhales, blinking rapidly, welling up. Here we go.

'Yep. Rough night.' I leave it at that. He knows. His mouth
curls at the corner in a half smile, half apologetic grimace.

'Reminds me of that disastrous New Year's Eve you ended up
in A & E. We got off our faces on cans of Red Stripe, on the dance
floor at Camden Palais. You thought I was flirting with someone
else and stormed off.'

'Did I? All I remember is standing in the pouring rain for two
hours waiting for the night bus, don't really remember much else.'

'Right. I took a mini cab and drove around for hours; thought
I'd lost you.'

I never knew that. Is that true or is he embellishing the past
with his heroics?

'I always admired how wild you were. Passionate. Carefree.'

'Or careless . . . Well, not any more, Daniel.'

His clenched smile drops and his expression darkens; he is
either about to confess or spin me a tale. The thing about marriage is that over time you learn so much about your partner. You
hear the conversations they have in their sleep. You tolerate their
habits and watch them when they think they are alone. I know
every flicker and every tell. Or at least I thought I did. He pulls up
a chair next to the bed, sits like a bad actor in a medical drama
and clasps my hand.

'I thought you were dead; you were just lying in the road not
moving.'

The scream of the car horn courses through me again and I
squeeze my eyes tight. 'How did we get here, Daniel?'

'Sarah, you were hit by a car, don't you remember?'

'No, I mean, how did we get here? How did our marriage arrive at this point?'

His face is blanched and he opens his mouth but nothing comes out. I look at him, searching that face, trying to find the man I once knew.

'I know about you and Helen, Dan. I know you've been having an affair.'

I want him to deny it. I want him to show me irrefutable proof that it never happened, that our marriage is still intact. But before any words form, I can see the muscles in his face betray what's really in his heart, then the mind kicks in. He looks at me and smiles, his knee judders up and down. There's the tell.

'It was a mistake. I was drunk and we had a one-night stand, it was nothing. It *is* nothing. I've been so worried about you, so stressed. The illness is a lot to cope with. And then on top of that the pressure of me being the only one earning any money. I've had a lot of shit to deal with.'

At first, I'm pleased that he's being honest and relieved that I'm right, that I'm not crazy. But then the weight of disappointment yanks me down. For a split second, everything is over. We've separated, our lives have divided, our daughter is splitting her time between us. I see exactly how it will be, how I will get out, move on and survive. A life without him. But then I remember that I am not likely to survive. I don't have much of a life left, with or without him. The penny drops.

'I understand, Daniel. No one wants to fuck the patient, right?'

Neither of us speaks for a second; the silence is full of truths that neither of us wants to confirm.

'Daniel, I think you should go. I can't forgive you for this.' My voice is unnaturally calm and measured, but even as I say the words, I don't believe them. I hate what he's done but I can't hate *him.* The roots of love are just too deep to rip out in an instant. I want us to leave, to go home and rid ourselves of these poker-playing vultures, these highfliers with their deals and schemes and clever moves.

Daniel's hand is now over his eyes in shame. He's crying. I hold on to my resolve. This is the strange currency of deceit. For him, relief has come with his confession, the weight has been lifted. But for me . . . Well, I'm left straining under the burden of confirmation.

'Is it over with her?'

'Yes. It was just once. I nipped it in the bud and since then we just meet professionally when I come here to the Schiller Institute. It's business, nothing more.'

Oh Daniel, you were doing so well. He nearly had me. His lie within a lie is well rehearsed, as I knew it would be. I gaze into his lying eyes and smile.

'And where is she now?'

'I don't know, I haven't seen her since the launch this afternoon.'

I know what I saw. Helen was driving the car that hit me. Daniel was with Helen and my husband is still lying to me.

He takes my hand and kisses it. 'I'm sorry, Sarah. I never meant to hurt you. I am here for you. Now you need to get some rest, love. Everything will feel better in the morning.' He places his hand on my bandaged head.

The warmth of his lips on my skin and his comforting familiar smell envelop me in a shroud of love and safety. But it is all a façade. He's wearing a mask. He smiles at me and I smile back. We mirror each other, both deceivers now.

I'm wondering how deeply my nails will have to dig to prise that mask away. To tear it off and reveal the true face of betrayal.

CHAPTER 42

DANIEL

Heart pounding, I drive back down the road from the Institute towards the bend where the car hit the crash barrier. The car I've borrowed from Schiller smells of stale sweat and cigarettes. Echoes of the crash jolt through my body as the road pitches down, tracing the river in the deep ravine of the valley. I play out every possible scenario in my mind: was she thrown from the car and badly injured? Did she stagger down the road to call for help? Is she in some emergency room fighting for her life? Did she fall to her death? My mind is all over the place and I feel sick to my stomach, but I have to know what's happened to her. I have to find her.

In the hazy light of the cold morning, the road seems different. A tractor ploughing the snow from the narrow mountain pass chugs its way ahead of me, slowly clearing the route. The road becomes a single track and the vehicle grinds to a halt. The plough blades shift snow to the side as an old, bedraggled ram clambers over the piled drift and stands in the centre of the road. The vehicle moves off and the ram leaps over a ditch. As I creep past, it stares at me from the verge, challenging me, ready to charge. It's no less than I deserve. In the rear-view mirror I see him regain his rightful place in the middle of the road, the condition of his battered horns a testament to all the fights he has won. I realise how tired I am, how little fight I have left in me.

I don't think I love Sarah any more. If I do, then why am I here looking for Helen and not sitting by her bedside? We both nearly died last night and still that wasn't enough to shake me out of this obsession. I don't expect anyone to understand unless they have lived inside a marriage that's dying. I've hung on for as long as I can, but that's the problem, I've been hanging on. Hanging on to her fame and her achievements. Trying to carve a path for myself but failing. It might be hard to hear, it's hard to say, but my self-worth is completely wrapped up in what I do. It's hard to live with a winner when you're not even in the game, especially as a bloke. Helen never makes me feel like that, she makes me feel like anything is possible: because it is. Even with what we are about to do, she would say, 'There is always a way.'

I approach the sharp hairpin bend and pull into a lay-by further down the road. I can see the torn crash barrier, rippling and bending over the sheer drop below. Her mangled car is down there. I feel sick, picturing what's left of it: a wreck of twisted metal at the bottom of the ravine. A flood of images flashes through my mind. In the moments leading up to the crash, her window was down. She looked over at me and then I saw Sarah in the road. I grabbed the wheel but we spun and struck the side. And then what? Was she flung through the open window? I can't remember if she was wearing her seat belt. I reach into the torn pocket of my jacket and try to turn on my shattered phone for the fiftieth time, still hoping somehow that it might power up, but it's dead. Shit, she has no way to contact me.

I get out of the car and walk back up the steep incline. To the side of the road is a footpath, with a sign that reads, '*Passerelle à Tourneresse*'. A route for summer hikers, following the waterfall and the stream as it wends its way to the Rhône. The damp morning shrouds the path in a blanket of mist and, like a fallen angel descending into Hades, the swirling fog swallows me whole.

It takes about thirty minutes to get to the bottom of the ravine. The path twists and turns, so steep in places I have to slide down on my backside, grasping at rocks to stop me cascading into the ravine. I clamber over stones and frosted winter vegetation, my feet sinking into knee-deep snow, slowing every step. Eventually, through the parting mist, I see the crumpled heap of metal that used to be Helen's SUV. The windscreen is shattered, the doors are dented and the roof has caved in. The whole chassis is twisted and buckled. I squint to see if Helen is somehow still in there, draped over the steering wheel, trapped between the airbag and the seat. Or her head dashed on a rock, teeth smashed in her bruised face. Bent-back limbs broken and twisted. I close my eyes and try to shake the terrible images from my head.

I approach the wreckage, dreading what I might find. Shards of glass crunch under my feet and in the trees jagged ribbons of steel from the crash barrier sway in the wind. But she's not here. I stand for a second, frozen to the bone, wet and shaking. There is nothing left for me in this place. I stand and look back up the trail. Helen is gone.

I don't know what to do without her.

CHAPTER 43

SARAH

I wake up in a hard bed with thin sheets wrapped tight around me and remember where I am. Then I remember what has happened. I squeeze my eyes closed, praying it's not true. I now know for sure that I can't trust Daniel. He lied to me and dressed it up as a sincere confession. But at least my instincts were right. Despite my illness, despite my untethered state of mind, I now know the one person I *can* trust is myself.

The door opens and Mauritz Schiller enters, taking care to close it gently behind him. The room is dark. It's like a morgue in a state of respectful mourning. But I'm not dead yet.

'Can you put the light on, please? I can't see you very well.' His shadow in the corner is unnerving me and I'm starting to feel like a prisoner rather than a patient in need of care.

I sit up as his chair glides slowly across the room towards me. He comes into view and I see a brown envelope in his lap.

'Sarah . . .' He hesitates as if unsure how to frame the question. 'Sarah, would you mind describing to me the diagnosis you received regarding your Alzheimer's?'

I search his face to see why he would ask such a strange question. 'I'm sorry, I'm not sure what you mean.'

'I need to understand what first prompted you to suspect that you might need to have an MRI scan.' Mauritz thumbs the envelope, turning it gingerly in his hands.

'Well, my father was diagnosed with dementia a few years ago. We had to move him into a care home. It's really taken quite a toll on our whole family. Then I started to develop similar symptoms; I needed to know if I had it too.'

He smiles and nods in sympathy, his bedside manner kind and understanding. 'The evidence for hereditary diagnosis is still quite vague.'

'I've been suffering from severe migraines, dizzy spells and memory loss . . . that kind of thing. The scan simply proved what Daniel and I both suspected.' Tears spring to the corners of my eyes as I remember the evening just a couple of nights ago when we read the email together.

'Dan was even more devastated than I was. I've never seen him cry so hard, he was really destroyed.' I wish we could rewind the tape and go back to that night. No. Further than that, go back to . . . Oh, come on, Sarah, there is no going back. 'It's been really tough on him, seeing me like this.'

'I see.' Mauritz shifts his chair forward slightly and removes a wad of paper and some acetate scans from the envelope. 'Aside from the symptoms you describe, can you remember what it was specifically about the scan that led you to believe that you were suffering from early onset dementia?'

My brow furrows as I rack my brains to remember the wording Daniel read out from my file.

'Um . . . Just that the scans showed evidence of amyloid plaques in my brain. It was so startlingly similar to my father's diagnosis that I wasn't really surprised.'

Mauritz leans forward and touches my hand.

'Sarah, we ran some blood tests and found a cocktail of drugs, opioids and some chemicals that will take a little longer to identify.'

'Yes, I've been taking cholinesterase inhibitors to delay the progress of the disease.'

'Sarah, what I am about to tell you is going to be a shock.' He bites his lower lip as he fumbles with the papers in his lap and pulls out a brain scan. 'You have a perfectly healthy brain. There is no scarring and no plaques, you have no evidence of any kind of brain dementia. You do not have Alzheimer's.'

I take the scan and stare at the image, running my eyes over the words on the page.

'No, I'm sorry, this can't possibly be right. I saw my scan: this one is incorrect.' I hear my voice and for a split second I catch the sound of doubt; a question mark in my tone. Somewhere deep down, a door is opening to reveal something that I have known all along. Something that is only just becoming clear.

'Sarah, I conducted this scan here and obtained a second opinion. There is no doubt, your brain is completely healthy. It's the drugs you have been taking that have made you feel unwell.'

I look down at my trembling hands holding the piece of paper, shaking with fear and a growing rage.

'But I have been seriously ill. Things have been . . . upside down, things haven't been right. I have had hallucinations and . . . blackouts . . . paranoia . . . memory loss. I'm all over the place; my brain is definitely not functioning correctly. I am my own evidence, no matter what the scan says.'

Mauritz squeezes my hand firmly. 'Sarah, look at me.'

I raise my head and look into his eyes, like my own father's, kind and sad.

'The medication we identified from your blood test is an extremely potent narcotic and is known to cause hallucinations and paranoia, depression, disorientation. We rarely prescribe it in this country except for extreme cases of schizophrenia, and even then it's a last resort.'

And then the door to the truth is flung wide open. Daniel has done this to me. *He* oversaw the scan, *he* prescribed the medication. *He* delivered my diagnosis. Daniel has been drugging me. No. It can't be true. My husband wouldn't consciously hurt me like this. Would he?

I look down at the scan again and I see the sheets of the hospital bed I'm lying in. Daniel persuaded me to come here. Why would he do this to me? I'm the mother of his child. If he was so unhappy, why didn't he just leave me? Why torment and torture me like this? As the facts and the evidence begin to fall into place, a coldness runs through me. Daniel has poisoned me. I'm utterly frozen in disbelief as tears tumble down my face and onto the scan.

Mauritz places his hand on top of mine. 'Sarah. You have my full protection. We must get you out of Geneva. I will arrange for my private plane to take you back to London this afternoon. In the meantime, you must rest. I will contact the embassy and take care of everything else. You have my word.'

I swipe the tears drenching my face and shake my head. 'I can't . . .'

'Please don't worry. He won't get in. He won't get through security, I will make sure of that.'

He holds my gaze, not letting me go until I concede.

'Please can I call my daughter?'

'I'm sure we can arrange this.'

As he leaves the room, I get out of the bed and stand in the middle of the room. I feel the floor with my feet and remove my gown, standing there naked. I look down at my body, the legs that have carried me all my life, the scar from the birth of Maddie, my breasts that fed her and my arms that dragged her to school. My hands ball into fists and I raise my head.

You want me gone? You're going to have to try harder than that.

CHAPTER 44

'Mauritz? It's Pavel.'

'I have nothing to say to you, Osinov—'

'Don't hang up.' Pavel's tone is different. There is panic in his voice, an uncertainty that is out of character. 'It's urgent that I speak to you, please just hear me out.'

The last person on the planet Mauritz wants to speak to right now is Pavel Osinov. He is in the process of arranging Sarah's journey home. When his phone rang, he answered thinking it was Jan Pager calling back with confirmation of her flight.

'I have nothing to say to you.' Mauritz bites down so hard he tastes blood.

'Helen Alder and Daniel Collier are plotting something highly illegal. I believe Sarah Collier is in danger. I have all the evidence. I've seen it with my own eyes.'

Mauritz chews the inside of his cheek and juts his chin forward. He has his own evidence: Sarah's brain scan and the analysis of her blood confirming the levels of narcotics in her system. But could there be more? He's curious but he can't risk any further co-operation with Pavel Osinov.

'Sarah Collier is now safely in my care. Her well-being is no concern of yours.'

'She is at the Institute?'

'I wash my hands of you, Pavel, and return you to your Russian comrades at the FSB. Good luck, you'll need it.'

'Mauritz, listen to me!' Pavel sounds desperate. 'I have evidence that her life is in imminent danger. I'm sending you an email, please open it, it's crucial that you—'

Mauritz kills the call. The phone immediately rings again but he ignores it, letting it go to voicemail. Mauritz already has the situation under control. But something that Pavel just said taps at the back of his skull. 'Helen Alder *and* Daniel Collier.' Co-conspirators? How does Helen figure in all this?

He manoeuvres his chair over to his desk and opens his email account. Mauritz's finger hovers over a message from Pavel with an attachment. Does he really want to open this can of worms? He knows there is no love lost between her and Pavel; maybe this is just bad blood. What could she possibly have done to compare to Pavel's betrayal? He's about to close the email without reading it when he sees some words in the subject line: 'Elysium Life Choice'.

He hasn't seen that name for quite some years but it's one that he recognises instantly. In the blink of an eye, he is lying on a stretcher, being airlifted from a mountain. Then he's in a hospital bed watching the grim faces surrounding him. He remembers the paper he held in his hands. Mauritz clicks on the email. He immediately recognises the logo. After his skiing accident, Mauritz had researched 'Elysium Life Choice', the famous euthanasia clinic in Zurich. He met with the doctors, he was vetted and approved, but something changed.

His breathing slows and his furrowed brow darkens as he reads the email. The document is an application for a patient with Alzheimer's disease to voluntarily end their own life. The name of the applicant reads, 'Professor Sarah Margaret Collier'.

Mauritz sits back in his seat. The plan is so appalling, so calculated, it is hard to comprehend. Daniel Collier deliberately misdiagnosed his wife with a terminal illness and with the assistance of his lover, Helen Alder, is conspiring to use her condition to end her life. They planned to use the 'Elysium Life Choice' euthanasia clinic to commit murder.

Mauritz waits, contemplating what he has just seen, letting the truth sink in. The evidence before his eyes of why Helen has been so focused all this time on Sarah Collier. The other shoe drops.

Very slowly, Mauritz feels for a small button under his desk and presses it. A high-pitched siren blares and a small light in the ceiling begins to flash. A fire alarm: everyone will now clear the building. He picks up his phone and Jan Pager answers the call.

'Professor Schiller, the alarm was just triggered from your office.'

'I know, I want the building evacuated and I need you to ensure the Institute is secure. No one comes in or out, we're on high alert.' There is a pause at the end of the line.

'Yes, sir.'

'If anyone tries to gain entry, you need to let me know immediately.'

Mauritz calmly reverses his chair back from the desk and begins to travel along the corridor towards the elevator. A flurry of technicians and administration staff moves quickly from their offices and the central laboratory, heading for the exit. His plan is to clear the building of everyone, including Jan Pager, until Sarah's flight is confirmed, and then he will escort her to the airfield in his personal vehicle. He presses his fingerprint to the touch pad that leads into the restricted area, towards the room where Sarah is being kept safe. As the door clicks open, he feels a hand on his shoulder.

'Mauritz? The fire alarm is sounding, I think we had better get you to safety.'

Mauritz turns in his chair. Looming over him is Helen Alder. She is dressed in a bomber jacket and black jeans; her blonde hair is tied back in a ponytail and a brown leather bag is slung over her shoulder. His eyes narrow as he scrutinises her, trying to figure out his next move.

'There is no emergency, Helen, I set off the alarm. What are you doing here?' He reverses slightly, putting distance between them. Helen's eyes flick to the door.

'Checking on our patient?'

'What patient?'

Helen smiles and exhales, inclining her head. 'Are we going to do this here in the corridor?'

Schiller slowly moves back towards his quarters; Helen follows and closes the door behind them. She stands with her back to the wood. Mauritz moves across the room to a cabinet and pours himself a drink. He decides to cut to the chase.

'I know about your affair with Daniel Collier and I know that he has been drugging his wife.'

Helen glares at Mauritz.

'God, that's awful. What an asshole.' She pushes herself away from the wood and saunters into the centre of the room. 'Wow! I feel so dirty now.' A smile is forming across her lips. 'But then, we only fucked a couple of times, he's not all that.' There is something very different about her. The tone of voice coarser. More brash.

Mauritz takes a sip of vodka and lifts his head, his chin firm in the face of his once-trusted employee.

'Tell me about Zurich, Helen.'

She doesn't flinch but instead moves closer towards him. 'Not gonna offer me one?'

Mauritz blinks very slowly, his blank face impenetrable.

'Guess not. Well . . . it seems we've both been busy.'

He grips the arm of his chair as she towers over him, suddenly feeling vulnerable. 'I don't care about your affair with Daniel

Collier, but you need to tell me what is going on. What has he forced you into?'

'Oh, Mauritz, your view of the world is so conservative, so old-fashioned. You are one of the greatest visionaries of our time, and yet . . . pfft.' She blows through her lips with a shrug, mocking him.

'I did a scan on Sarah, there is no Alzheimer's. But there *is* a licence for an assisted suicide to terminate her life. Why? Who has orchestrated this?'

Helen's mouth opens to speak but no words arrive. Instead, she leans in close, resting her hands on Mauritz's chair, and exhales pointedly into his face. He turns away.

'The document was found on your server, Helen. What have you done?' The rise in Mauritz's voice is one of anger, but the crack of panic betrays his true feelings.

'You know nothing. You have spent your whole life trying to prove to the world that you matter, trying to make a legacy for yourself. But you have been so focused on looking outwards that you have failed to see what's right in front of your face.'

'You bring shame to this institution. I trusted you and gave you opportunities and you betrayed me, just like Osinov.'

'Everyone is using you, Mauritz, even the investors of Neuro-cell. They don't want your "ethical life-saving technology", they're not interested in helping people. They just want to make money.'

'What have you done?'

'It's not what I've *done* . . . It's what I am *doing*.'

Mauritz slams his wheelchair into reverse and Helen stumbles forward.

'Get out.' He taps his keypad. 'I'm calling security.'

'I think they're all a little busy.' She grabs her leather holdall from the floor.

'Then I'll call the police.'

The threat doesn't register and she looks at Mauritz with pity. The barrel of the pistol appears out of nowhere, directly aimed at his chest.

'I realise this won't hurt you, Mauritz, because you can't feel anything, but it's necessary.'

'No, Helen, please . . .'

The bullet explodes from the barrel, passes through Mauritz's chest and exits through the back of the chair. It splinters the wall behind, the sound dampened by flesh and bone. She watches with intense curiosity as Mauritz Schiller slumps forward down into the seat. She then raises the weapon again and fires it straight into the side of his head. Blood spatters the tessellating pattern of the Escher painting that hangs beside him. She watches it trail from his lips and run down his neck to his chest as his shallow breathing slows to a stop. She tilts her head to the side and studies him, savouring the moment. Then she moves.

Taking care to avoid stepping in the pooling blood that is now spreading around the wheels of his chair, Helen pulls on a single black nitrile glove. She wipes fingerprints from the handle of the weapon she just fired, walks out of Mauritz's quarters and travels up in the elevator. She moves swiftly down the corridor and into the office of the gun's rightful owner; she only borrowed it after all. And it's only right that the gun responsible for Mauritz's death should be easy to find. After depositing it back in the bottom drawer, she returns to her office. She has a little breathing space now. Enough time to cover her tracks. The entire building is in lockdown, she will wipe her hard drive, shred every scrap of remaining evidence.

Then she'll deal with Sarah Collier.

CHAPTER 45

SARAH

A gunshot cracks in the distance. I jolt awake with a start. A hand clamps over my mouth. I try to scream out but the hand pulls tighter. I bite down hard as another arm wraps around my neck and I'm pulled forcefully into a headlock. The tangled bed sheets restrain my kicking feet as I explode in a frenzy of elbows, trying to butt my head back to catch the face of my attacker. A high-pitched alarm is sounding in the distance and a red light is flashing high on the wall.

'Sarah, stay still. Don't move, don't scream.' It is Pavel Osinov. I bring my foot up and kick back into his shin but he locks me tighter and pushes me to the wall, leaning in close. He puts a finger to his lips and hisses at me. 'Shhh, be quiet.' I crane my neck and see his face in the half-light. There is a huge wound across his left cheekbone and crusted blood runs down from his white hair onto his face.

'Please don't hurt me, my daughter . . .' I can't get the words out.

He relaxes his grip on me and sits back on the bed. I shuffle backwards towards the pillows. 'Sarah, I won't hurt you, I'm here to help you. But we don't have much time.' He glances over his shoulder to the door as he speaks. 'Can you walk? Are you injured?' I shake my head, still clenching back the desire to scream. He continues, 'We need to get out now.'

'I'm not going anywhere with you!' I kick both my legs out with great force into his chest and he tumbles backwards off the bed. I leap up and make a bolt for the door but he scrambles after me, catches my arm and yanks me back. I slip and my legs collapse underneath me. His whole body weight pins me to the floor. He hisses a violent whisper into my ear as I struggle violently.

'Sarah, stop. Listen, you *have* to trust me. I need to get you out; your life is in danger. She's coming for you next.'

The escalating anxiety in his voice and my inability to move stop me from struggling.

'What are you talking about? I *don't* trust you. You're a Russian agent, everybody knows who you are now. I said get away from me.'

'For God's sake, Sarah, listen to me. Helen Alder wants you dead. I have evidence to prove it. I came to look for you, I came to help you!'

I'm breathing heavily now, winded and hyperventilating.

'I heard gunshots down the hall.'

Pavel glances to the door. 'She stole my pistol, the whole place is in lockdown but she's still inside the building. We need to move.'

'Why should I trust you?' I stare into his eyes with defiance.

'After the Neurocell launch, when I drove you to the hotel, you were confused and disorientated. If I had wanted to harm you, I would have done it then. I have had your back the whole time you have been in Geneva. I've protected you, Sarah.'

'Get OFF ME!' I push him away.

'Look at me, look at my face. Helen attacked me.' He turns and shows me the head wound. 'She's a violent maniac, she's a psychopath. You know why she tried to smash my head to a pulp?' I look at the wound and shake my head nervously.

'No, why? What did you do to her?'

'I found out what she intends to do next and it involves you. I'll explain everything, but right now we need to get out of here.'

I look into his eyes and at the world of loss and pain that lives there. It was something I noticed the night of the presentation, when we smoked cigarettes outside the back door. I could sense then that he was a complicated man. I don't know if I should believe him but he's right, he's never given me reason to doubt him. He has never done anything but help me. I may live to regret it, but my mind seems clearer. I am my own person. I get to decide what happens to me, and I decide to listen to my gut. I nod and get myself up from the floor. I am taking a leap of faith but I still eye him with caution.

'So, what's the plan?'

Pavel squeezes my shoulder and nods. We both head to the door. Slowly, he cranes his neck into the passage beyond. The coast clear, he looks back at me. 'Wait here.'

He disappears for a minute and then returns with a bundle of clothing and some shoes. A pair of dark-blue protective overalls and plastic hospital slip-ons. 'Put these on. Quickly.'

The overalls swamp me and the shoes barely fit, but beggars can't be choosers. We move off at speed down the corridor towards the exit. The distant fire alarm is wailing and the red lights on the ceiling are flashing in warning. Pavel swipes his key card over the sensor, but the door doesn't open. He pulls out his phone and taps in a code, waits a few seconds and then the door unlocks.

'I designed the security grid so . . . not such a bad date after all.' The bad joke doesn't quite put me at ease. We move out of the 'restricted access' corridor and start to head towards the elevator, when Pavel suddenly stops.

'Mauritz's door . . . He never leaves it open. Something is wrong.' We walk slowly and silently towards Mauritz Schiller's private quarters. There is a faint whirring sound coming from the other side of the door and Pavel gently pushes it open a little further. The room is dark save for the flashing red light. And then I catch a glimpse of him. My hands shoot to my face with a stifled cry of shock.

Pavel touches my arm, urging me to stay where I am. He moves closer and shines the light from his phone onto the wheelchair. Mauritz is slumped in a pool of blood, with half his head missing. I bend forward and hold my knees, about to vomit. Pavel takes off his coat and gently places it over Mauritz Schiller's face. He bows his head in silent prayer and, his eyes full of tears, moves away from the corpse of his friend.

'She did this, I'm sure of it. It's you she wants, Sarah.'

Pavel moves across the room to the Escher painting on the wall. Blood drips down the surface of the canvas. Pavel feels behind the edge of the frame. A panel in the wooden wall clicks and a small door, perfectly formed and concealed within the grain, opens outwards.

'Mauritz's wine cellar.' With a sad smile on his face, he steps inside and we descend a winding stone staircase carved into the rock. We pass through a dark cavern with locked cages piled high with dusty bottles of vintage wine. At the end of the passage is a small trapdoor, like some kind of access hatch. Pavel drags an old wooden box and pushes on the metal door, flipping it open. He clambers out, reaches his hand down to me and I scramble up after him. A small flight of stone stairs leads us to the base of the building, inside the underground car park.

We head towards a banged-up old Renault, and I look over at the Russian. He sees me hesitate.

'I know, I'm sorry, it's a rust bucket.' He gets in and turns the key in the ignition as I open the battered passenger door. 'Not really my style but I had to slip in unannounced.'

I fasten my seat belt. 'And now what?'

'And now we slip out.'

We ascend the spiral driveway of the Institute, concealed by the white-rendered curtain wall. I see a gaggle of people huddled out-side as the fire alarm continues to blare. A number of other cars are lined up, slowly leaving the complex in a kind of exodus. My eyes scan the windows of vehicles looking for Helen Alder, but she's not in any of them.

Pavel turns to me, his face full of focus and determination.

'I have a plan but I need your help. Sarah, can I trust you to do everything I ask?'

I stare out at the road ahead. 'Yes, let's make her pay.'

Pavel looks across at me, his eyes on fire.

'*Prinesite suku vniz*. We're going to finish this.'

CHAPTER 46

Helen Alder stands in the doorway of the Alpine cabin, beside a children's playground, in the centre of the Parc La Grange, on the Cologny side of the lake. Things haven't quite gone to plan. This will be the last time she will come here. Her position has been compromised and now she must leave it all behind. It was always temporary, this run-down old shack, hidden in the trees. A place where she could come and go without anyone noticing. Her departure is a little earlier than scheduled; she hasn't quite seen things through. The loose ends remain messy and untied, Sarah has managed to slip through her fingers, but there is no time to deal with that, she has to move fast. They'll be coming for her.

She headed for the cabin but as she approached, she knew something was wrong. The door was open and the old hatch windows were off their hinges. The place has been turned upside down. Items of clothing are strewn across the floor and papers scattered everywhere. The hideout has been ransacked. She now walks slowly into the middle of the room and to the section of broken floor where the armchair has collapsed into the gap. Is he dead? She sniffs the air, the smell of gas now just a faint aroma. There is a dead rat in the crevice of the floorboard where Pavel was lying. He is gone. She steps very carefully through the detritus and pulls on the back of the chair, tipping it over and looking into the crawlspace under the house. The earth is dark with blood where his head lay. She glances over to the fireplace. The cut zip ties around the feet of the stove confirm his escape. It appears the man is as good as his reputation. He has the persistence of a cockroach.

She picks her way across the room towards her desk; the broken whisky bottle on the floor crunches under the soles of her Prada snow boots. Pavel Osinov knew exactly what he was doing. She has no doubt that he has tried to access her computer. No matter, soon all of this will be over. The whole place is starting to feel like the past; something has shifted. Even the cabin knows, rotten and collapsing in on itself. The ruins of a place that was once useful but has served its purpose.

All evidence of her time here needs to be dismantled and destroyed. But first, she has business to attend to. She switches on her computer and the screen flickers to life. Before she writes, she pulls out a pack of her favourite Canadian Du Maurier cigarettes from the drawer and lights one. This time she will smoke it all the way down to the filter. As she logs on, a security warning flags up a download. She scans the files and notes what was opened and when. She sits back in her chair and drags on the cigarette. So, he did get into her private server. He saw everything. But he doesn't *know* everything.

She settles into her chair and prepares to write one last blog post. The last entry will be an obituary. It is a piece that she has had in her head for a while now, only with a few added extras. After the unexpected events of yesterday, a little embellishment was necessary. There is a sense of sadness as she types. Satisfied, she publishes the last ever *Landau Report*.

She smiles to herself, imagining Pavel Osinov gloating over all the evidence he thinks he has found. Evidence that would condemn Helen Alder to prison, possibly for the rest of her life. But the thing is, Osinov has nothing. The evidence is worthless. Because Helen Alder doesn't exist.

She reaches into her pocket, pulls out a passport and lays it on the desk, opening it on the identity page. Sarah Collier. She reaches into her leather holdall, pulls out another passport and opens it alongside. Terri Landau. She looks from Sarah to Terri and Terri to Sarah. There is a similarity, at least there will be. Helen stands and moves to the small kitchen sink at the rear of the shack, where a cracked mirror is nailed to the wall. A dribble of rancid brown water runs from the rusty tap and fills a plastic bowl. She takes scissors from her bag and starts to hack at her hair, just a few inches. Helen stares at herself in the mirror for the last time and smiles. She was useful, well groomed, well spoken. Expensive. Everything she wanted her to be, it will be sad to say goodbye. Helen reaches for her bag again and, taking a small bottle of dye, she carefully squeezes the auburn colour through her blonde hair and massages it in. After a few minutes she tips the bowl of water over her head, grabs an old T-shirt left by the sink and towels her hair dry. She lifts her face to the mirror. Terri Landau stares back. It's time to go, there is someone waiting for Terri who she hasn't seen for a very long time.

She sets about covering her tracks; piling everything into the collapsed armchair in the centre of the room. She carefully pockets Sarah's passport and dumps her own Canadian one on top of the pile. She opens the door to the log store and drags out a jerry can. Heaving it inside the cabin, she prises off the lid and douses petrol liberally over the desk, the bed and the armchair. She then pours the rest of it over the floorboards and the torn curtains and trails it all the way back to the door. She holds her arm over her nose as the heady fumes rise into her nostrils. Every last scrap of evidence must go up in flames. Everything must burn.

Terri heads to the door and turns back for one last look. Taking the lighter from her pocket, she flicks the Zippo open and throws it to the ground. A hovering blue flame moves quickly to the centre of the room. Before long, a raging bonfire crackles as the mound of papers and clothes is devoured by an orange flame, spreading quickly across the desk. But then the hose of the small gas fire, wedged in the floor, suddenly catches and the flame rips through the rubber, charging up the hose towards the gas canister. Terri darts for the door. She grabs her bag as the whole cabin explodes like a bomb.

A massive blast echoes around the woods, setting off car alarms in the distance. Terri sags with exhaustion and shock. She watches her entire life – Helen's life – collapse into burning ash. Helen is no more. In the distance she can hear sirens, she must get out of here. She pushes herself up from the snow, grabs her bag and staggers away. This is the moment she has been working towards, but the clock is ticking. She knows they will be watching and waiting but if she can pull this off then she will finally be a free woman.

CHAPTER 47

THE LANDAU REPORT

Dear faithful followers,

After my shocking exposé of Russian interference at the Schiller Institute, I have had to lie low. They always come for people like me – truth tellers – either through the courts or personal media attacks. And in some cases, they come in harder. Let's just say I'll be keeping away from windows in high buildings. But as you know, I am incapable of leaving any stone unturned.

We have a right to know what the Russians intend to do with Neurocell, assuming, as we should, that Pavel Osinov has now delivered the prototype to the Kremlin. But there are more immediate things I need to deal with. I am about to break my own rules and reveal my source at the Schiller Institute. Over the past few months, I have been able to keep the public informed of everything that has been going on at Schiller thanks to the assistance of someone on the inside. Helen Alder, who ran the Schiller Institute's PR and marketing department, brought Schiller from obscurity and into the public eye. She put the brand of 'Schiller' on the map. At every stage of Neurocell's development, she has kept me informed of its progress. She has been your eyes and ears, ensuring full transparency. It was Helen Alder who must be credited with exposing Pavel Osinov. She feared for her life should his identity be exposed. She warned me that both she and Mauritz Schiller had received death threats. And it seems it wasn't merely a threat.

I regret to inform you that Helen Alder was killed this morning in a car accident. Witnesses place Alder at the wheel but both the wreckage of the car and Helen's body are yet to be recovered. Her fears were not unfounded. This is how they operate: the whistle-blower is always disposed of. Countless journalists and critics of oppressive regimes have lost their lives before, and now Helen Alder is just another name added to that list.

Pavel Osinov is armed and dangerous. He is a man willing to sacrifice anything or anyone to achieve his aims. Now my fears fall upon Mauritz Schiller, who must surely be his next target. I have tried to contact Professor Schiller to warn him but have been unable to make contact.

Helen Alder will always be remembered as a fallen hero, someone who tried to reveal the truth, who tried to do the right thing with respect and dignity. A woman of honour whose legacy may well die with her.

The Landau Report must go to ground, it's too dangerous for me to carry on. There is now a target on my back and I genuinely am in fear for my life. I must go into hiding. But perhaps one day, we will meet again. Just remember:

A spy is a liar who believes their truth, until they are wholly deceived by themselves.

Stay strong, stay safe.

Terri Landau

CHAPTER 48

DANIEL

The door to the hotel room is ajar; someone has been in here. I slowly push it open and step inside. The room appears to have been trashed; the place has been turned over. I scan the room, looking at my strewn clothing and documents, my laptop open on the desk, a broken lamp on the floor. I survey the damage, wondering who has done this. I feel numb. Just like this room, my insides have been ransacked. I step through broken glass and crouch down to inspect my bag, which has been tipped out onto the floor. I pull it up onto the bed and for some reason I start to gather my belongings. I'm not sure where to go now. My hands and body are on autopilot, while my mind is in an absolute frenzy, totally without direction.

I thought there might be a message from Helen here at the hotel, that maybe she'd be waiting down in the bar with a pair of martinis by the pool table. Memories of her crowd my mind, all of them versions of different fantasies we've played out. With my phone destroyed, we have no way of communicating unless I stay here, in the hotel room. I could walk to the cabin but what if she calls? And of course, I never made any note of her number, not even on my computer, always keeping that one secret. It's funny, isn't it? That small device provides information to access our entire existence, and without it we are well and truly screwed.

I had reception call all the hospitals; no one by that name had been admitted, which is a blessing really. I have no way of knowing if she is dead or alive. The silence is deafening until a church bell begins chiming in the distance: noon. What should I do now? I don't know what to do without her. This plan we made is unfulfilled but without Helen it has no purpose. Without Helen, *I* have no purpose. The pain of loss is clouded by panic. Who am I now without her?

As for Sarah: I've abandoned her. I left her at the Schiller Institute. There is a version of this where I pack up my bag, check out, pick her up and jolly along to the airport as if nothing has changed. Back to London, back to our lives. Pretend none of this has happened. She may forgive my affair but how do I explain everything else that I've done to her? No. There is no going back. And to be honest, I don't want to go back. I can't go back to living like that, a shadow of who I want to be. Helen drew me into the light. That's where I belong.

It wasn't supposed to be like this. It just felt like a silly game to begin with. When Helen first planted the seed, we were drunk and playing 'What would you do if you won the lottery?' You know that one? It was just fantasy. But the seed germinated and grew. 'What ifs' turned into hints and nudges, which became theory and then before I could catch up, we had made a solid plan with roots. Just get Sarah to Geneva and we will roll the dice.

The church bell is still ringing. I stand at the window, stuck in the room with nowhere to go. My child brain wonders, if I fell to my knees and asked for God's forgiveness, would he listen? – but it's the other one who has hold of my soul.

The hotel room phone rings. I scramble through the mess on the floor towards the side table and grab it with both hands. My prayers have been answered.

'Helen?'

'Monsieur Collier?' It is a voice I don't recognise. My heart sinks.

'Er . . . Yes?'

'This is the reception desk. We have received a call from one of your colleagues. She asks you to meet her at . . . Do you have a pen? I will read out the address.'

She's alive. Thank you, God. I step over the bed, dragging the phone cord, and I grab a pen and envelope from the desk to scribble down my instructions. This is it. Helen's alive. My despair vanishes in the blink of an eye.

I take the mountain road towards Les Diablerets, the same route I rode with Pavel Osinov a few days earlier. Today the weather is calmer but the gathering low clouds suggest that at higher altitude it will be a little rough. There is a trembling within me. That shiver of ecstasy that comes with depravity. I should fear the future but I'm just living for the next moment and blocking out the rest.

As the road starts to ascend, the car begins to slow and I drop the gear and step on the gas. I grip the wheel and conquer the bends, taking control of my destiny, willing to accept my fate.

Eventually, I reach the lift station of Col du Pillon. The grey cable car emerges out of the descending storm clouds and I pull in and park. A few skiers are exiting the lift as I approach the booth and purchase a return walking pass. I zip my coat up tight around my face and head up to the glacier. The ascent to 3,000 feet clears my head and I rise in body and in spirit with the thought of Helen waiting for me at the summit.

The lift swings as the wind picks up, trying to dock at the top of the station, hovering just out of range. The operator makes several attempts, but the buffers knock and bang against the sides of the car. My hands grip the side bar and eventually the lift makes contact with its guide runners and slowly moves into position. The doors slide open and a chill of biting wind slaps me in the face. I raise my hood to protect myself from the whiteout. I step out of the lift and stand for a moment, watching the skiers descend. Across to the side of the piste, I can see the outline of a cabin. A broken wooden sign points me towards my destiny: 'La Grange.' As I start to brave the walk across the piste, the wind picks up, blasting the powder from the surface and sending it spinning into the air like millions of tiny diamonds, their facets caught in sunlight.

As I approach the cabin, I notice a figure standing out on the veranda, their hood pulled up to shield their face from the storm. As I move closer, they turn and drop their hood. I find myself looking into familiar green eyes.

'Hello, Daniel. You don't look very pleased to see me, maybe you were expecting someone else.'

CHAPTER 49

SARAH

We face each other. Daniel doesn't speak, the shock on his face tempered with shame. The look in his eyes when I removed my hood and he saw that it was me and not his lover is a look I will never forget. Stripped of all the layers of deceit, I see the truth. He can no longer hide it from me. At least that's something.

We move inside the cabin and he follows me obediently. It's empty inside, it's been planned that way. Pavel made the arrangements while I left the message with the hotel. I'm the bait and now before we land the fish, I need to hear everything from his mouth. *They* need to hear.

'Shall we have a drink?' I ask for my benefit more than his. I need the courage. The lone barman catches my eye and brings over a carafe of red wine and two glasses. The table is set for lunch, but I doubt either of us has an appetite. I nod to him and he exits through a small curtained door, leaving us alone. I pour the wine into the glasses and hold mine up.

'Cheers, Daniel. To old times?' He sits in silence, his face grim, his drink untouched.

'You have nothing at all to say to me?'

His eyes finally meet mine, filled with the predictable tears that I'm so used to seeing. Once, not so long ago, they would have pulled at my heart strings and my empathy would have been triggered. But now, I feel only pity. I'm not cruel. I don't think I want him to suffer – but I want the truth before I decide.

'Shall we start at the beginning? Why don't you tell me how

much I was worth?' He doesn't answer. I'm not going to do this for him. I refuse to hold his hand any longer. 'Daniel, look at me, we may not have much time left. Do you understand what I'm saying? If you don't tell me now, I can't help you.'

After another moment of silence, he finally speaks.

'I've always lived in your shadow, Sarah. From the second we met, you were better than me. Do you know what it's like to live with someone who makes you feel inferior every day? It was killing me. Death by a thousand cuts.'

'Daniel, everything I did was for you, for Maddie, for us. You *know* me, when did I ever bask in glory? Let alone rub it in your face?'

'The Nobel Prize just changed something in you, I can't explain it. It was as if you disappeared behind a door that was locked. I was barred. I was happy for you, but it started to dawn on me that I would live the rest of my life in your shadow, as Sarah Collier's husband. It was a life sentence. One that I didn't choose. One that I hated you for.'

'I didn't do *anything* to you. Was my success such an affront? For fuck's sake, Daniel, I retired to spend time with you and Maddie! I gave up my career. You got what you wanted.' I decide to cut to the chase. 'You didn't answer my question. How much was I worth?' I wait.

'A million.' His voice is cold and cruel. I start to laugh, I can't help it.

'Oh, Daniel, you're a fool.' His stupidity is worthy of ridicule.

'What's so funny?' His eyes are dark, hatred brewing before me.

'Helen told me the endorsement fee was ten million pounds and Mauritz Schiller confirmed it.' The look on his face tells me everything. 'Christ, you didn't know, did you? She played you,

Daniel.' I wait and watch. 'So, what was the plan?' He is silent again, slowly working everything out. His face is pale and his eyes are darting from left to right as he untangles the knot. In my wildest dreams, I never pictured us here. 'Daniel. What . . . was the plan?'

Then he starts to talk.

'The endorsement fee would only be paid if your name was attached. Persuading you to come to Geneva was the only way to get that signature on the line. You had to become the face of Neurocell: it would guarantee maximum publicity and with you behind it, the launch of the product would be infallible. I knew you would never agree to it, so I had to . . .' His voice trails off. He can't say it; the coward can't admit what he has done to me.

'So, you had to . . . what?' I take it slowly. 'Pretend I had a brain disorder and drug me to induce confusion and hallucination? Emotionally blackmail me by using a fake illness to persuade me to endorse its cure? Wreck my confidence, tear me down, make me actually need you for once?' I'm spitting out the words. Saying it all out loud makes it all the more real and all the more devastating. What my husband chose to do to me. He has to say it, he has to admit it. We can't go further without his confession.

He looks up and stares at me coolly as he says, 'Yes.' That's it. Just one word.

'I know everything, Daniel. I know about the affair, the drugs, the fraud. But what about Karima? She conducted the scan, is she in on this too?'

He's breathing hard and shaking his head.

'No, she knows nothing. I went into the system and switched scans with another patient. Karima believed they were yours.'

I'm sickened. I watch him writhe in his chair.

'It was all Helen's plan.' Coward. It's predictable but believable.

After all, it is characteristically Daniel: following in other people's footsteps, surrounding himself with people who will elevate his prospects. Oh God, was that us? Of course, I was that girl. I was flying high even then; he captured me and tried to clip my wings. Well, he hasn't succeeded.

'Sarah, please. I never intended for things to go this far, to get so out of control. I would never let anything bad happen to you. You have to believe me.'

I can't believe what I'm hearing. 'But you *have* let bad things happen to me, Daniel. You've hurt me in every possible way. What was it all for? For love? For money?'

He casts his eyes to the floor. I take a sip of wine, waiting for an answer.

'Love. Yes. I wanted . . . I *want* to be with her. I want a new start.' His voice is so thin he can barely say it and he can't look me in the eye. Even though I knew this was coming, every word slices into my heart. But now I need to ask the most painful question of all.

'And what about Maddie?' My eyes burn as I say her name. His face flushes red. He has no answer. We sit across the table from one another, only a metre away, yet never so far apart. 'Do you want to know the worst part? The person you think you've fallen in love with. You don't even know who she is.'

He shifts in his chair; his eyes flick up to mine in curiosity.

'You haven't worked it out yet, have you? Helen used you. She used you to get to me. She used you to steal ten million pounds. Her real name isn't even Helen Alder. It's Terri Landau. She has been using *Landau Leaks* to extort money from different pharmaceutical groups and this time Schiller was her target and I was her victim. I've seen documents. You were just a mechanism, a conduit, a way to make it happen.'

The rusty cogs in his tired brain begin to turn and very slowly, like watching somebody emerge from a deep sleep, I see the penny drop.

'No, it's not possible.'

'It's the truth. She's quite the architect. She's using her blog to pin her crimes on Pavel Osinov. She doesn't care about anyone but herself. She never loved you; she just used you.'

The cruelty is starting to feel like a warm bath, I'm all in. I want to watch him squirm. He stares at me in silence. Then his face develops an indignance, a defiance.

'It's not true. Helen loves me.'

'Helen?' I take out my phone, pull up a news article and pass it over the table.

'A criminal trial in Toronto. A woman accused of kidnapping her estranged daughter. She was arrested and sentenced but as you can see, she somehow escaped. It's a cold case. Recognise the face in the photo, Daniel?' His head is shaking side to side in an unconscious reflex. 'Now look at the name.'

He looks at the screen and the horror of realisation clouds his face. A broken whisper emerges from his dry mouth.

'Terri Landau.'

I watch him as he replays the last days and weeks and months in his mind, trying to work out all the moments of deceit. I take a large quaff of the red wine, draining my glass and letting the liquid warm me and rouse me for my last bombshell. Then I release the grenade. Reaching down into my bag, I pull out a document and slide it slowly over the tablecloth towards him.

'Elysium Life Choice. Do you know what that is, Daniel?' He slowly shakes his head, the blood draining from his face. Then I can see the dawning realisation of the evidence I have in my possession.

'It's a euthanasia clinic.' I spell it out for him.

I watch his hands clench and beads of sweat form on his brow; his chin quivers and his whole body begins to tremble.

'She was planning to murder me. And you helped her every step of the way.'

He doesn't want to hear any more. His face coils up in rage and he directs all his hurt and frustration at me.

'All we wanted was to be together. I would have done anything to be with her. Anything. Living with you was like *my* death sentence. You have sucked the life out of me for years. Nothing I did was ever good enough.' His eyes are gleaming with hatred as he spits out his insults. 'Helen showed me a way out of my misery and I grabbed it with both hands.'

My heart hurts as he speaks but most of all, I feel exhausted. I don't recognise this man sitting in front of me. The lies and the deceit are hard to handle but the worst part is seeing clearly for the first time just how pathetic he is. I've heard everything I need to hear. I turn my head and speak towards the curtain obscuring the kitchen door. 'If you have everything you need, you can arrest him now.'

It happens quickly. Daniel's eyes flick to the door behind me where the Swiss police are waiting. He suddenly grabs the edge of the table and slams it into my stomach, winding me and toppling me backwards out of my chair. The contents of the table clatter across the floor and the wine glasses shatter. He falls and scrambles backwards across the room, trapping himself in a corner. He grabs at the broken glass that has tumbled off the table and thrusts it out at the two men who are calmly advancing towards him. His head whips around, looking for an escape route, but there is none. He presses himself into the wooden logs of the wall, his feet digging hard into the floor as if by sheer strength he might push the wall down. The strangled moan of a desperate man escapes from his throat. It is unbearable. I have to end this. Once again, it's down to me to sort out the situation. 'Daniel. Stop. It's over.'

Pain then becomes desperate insanity; he turns the shattered stem of the wine glass on himself. First to his wrist and then to his throat, pushing into the artery of his neck. I can see the skin about to break. For a second, I can't breathe. The appalling sight of this man ready to take his own life is pitiful. I bring myself slowly to my knees and crawl towards him.

'Daniel . . . Daniel . . . please . . . for Maddie.' I hold out my hand.

The poor man is unable to finish what he has started. He collapses, sobbing into a heap on the floor, and the two policemen restrain him. I'm torn apart. Half of me wanted a remorseful confession, half of me wanted the skin to break and the blood to flow. I have always been someone capable of forgiveness, but remorse must come first.

I want punishment and retribution for what has been done to me. The feeling is overwhelming. But it isn't just Daniel who must feel the wrath of my revenge. Helen's next.

CHAPTER 50

The line for the first-class check-in desk at Terminal 1 is long. The bored airline attendant at the desk surveys the crowd and cracks his neck. This is turning out to be a long afternoon. The family in front of him haul their overweight bags onto the conveyor belt and fumble around for their passports. He blinks slowly, holding his patience. Boarding passes are issued and a tight smile sees them on their way to the security gate.

'*Suivant.*'

A woman with short auburn hair and a baseball cap pulled down over her face steps forward. She is travelling light, hand luggage only. The airline representative takes her passport and surveys it with pursed lips.

'Bonjour . . . Madame Collier.' As he says the name, he glances up and eyeballs her. 'Ah, it is a pleasure, Professor. How was the conference?'

Terri's heart leaps into her mouth. This man knows who Sarah Collier is. A fan, that's all she needs. She struggles not to betray her panic and forces a smile onto her lips as her palms begin to sweat.

'Very good, thank you.' Her English accent has been practised and is passable. She gets out her phone, pretending to attend to something urgent to prevent further conversation.

The attendant taps on the computer keyboard. Seconds feel like minutes as he continues to type. What on earth is the delay? He then swipes the passport through the scanner and an ominous beep of rejection sounds. Terri's nerve is being tested. It's rejected again and she leans on the side of the desk, steadying herself. Her face is a mask of calm annoyance, but inside her stomach is turning. He picks up the phone and dials a number. As he waits for the call to connect, he watches her.

'*J'ai un problème avec une biométrie . . . oui d'accord.*' He replaces the receiver and continues to work on the computer, without looking up.

Terri's face drains of blood and her palms grow damp. She must board this plane. She must get out of Geneva. She glances sideways at the queue of other passengers starting to glare in her direction. They can wait, they have no idea of the ordeal she has been through.

'No baggage?' The attendant looks at her curiously; her mouth is dry, the tongue stuck to the roof of her mouth.

'No.' Her voice does not betray her discomfort.

After a few minutes a grey-haired woman arrives at the desk and whispers something to the man, who then vacates his seat and stands behind her as she proceeds to enter more information.

'Pardon, Madame. According to our records you flew out from London and were due to return on Monday.' The woman speaks slowly and with authority.

'Yes, my plans have changed.'

'And your companion is no longer travelling?' Eyes look over a pair of half-moon reading glasses.

'No.' There is no need to divulge anything more, the simpler the better.

'Could you remove your cap please, Professor Collier?'

Heart thudding in her chest, the woman pretending to be Sarah Collier gently takes off her hat and runs her hands through her hair. She gathers her strength and looks directly into the face of the desk clerk and smiles. The attendant smiles back and turns back to the keyboard.

'*Merci bien*. Would you prefer an aisle or window seat?'

'I really don't mind.' Terri watches the attendant like a hawk and eventually the printer surrenders the boarding pass. It is placed into the passport and then pressed into her hand. The pins and needles in her fingers subside and she replaces her baseball cap.

'We have a note here on the computer for a chaperone to escort you to the lounge and the gate. If you would like to follow my colleague, he will assist you. *Bon voyage*, Madame.'

Sarah's VIP status is in the system. Special arrangements made for the Nobel Prize-winning celebrity guest, Professor Collier. She nods and places a pair of sunglasses over her eyes. Playing along. Playing Sarah.

She follows the man from behind the desk and proceeds to the fast-track security line. Her hand luggage, outer coat, baseball cap and boots are placed on the conveyor belt and glide into the scanner. With her shoes off and without the hat, she suddenly feels exposed and vulnerable, everyone can see her, everyone is watching her, and she has nowhere to run. Passing through the X-ray without a hitch, she watches as her bag moves slowly through the machine. Eventually, it emerges; she snatches it from the belt and walks on. She's through. One step closer to home.

The chaperone is waiting on the other side of security and leads her through the crowds, who are killing time, shopping and eating. She has no appetite for either. She keeps her head down and grips her bag tight, unable to relax until the wheels of the plane leave the tarmac. They arrive at the lounge and the chaperone walks her through.

'You will be collected shortly before boarding. Would you prefer to board first or last?'

She pauses. Her seat is at the front of the plane in first class; boarding last will mean that she will not have to face any scrutiny from the other passengers as they file past.

'Last, please.' The attendant smiles and holds out his hand. She looks at him, confused.

'Your boarding pass?' The hand hovers, waiting to take her precious ticket to freedom. She hands it over. The man smiles and guides her to a comfortable sofa in the corner with a view of the runway. She watches him walk away in the reflection of the glass and breathes a deep sigh. The Air Canada plane is standing on the tarmac, being refuelled and loaded with luggage. It's not parked at the gate. That will mean boarding the plane from a transfer bus with other passengers. Damn. She gets up and walks over to the drinks table. She pours herself a glass of champagne to steady her nerves and looks over at the flight departures board. Just another twenty-five minutes to wait, and everything she has been fighting for will be hers. She sits patiently, safe in the knowledge she will be returning home a free woman.

Eventually, the announcement for final boarding for Air Canada flight 176 to Toronto cuts through the silence of the empty lounge. Terri notices a man hovering in the doorway, holding a piece of paper in his hand, a phone to his ear. It isn't the attendant from before but this guy is wearing the airline uniform. He hangs up the call and waves to her. She snatches up her bag and moves quickly towards him, her jaw clenched and her eyes focused.

'Professor Collier?' He smiles as she approaches.

Terri looks down to the boarding pass he is holding. 'Yes. I can take that.' The man smiles at her. He does not pass the paper to her but instead holds out his hand to receive her bag.

'*Puis-je vous aider?*' She has no intention of giving the bag over.

She grips the handles tight, as tight as the smile now forming on her lips.

'*Non.*' The edge in her voice is sharp but then softened with a forced smile. '*Merci.*'

'As you wish. Please follow me.'

The man leads the way. They pass two ladies on the desk by the door who barely glance up, their over-manicured nails tapping away on their phones. No one is really paying attention to the world around them. No one except Terri, whose intense focus is on every ticking second of the next few minutes. Her life is moving in slow motion on her final walk to freedom. There is a little girl called Josephine waiting for her, somewhere, back home. Finding her will be her next challenge, but the thought of finally feeling those arms around her fills her with courage. She is on her way.

'Your car is waiting, Madame Collier.' The man is pointing down the stairs, away from the queue of passengers descending the escalator, ready to board the bus.

For a split second, Terri considers taking the bus along with everyone else, safety in numbers. But the man still has her boarding pass. She obeys and follows him down the stairs.

The wall of glass slides back to reveal a blast of cold air and the loud roar of the waiting plane's jet engines. The chaperone guides her towards a limousine and opens the door. As Terri slides into the car, the rep bends down to meet her eyes with a smile.

'*Un plaisir de vous servir*, Madame Collier. Enjoy your flight.'

All is well, everything is normal, as it should be. The door is pushed closed and the mechanical sound of the lock sucks the noise of the airfield from her ears. The back of the driver's head, in a smart peaked chauffeur cap, turns slightly to check that the passenger is ready. The car pulls away and they glide across the tarmac.

The enormous wheels of the plane pass the side window, and the tip of a wing and the blades of a giant jet engine loom across the glass roof of the limousine. She's made it. The car pulls up alongside the staircase to the front doors and Terri looks out to see a member of the cabin crew in a red uniform standing at the top. It's time to go. She reaches down to the door handle and tries to pull it open, but it is locked. She pulls harder and still the door won't move. Leaning forward, Terri taps on the glass to the chauffeur, who continues to stare forward.

'Hi there, could you open the door, please?' Her voice trembles with anticipation.

The door remains as locked as the driver's unflinching forward stare. Something is wrong. A sense of panic begins to rise in her chest.

'Hey!! Hello? Open the damned door.'

Terri watches as the staircase to the plane withdraws from the tarmac. Her heart is punching through her chest as she watches the emergency exit door of the plane close. Her escape route, her lifeline is slipping away before her eyes. She hammers on the glass.

'Hey! Open the fucking door, asshole!' Then slowly, the car begins to creep forward, pulling away from the plane, away from her freedom. Terri watches as the red and white maple-leaf emblem on the tail of the plane passes over the glass sunroof. She turns to look out of the back, her hands on the glass as the car speeds towards the other side of the airport. She sits back in her seat, pulls her knees up to her chest and with the unbridled force of sheer rage slams her feet into the privacy screen.

'STOP THE CAR! STOP THE FUCKING CAR!' Her screams are muffled from within the sealed prison of her bulletproof executive limousine. She continues to pound her feet against the security glass. Kicking and screaming, slamming herself into the impenetrable pane. The driver continues to look forward. He removes his cap to reveal his buzz cut of white hair. Pavel Osinov accelerates out of the terminal, whizzing past the airfield chain-link fence and away.

CHAPTER 51

SARAH

I have returned to the place where it all began. I should never have let Daniel persuade me to come here, and after today, I will never set eyes on the Schiller Institute again. They have Daniel in custody but now it's her turn. A limousine pulls up outside the concrete pillars of the main gate. I trudge through the deep snow of the driveway towards the car. I take a final deep breath of clean pure air, open the car door and step inside.

'Sarah, I think you have met Terri Landau before.'

Pavel is in the driver's seat, the glass partition lowered. I look over at the woman I knew as Helen Alder, dressed in a black bomber jacket, jeans and sneakers. Her hair is no longer blonde but has been dyed a soupy orange, hacked into a crude bob. Terri Landau is considerably less well put together than Helen. Her face is expressionless and she says nothing. The car moves down the single track from the Institute and takes a sharp corner into the dark narrow tunnel carved into the rock that keeps it isolated from the rest of the world. Pavel slows to a stop and kills the engine, cocooned inside the darkness of the mountain.

There is a long silence between us all. The mask has dropped, no need for any further pretence. Her hand moves from her lap to the handle of the door; the locks click. She isn't going anywhere, but then neither am I.

'Daniel confessed.' My voice is shaking. 'He told me everything.' I watch her nervously, waiting for a response. I know what this woman is capable of.

'Daniel doesn't *know* everything.' She turns her head slowly, as if it's disconnected from her body, and looks me in the eye. 'He barely knows the half of it.'

'He told me the clinic was your idea.' I'm not wasting my time. I want a confession. Terri blows air through her lips with a smirk. She's laughing at me; this is all just a game to her.

'What can I say? Daniel made his choice.' The self-satisfied shrug is so nonchalant that my fingers clasp into fists.

'A choice to end my life?'

The corners of her mouth curl. 'Well, there could only be one Sarah Collier.'

'You honestly believed that you could just wheel me into that clinic and no questions would be asked? People need to make that choice themselves, in sound mind.' Surely she can't be that naïve, this is a woman who does her homework.

'Your inevitable overdose would need paperwork to verify a suicide. Your diagnosis announced to the world, the application to Elysium Life Choice; the decision for you to end your own life needed to be watertight.' She is smiling in triumph, proud of her sick plan. I'm speechless.

I swallow hard, tears threatening to spring forward. I can see Terri is enjoying the pain she's causing but I refuse to give her what she craves.

'"Put her down like a dog." I think those were the words he used . . .' It's too much to bear, my hands rise and I can feel myself recoiling, ready to strike her.

'But Daniel didn't have the balls to go through with it. He wasn't coming with me. I could tell.' She turns back to me, pausing for a second, and her pupils dilate as she holds my stare. 'The last time he fucked me, his heart just wasn't in it. You know what I mean?'

I want to smash her gurning face through the glass. The feeling is so overwhelming I can almost feel her skull in my hands. I hear a click, then the barrel of Pavel's pistol emerges from behind the headrest of the front seat, aimed point-blank in Terri's face.

'Thanks for returning my gun.' His voice is calm.

'We both know you're not gonna shoot me,' she hisses through bared teeth. I want him to pull the trigger. I want *this* dog to be put down. But we need more. I want this pinned on her. All of it on her.

'Why did you do it?' It's a simple question but I don't expect a simple answer.

'I just told you.'

I hold her gaze, no more prompting, it is her last chance and she knows it. The smile fades from her face and her head drops forward.

'I have a daughter. Her father wanted me out of her life. He was granted custody and when I tried to get her back, he had me arrested for kidnapping. I'm a wanted woman.' As she starts to talk, Pavel lowers his gun. Terri's eyes move to the window, and she looks up at the light pouring in from the now clear sky. 'They removed my citizenship, stole my life. I haven't seen my little girl for nearly six years.'

Am I buying any of this? I watch her choking back tears, or is she forcing them to the surface? She raises her head and stares directly into the sun before turning to me.

'You're a mother, what wouldn't *you* do to protect *your* daughter?'

I watch the tears falling down her face.

'What about my daughter? Did you ever think about what would happen to her?'

She looks at me with imploring eyes. 'I knew you would understand, Sarah. I had to go home, I had to see her. I couldn't do it as

Terri Landau so I had to become someone else. I had to become you.'

'But why me?'

Terri's face changes. A darkness descends in her eyes and the tears suddenly evaporate.

'It *had* to be you. Your life was the most valuable and I needed money to secure my future. And it was really quite fascinating. You were like an insect pinned under a lens in the scorching sun. I enjoyed watching you burn.'

My voice is shaking. 'Thank you for your honesty.' My trembling hand climbs to the collar of my coat and I pull it back to reveal the small microphone wired into the faux fur. 'I guess you're the one who's going to burn now.'

Without a millisecond of reaction, Terri's voice changes; her flat expressionless words flow out at speed, like a prepared disclaimer.

'Daniel coerced me. He sexually harassed me the first time I met him in Frankfurt. He threatened me, forced me into a relationship with him. It was entirely his plan. He beat me. I have photos of the bruises. The bank accounts are in your name. *You* did this to *me*. You forced me to set up the endorsement for your own financial benefit. It's never gonna hold up in court.'

'The murder of Mauritz Schiller will certainly hold up in court.' Pavel pushes the gun back up to her face.

Terri remains very still, watching us both, considering her next move. Then, in a flash of movement, Terri's hand lashes out and grabs the barrel of the pistol. A gunshot erupts and glass explodes all around me. Pavel cries out in pain, holding on to his shoulder. I duck down with a scream. Terri wrenches at the pistol again and launches herself into the front of the car. A second shot explodes as she kicks out, smacking me in the face. She bites down into Pavel's hand and the gun clatters into the footwell. Terri raises her feet and smashes Pavel in the face. His head thuds against the windscreen with a sickening crack and he slumps in his seat, out cold. She scrambles out of the car through the shattered window, shards of glass ripping her clothes and skin as she breaks free. I reach forward into the front seat, fumbling to find the gun on the floor. I grab it, release the door locks and I'm out of the car after her. She darts off around the corner of the tunnel in a sprint.

She has a head start but I'm after her like a wild cat hungry for its prey. She breaks out of the dark tunnel and into the light, turning back to see me following her. I raise the gun. The crack of the gunshot slices through the silence but she ducks sideways off the road. I follow after her into the pine forest, my feet digging deep into the snow, keeping her in my sights. My legs burn as I push through the now waist-deep snow, branches whipping me in the face as I duck and weave after her. I hear the shriek of a bird high in the sky. Then a flurry of mountain chamois burst out of a dense thicket, startling me. I crouch down. There is silence, just the rushing wind and the thudding pulse of blood in my ears. I wait and watch. Suddenly I spot her through the trees, crawling like an animal towards a clump of trees. She's bleeding. I can see the trail of blood in the snow. I watch her as she rolls sideways under a covering of low-hanging branches. I raise the gun, unsure of how to even aim this thing, but I look down the barrel to where I think she is hiding and pull the trigger. Splinters of wood and snow explode from the trunk of the tree and Terri darts out of her hiding place. I shoot again and follow. She's limping and bleeding. I'm up and after her. As she reaches a plateau in the terrain, she loses her footing and skids towards a bank of trees, crashing through them. I pick up my pace: I have her now.

As I gain ground I see her, teetering on the edge of a sheer drop, her arms flung wide. She turns and drops down, holding her bleeding leg. Then with a startling explosion of energy, she charges at me. I raise the gun again but she slams into me, hurling us both over the side of a jagged outcrop of rocks. The gun flies over the edge. I grab her hair and pull hard. She screams and tries to sink her teeth into my face. I claw at her, trying to find her eyes. My nails find the soft flesh of eyelids and I push down. Her fist smashes into my cheekbone as we stumble over the edge of the ravine.

My hand digs deep into her eye sockets, holding on to her face like a bowling ball, as we fall. My body slams into a rock but I manage to catch the branch of an overhanging tree with my other hand. We're both caught in a brittle cradle of branches, gasping for breath. I release my hand from her face and hook it around the branch, my left foot jammed into a crevice in the rock face. She is further out than me, hanging on to the tree branches for dear life. They bend and crack under the weight of our bodies.

I want to let her fall, but there is something in me that can't allow that to happen. This woman must be brought to justice. She has destroyed everything I ever cared about and she must atone for what she's done. Terri's wide eyes look up at me as the branches crack and the tree drops suddenly. If I move down to her, we'll both fall.

'Grab hold of my hand.' The fear in her wild eyes suddenly dissolves into hatred.

'Get away from me.' She would prefer to fall than allow me to save her.

I reach down as the tree roots begin to tear themselves away from the bedrock. She yelps and scrambles further up the trunk towards me. The tree sways precariously in the breeze. For a second we are both flying over the edge. Towards certain death. My foot in the rock digs deeper and my arms find strength they never had.

'For God's sake, Terri! Take my hand.'

She slowly reaches her hand towards mine and grasps it in hers. Her hand grips on tight as she begins to slowly pull herself up. But then, just as her foot finds the edge of the rock, I feel her hand pulling on mine. She pulls harder and then yanks at my arm. She still believes she can end this her way.

Terri looks up at me. Slowly the corners of her mouth curl and her lips part. Her mouth opens wide as she bites down hard into my hand. Pain shoots up through my arm and I cry out, pulling my hand back and releasing her from my grip. Terri arches backwards, spreading her arms wide, throwing herself into the broken branches. She is held there for a second before the branches snap and she drops out of sight, plummeting into the ravine below. A scream rips through the silence of the valley before an eerie silence descends. She is gone. I push myself back up through the tangled roots and over rock. I lie back in the snow, panting, utterly spent but alive.

A kestrel spirals down towards the broken tree and hooks its talons around a branch. It watches me lying there, its head flicking and turning, surveying the scene. Then, in a flurry of feathers, the magnificent bird dives over the edge in glorious flight, wings spread wide, soaring in silence.

The nightmare is over. It's time to go home.

EPILOGUE

SARAH

The increased morphine dosage has made Dad a little more disconnected than he was before. It's been sunny and the staff have had the windows open. I can see the tulips are starting to bloom in the garden. Spring is early this year. I sit next to him on the bed with my head on his chest, his hand tapping my hair without feeling; it's an empty gesture. He doesn't really know who I am. But at least I do, finally. I know exactly who I am and what I want. The time for crying is over. I have no tears left.

Maddie is playing out in the garden with a younger girl. I watch them both as they sit at a small plastic table, pouring pretend tea into cups. She's too old for a game like this but she's humouring her playmate. My dad leans over and whispers, 'Are we going to the garden party again?'

'What garden party, Dad?' He's staring out of the door at Maddie and her new friend. I think he's rambling but then I remember that the nurses wheeled Dad's bed out into the garden last Sunday. I smile, get up and walk out of the room towards the nurse, who understands exactly what I'm about to ask.

'We'll take him outside again. Why don't you get yourself a cuppa?' She can see the exhaustion in my face. These amazing people who work in end-of-life care must have nerves of steel, or enormous hearts of gold. Or more than likely, both. I'll never reconcile the fact that human beings can be capable of both extreme acts of love and extreme acts of cruelty. But I've seen both, I've experienced both.

I move through the ward and out of the double doors to the dining room, where other residents' friends and families have brought homemade cakes and put them all on the table for everyone to enjoy. I pour myself a tea, and out of the corner of my eye I'm suddenly aware of a man standing outside the glass door, looking in. I lift my head and, through the glass, I see the last person I expect to see. I nod in recognition and Pavel Osinov enters the room. He's dressed in jeans and a knitted sweater, with Nike trainers and a blue baseball cap. He looks like a fish out of water.

'How did you know I was here?' It's a stupid question; the man is a spy. He just smiles. I try again. 'How's your shoulder?' I ask, scanning his clothes for signs of the bullet wound Terri Landau gave him.

'Alright, how's your face?' The bruises have all healed, on the outside at least.

I laugh. 'Tea?' He shakes his head. 'I'm afraid my father is . . . deteriorating.'

'I'm sorry to hear that, but at least you are with him. He brought you into this world and now it's your turn to guide him on his way home.'

It's a beautiful sentiment but I want to know why he is here.

'What do you want, Pavel?' It's blunt but I'm tired and I'm trying to put what happened in Geneva behind me. His face is a reminder of the horror I've been through. His eyes drop to the ground. It's as if he wants to tell me something but can't quite find the words.

'I had to get out of Geneva in a hurry but there were some financial loose ends to tie up in London. How is Daniel?' Pavel enquires, inclining his head.

'He's still in Switzerland. They're building the case for fraud and extortion, but I don't want Maddie growing up with a father

278

who is in prison, so I'm not pressing any further charges. It's between him and the Swiss police now.'

Pavel nods and, reaching into his bag, he pulls out a manila file, which he hands to me: a birth certificate, photographs and the documents for Elysium Life Choice.

'I wanted to give you your identity back, this is everything they had. *Everything*. It's all there.'

I smile in sad gratitude. 'What about you? Back to your idyllic life in Berlin?'

'Ah . . . yes . . . Well, that was really a little pipe dream, I'm afraid. I don't actually live in Berlin. I'm . . . well . . . I'm not really who you think I am, I'm no hero.'

'Don't flatter yourself, James Bond, I never thought you were. Even though you did save my life a few times.' He laughs, shakes his head and tightens his lips.

'I am going home. I just came to say goodbye.'

'Home?'

'To Moscow.'

'I thought . . .'

'Yes, I was exiled. On an FSB hit list, ostracised by the Kremlin, that part was true.'

'So how can you go home?'

'I . . .' This seems hard for him to say. It is a confession. 'I eventually paid the price that they were asking.' The ground beneath my feet suddenly feels soft; I have an awful feeling I know what he's about to say.

'I delivered Neurocell to them.'

So, after all this, Terri Landau was right, he was a Russian asset.

'They would have copied the prototype anyway, they always do. But by being the person to secure it for them, I am able to go home to see my family.' He pauses for a second, tears in his eyes.

A heavy weight hangs over him and his tone is sombre.

'I am here to say goodbye. A new iron curtain is falling, Sarah. True Russians are returning to the motherland and I am Russian to the core. It's beyond my control, it's the blood in my veins, for good or bad. I know I will never leave once I have found my way back.' There is guilt in his voice. 'Please don't judge me. I think ultimately, we are *all* trying to find our way home, aren't we? You understand.'

And I do. There is nothing more to say.

He stretches out his hand and I take it. He squeezes mine firmly and we hold on for a second longer than we need to. It's hard to part, after all. But then he turns and is gone. I watch his back as he leaves, knowing I'll never set eyes on him again. The man who saved my life and brought me home to my daughter and my father.

I return to the ward and watch Dad through the window outside. The nurses have wheeled him out onto the terrace, into the sunshine. Maddie has climbed up with him and they are cuddling, he's whispering something in her ear. I move closer and realise he is singing a song to her. He used to sing me to sleep with made-up songs when I was Maddie's age. As I approach, I catch the faintest whisper of a lyric, lifting on the breeze into the air:

> *'You and I have memories for the long road ahead.*
> *Lying solo in the sun, with an angel by the bed.*
> *Tell me in a letter and you'll never be alone.*
> *Throw it to the wind and let it guide me home.'*

I think he's on his way.

ACKNOWLEDGEMENTS

With thanks to Jim Gill and Amy Mitchell at United Agents. Robin Morgan-Bently, Nicola Wall and Harry Scoble at Audible UK for embarking on this literary adventure. Josephine Lane for being the most innovative and patient editor I could have wished for. To Harlan Coben for unknowingly inspiring me to run with an idea no matter how crazy. And finally to all the team at Faber – Louisa Joyner, Hannah Turner, Hannah Marshall and Sara Helen Binney – for their enthusiasm and commitment to my debut novel.